W9-BZP-402

THE BANKS SISTERS

THE BANKS SISTERS

NIKKI TURNER

THORNDIKE PRESS
A part of Gale, Cengage Learning

GALE
CENGAGE Learning·

Farmington Hills, Mich • San Francisco • New York • Waterville, Maine
Meriden, Conn • Mason, Ohio • Chicago

GALE
CENGAGE Learning®

Copyright © 2015 by Nikki Turner.
Thorndike Press, a part of Gale, Cengage Learning.

Thorndike Press® Large Print African-American.
The text of this Large Print edition is unabridged.
Other aspects of the book may vary from the original edition.
Set in 16 pt. Plantin.

LIBRARY OF CONGRESS CATALOGING-IN-PUBLICATION DATA

Turner, Nikki.
  The banks sisters / Nikki Turner. — Large print edition.
    pages cm — (Thorndike Press large print African-American)
    ISBN 978-1-4104-8098-9 (hardback) — ISBN 1-4104-8098-4 (hardcover)
    1. African American women—Fiction. 2. Large type books. I. Title.
PS3620.U7659B36 2015
813'.6—dc23   2015011979

Published in 2015 by arrangement with Urban Books, LLC, and Kensington Publishing Corporation

Printed in Mexico
1 2 3 4 5 6 7 19 18 17 16 15

This book is dedicated to my greatest creation, my everything, my only son, Timmond Turner, I could not imagine my world without you! As I watch you turn into a young man, you continue to make my heart smile as you grown into your own. Our bond, and my undying, unconditional love for you, can never waiver! Always know that you have the power to do anything you set your mind to do and without a shadow of a doubt, Mommy always has your back! I thank God for blessing me with you and I thank you for our bond!

&

Every Nikki Turner die-hard reader! Thank you for picking up book after book after book, allowing me to continue to create and share my stories with you! I can't express my appreciation for you enough and I will never take you for granted. Without you none of this would be possible. I love you soooo much! Thank you! Thank you! Thank you!

1

"God always gives His toughest battles to His strongest soldiers."
— Mildred "Me-Ma" Banks

A black van had been squatting on the corner of Jefferson Avenue for the past twenty minutes. It was an older model cargo van with limousine-grade tinted windows. It easily blended in with the other vehicles on the busy street so that no one paid the van much attention.

A mistake that would cost everyone dearly.

Inside the van, behind the dark glass, were five guys on a major money mission. Each man wore all black and was skeed up on a mixture of cocaine and heroin. All of the men, besides the driver, were in possession of two things: masks that their faces would be concealed by and an AK-15 assault rifle, which rested inside of gloved palms.

"You think we should bounce?" asked the

passenger wearing a George Bush mask. "Maybe that shit's an omen." George Bush was referring to the police cruiser parked in front of the bank that they'd been casing for the past week.

The driver wearing a Queen Elizabeth mask said, "Fuck that. Police gotta cash their paychecks too. We sit tight, we wait this shit out," he said firmly.

Freddy Krueger, in the back of the van, next to Jason, from Friday the 13th, agreed with his longtime friend, Queen Elizabeth. "We sit tight and we wait this shit out."

Jason was about to toss his vote into the hat when the cop strolled out of the Metropolitan Savings and Loan National Bank, with a big smile, got into his cruiser and peeled off.

Once the cop beat the corner, it was a few minutes before Queen Elizabeth said, "Let's go get this fuckin' paper." He reminded them, "No one gets hurt unless it's unavoidable. But, understand," he looked in each individual's eyes, "nothing is going to stand in the way of us getting this money."

The clickety-clack of the assault rifles being cocked echoed off the van's bare interior. That was the unspoken communication that everybody was on the page and was ready.

Freddy Kruger opened the sliding door,

"Now let's go get this motherfucking money!"

On that note, everybody got out and they sprinted across the street, toward the back.

Meanwhile, inside the bank . . .

Fate would have it that it was Simone Banks' first official day on the job, and she was just getting the hang of things.

Jackie, the bank's assistant manager, and the person responsible for training Simone said, "You doing real well to be a newbie. You are such a natural at this," patting her on her back, "what do you do to make this seem so easy?"

Simone was in training to be a manager, and her first lesson was learning to operate one of the bank's seven windows.

"I stay positive and I pray to God," Simone said holding her breath hoping that this new endeavor would work out for her. More than anything, she really needed the job to support herself.

"Prayer always goes a long ways," Jackie said in an angelic harmony.

"You're right about that." Simone gave a smile with a nod, warming up to Jackie as she balanced and refilled her drawer.

"Are you sure that you never worked in a

banking institution?" Jackie asked with a compliment.

Jackie seemed to be in her mid-fifties. She wore her hair in a tight bun and had an overall good spirit. Simone and she had clicked almost immediately.

"No, just many years of business school combined with a lot of other courses," Simone responded. In fact, Simone was twenty-nine-years old and had never had a job in her life. When she was ten Simone and her father made a deal. As long as she went to college, he'd take care of her. And she took full advantage of the opportunity her father afforded her, getting degree after degree.

But over the past six months a lot had changed in Simone's life, mostly for the worse. And things wouldn't be getting better any time soon . . .

At 12:13 p.m. four masked men stormed through the bank's doors.

A man wearing a ski mask was the first one through the door of the bank, immediately raising his weapon and firing on the security guard. "Fuck on the floor."

Before the security guard, a father of two, could reach for his weapon, he ate three slugs to the chest and died immediately.

"Blah . . . blah . . . blah." Fear gripped

the entire bank. Customers screamed and the employees were mortified filling the bank with screams, squeals, and madness.

"Keep fucking calm, and nobody will get hurt," he said, waving the gun. "Don't fuccckk with me," he ordered. The patrons did exactly what they were told. After all, he'd just murdered a father in cold blood, it didn't seem like he was taking any prisoners.

The masked man ordered everyone, "Keep your hands in the air. No fucking heroes!" he said.

Simultaneously, the rest of the gun wielding crew followed suite. They came into the bank, guns blazing on some straight gung-ho style, firing shots into the air, and the customers dove on the floor or hid for cover.

"Rad-da-ta-ta," roaring bullets blazed through the air like fireworks. Next came the high-pitched screams from the patrons. Some automatically hit the floor and ran for cover while the others were stunned. A few just stood still in freeze mode, and waited for instructions from the guys in charge.

Then another man wearing a George Bush mask was smacking anybody in his way. "Shut the fuck up!" he said, wanting the patrons to fear him more and cease their screams of terror.

The shooting ceased and the robber in the ski mask shouted, "Everybody put ya hands on ya fuckin' heads! If you move 'em I'ma put a bullet in your fuckin' head!

Simone prayed to God over and over. But even while praying and being scared shitless, her brain continued to process the horrific scene, taking place in front of her very own eyes. Four bank robbers, ten customers and eight employees, alive. One — may he rest in peace — already dead. God, she silently prayed, don't let there be any more.

"Awwww," an ear piercing scream.

The outburst spewed from a woman with bleach-blond hair and red lipstick. The butt of an assault rifle slammed into her face, knocking one of her front teeth out. The tooth caromed off the marble floor and up against a wall.

"Last warning," Jason yelled at the lady as she silently wept.

The oldest of the four men robbing the bank and killing innocent bystanders was only twenty-four years old. This was the first bank any of them had ever tried to knock off. They were nervous, but the drugs did a good job at helping them hide it. And the more fear they instilled into their victims, the more emboldened the young killers became.

Ski-Mask jerked the trigger of the automatic weapon. *"Barratt . . . Barratt . . ."* he let loose a barrage of bullets again. The drugs had him on some renegade, strong-arm, power trip. He was feeling untouchable and invincible.

"Let me be clear. Do as we say, when we say it. If you can do that we gon' take this money and leave without anyone else fucked up. Get it?"

Heads slowly nodded.

Jason, Freddy, and George hit the first three tellers while Ski-Mask maintained control of the room.

"Please don't fuckingggg push me."

The teller at the second window got too close to the silent alarm, "Bitch, you touch that button, and I swear on my grandma holy drawers you gone die today!" Jason threatened. He backhanded the teller so hard, her legs wobbled, before giving out on her. It was still in question which was harder, the actual smack or her hitting the floor.

Simone still couldn't believe this was happening. She wasn't one to pray in the middle of a room but with what was going on right in front of her, praying seemed like the best thing for her to do right now. Though things were not looking too good for her, her colleagues or customers, it didn't stop her. She continued to silently call upon God.

Simone also prayed that nobody made any hasty moves because she knew these guys were dead-ass serious. The slightest move from her or any of her coworkers could and would cost somebody their life. As her thoughts continued to run wild, out of the corner of Simone's eyes, she saw Jackie's finger inching slowly toward the silent alarm. On one hand, Simone desperately wanted help to come and rescue them all from the bad guys, but she wasn't willing to risk her life trying to be anyone's hero. Better Jackie was a braver woman than her.

"Clack, clack, clack." More gunfire erupted startling her. The guy with the George Bush mask was in the face of teller three.

"Don't give me that fucking look," Jason-Mask ran over and jumped over the counter and bashed the next teller in the face, she grabbed her face with both hands and screamed. He grabbed her by the back of the head and rammed her face first into the counter. The blow was so powerful that she went unconscious instantly.

14

This sent everybody else in another frenzy.

"Shut the fuck up," Jason silenced the hostages who were in uproar over the heinous act.

While Bush-Mask and Ski-Mask waved their huge weapons around looking at everyone inside, Jason-Mask grabbed another teller by the hair and manhandled her. The poor woman was timid and couldn't help herself.

"Bitch put the money in the bag and no fucking dye packs! Hurry the fuckkk up! Bitch!" he shouted as he controlled her movements by her hair. Tears rolled down her face as she tried her best to place money inside a bag, her hands shaking badly. She managed to empty the money out of the first drawer.

The novice crew emptied the first three stations and moved on to four, five, and six.

"Come on man!" Bush shouted out. "Make that bitch hurry the fuck up!" Just as he saw the man move his hands from his head, Simone saw it too. She wanted to scream out and warn him not to move, "No, put your hands back up," but the words didn't come out.

The bank robber with the ski mask aimed, fired, and blew the back of the man's head off. The powerful slugs ripped through

15

the back of the man's head and exploded his face across the bank. Brain and blood decorated the shiny marble floors. Blood and brain splatter were everywhere and the place was becoming a massacre.

Everyone's face shared the same expression: disbelief. Betty scooped the money from the drawer as quick as her nervous hands would allow. Simone prayed that it was fast enough. Tellers operating windows five and six had learned from the others' mistakes, scooping money up in her hands and dropping it inside the bag and moving on to the next drawer of the other teller that was laying on the floor.

They quickly did as they were told and kept their mouths closed.

The innocent bystanders were horrified and only wanted this nightmare to end.

Window seven, which was Simone's window, was the only drawer that hadn't been hit.

"Bitch you know what's up." A small amount of spit came seeping out of his mouth as he spoke. The man standing over her screaming in her face with the gun in his hand was over six feet tall, yet several inches shorter than his lanky friend with the ski mask.

Simone froze, her feet became like blocks

of concrete and she couldn't move. In her head, she recited her earlier prayer. She kept praying to God but no matter how hard she prayed that God make her invisible, Jason and his friends could still see her. God either didn't see fit for whatever reason to make her invisible or he had better things to do. Either way, Simone thought she would soon be dead.

Calmly Ski-Mask said with the gun in her face, "Bitch, if you want to be the world's flyest corpse, keep standing there like a statue and don't you dare think I'm playing."

Though her face and eyes were filled with desperation and tears, you'd better believe they didn't have to ask her twice.

Point taken, she wasn't about to die for somebody else's insured money. She started stuffing money into the bag, like it was an Olympic event, and she wasn't settling for anything less than a gold medal.

He stood over Simone mean mugging, as she put the last of the cash from her drawer into the bag. After Simone was done, he hesitated.

"Don't fuck with me bitch!" he yelled at Simone, "I'll shoot your pretty little brains all over this counter!" He looked at her with disgust as if she was holding out on him.

She had no clue at all what more he wanted, she had given him everything she had in the drawer but he still wasn't satisfied. For a split second, she honestly thought that it was over for her.

All she could think of and hear in her head was a vague voice saying . . . *Here lays Simone Banks, may she rest in peace over* . . . she envisioned herself in an all white Donatella Versace gown in an all white, gold trimmed casket.

She convinced herself that she would be all right if she just did exactly as she was told. She was not ready to die and she still was praying to God that he let her live through this. She was taught that if she had the faith of a mustard seed, then God would deliver. But as soon as that thought crossed Simone's mind, she began to see bits and pieces of her life flash in front of her. Could this really be the end for her?

Simone couldn't understand, why her? She did exactly what he asked for and now he was going to kill her?

She felt a hard hit on the side of her abdomen and it took her a second to realize Jason-Mask had just hit her with his gun.

"Please don't shoot me! I did everything you asked me to do!" Simone pleaded. Indeed she could feel her life on a crash course and all she could do was beg for mercy.

"Bitch! Why in the fuck you playing with me?" he screamed at her, she could see his saliva seeping out of his mouth and then put the gun to her head and cocked it.

Her heart dropped at the realization that she was about to die. Then out of nowhere she got the strength and boldness to calmly speak out, "I gave you everything and I don't have any codes to anything," she wasn't going down without a fight.

He gave a long hard look into her eyes, with the mean mug and the gun still to her temple. Then said to her, "That that-there is your Chanel bag right? That there dat boy bag right?"

"Yes!" She nodded.

"Shit's real?"

Indeed it was. Simone nodded again. At this stage even if it was a bootleg replica, she would've still given the same answer. "Of course!" she proudly said.

"Well, that shit just saved your life, my bitch been asking for that shit," he informed her.

Simone stared at the purse. It was the hottest bag out and an expensive gift from her father. The matching wallet inside was one of the last purchases she made before all the credit cards were canceled and her once lavish lifestyle was pulled from under her feet. Though she loved that bag a lot, she loved her life more. Without hesitation, she shoved it too in the duffle bag with the money. There was no way in the world that she was getting hurt over a pocketbook, no matter how hot, expensive or authentic it was.

He grabbed the duffle bag, clutched on to it tight, one would have thought that he was Usain Bolt fleeing from a stick-up.

"Nigga you stealing ladies purses now?" Bush asked, shaking his head at his home-boy. Not waiting for an answer he just gave the demand, "Let's roll." He backed up toward the door and Ski-Mask followed. Jason flipped over the counter and hurried toward them making up the rear. He turned around and seen one of the remaining tellers press the silent alarm button. He aimed in her direction and squeezed the trigger. Bullets flew like a swarm of bats coming out of a cave. The slugs found permanent homes inside of her face, neck, breast, and stomach. Her body dropped and the masked men rushed for the door.

More screams of fears erupted from a couple people, scared shitless and worried that they could be next. But the guys kept heading to the door.

They were home free and Simone was still alive.

Finally, the nightmare is over! She looked up to the ceiling as if she could see God. *Thank you Jesus!* Simone thought as the last one of the deadly crew had one foot out of the door and one foot still inside. As she was about to exhale — grateful that she hadn't been too physically hurt but saddened for those who had, the unthinkable happened.

The dude wearing the Jason mask stopped at the door and turned around. Then he randomly pointed the AR-15 into the bank, for no apparent reason.

Simone's breath froze into a block of ice, trapped in her lungs. She found herself staring down the muzzle of the assault rifle like a deer paralyzed by the headlight of an oncoming speeding truck before the fatal collision. There was no time to duck or move out of the way and even if there had been a beat or two to get out of the line of fire, the suddenness of the act combined with her reincarnated fear of dying, held her in place like a straightjacket.

God help me! she prayed!

But it was too late . . . With a diabolical

look, Jason pulled the trigger.

Boom!

2

Bush shoved the bank's door open, leading the bloodthirsty crew across the street through the moving traffic to the waiting van. Once inside, the crew felt they were home free.

"We did that shit, man! We fucking did that shit," Ski-Mask said with a big smile on his face as he pulled his mask off. "Told you motherfuckers, we were going to make this shit do what it do."

"Go! Go! Go" Bush slapped the back of the head of the driver, putting pressure on him, "Get us the fuck from round here."

The driver in return, put the van in gear and pressed on the accelerator. He moved into traffic. They'd done it. They'd robbed the fucking bank and was going to be a'ight . . .

"We up now!" Ski-Mask said.

But before the celebration could get in full bloom, Bush noticed the two police cars.

"Shit!" He looked again, "Fuck!"

At the same time, to intensify things more, as Jason opened the bag and dug his hand inside, a dye pack exploded. He quickly removed his hand and shouted, "Fuckin' bitch! No! No! No! No! No! Not, a fuckin' dye pack!" Jason looked hurt as if someone had just taken his manhood.

"This shot was all for nothin' man?" Freddy shouted out of frustration.

The others looked down at the bag, just as two police cruisers turned the corner and blocked off the street. They exited their vehicles and leaned over their hoods with their weapons aimed at the van.

"Fuck, man, what the fuck we gone do?" Freddy got a bit antsy when he noticed the cop cars were blocking the one-way street. Two more black and whites bent the corner behind the van, hemming them in.

The vibe inside of the van flipped from jubilant to morose in the blink of an eye. Two black and whites parked nose to nose in the middle of the street blocking their van from continuing forward.

The driver tried to quickly diagnose the situation to figure out the best way out.

Jakes crouched behind the makeshift barrier, guns in hand and ready to earn their pay. The two cop cars behind them had now turned into six, and eliminated the option of backing up.

"It's work shawty! My turn now to put in mine! Buckle up my niggas!" the driver shouted out. He seemed to be getting an adrenaline rush off it as he put the pedal to the metal.

Underneath the George Bush mask Dougie freaked, "What the fuck we gon' do now?" he said with a shaky tone. The youngest of the four, Dougie was eighteen.

Ski-Mask — a.k.a. Mike — looked his cousin Dougie in the eyes, "We gon' get it on 'em," meaning go to war, "or die trying," Mike declared.

Mike was nobody's fool, he knew the odds of them winning a shoot out with the RPD were against them. But growing up black and broke, being the underdog was nothing new, it was their daily day-to-day norm.

Freddy Krueger a.k.a. Bennie was twenty-two years old and had already spent two stints upstate, going back this time was no option. He knew if he was even caught with a piece of stolen bubble gum, this time, they'd fry his ass for sure. "Court is in session," he said, "and it's being held in the street."

"Then let's get it poppin'," said Jason whose real name was Jason Kill. Jason slammed a fresh clip into the assault rifle. His boys did the same. Then Jason swung the door open. Doug, Bennie, and Jason hopped out the van.

Gun blazing.

Jason put a new clip in the gun and slid the back side door open. He let loose firing on anything in sight. The shots rang out loudly sounding like a warm night in Iraq.

The slugs from the AR's blew huge holes through the police vehicles shattering windows, knocking the sirens off the roof. It was a shame he hadn't joined the army because he had a great aim and plenty of heart.

The police returned fire. Both sides put it down hard.

A police officer stood up and caught three slugs to the face. His partner fired back multiple times at the man who'd shot his friend and coworker.

Meanwhile other shots were aimed for the driver. The front windshield of the van shattered, slumping the driver over dead. His head fell on the horn causing it to continuously sound. The men knew it was do or die and didn't have any time to waste. The team witnessed their homeboy, Mike, go down but there was no time to mourn. They would have to pay their respects to him with their war game.

The three masked men jumped out the vehicle and rolled into the street and were gunning like skilled soldiers, at war with the boys in blue. They were fueled as they opened fire on the police officers non-stop. The volley intensified. Both sides had lost a man and neither wanted to drop another, but knew there was no surrender or retreat. In no time, mixed with the sounds of guns going off, the air was filled with approaching sirens and first response vehicles.

The fella's bullets tore the cruisers apart. Huge holes popped up over the vehicle, sending two of the cars into flames. That gave the robbers that extra push they needed as they reloaded and continued gunning.

The gun exchange went on for a few minutes.

Being outnumbered and outgunned neither intimidated nor deterred the crew from firing their weapons. Two more boys in blue kissed the asphalt as blood leaked from their bodies. The AR-15's bites were as vicious as its bark.

Bennie tried to take cover behind a parked BMW and got chopped down like an oak tree. His body hit the pavement like a drunken monk. Pain soared through his body as if he'd been struck by lightning.

Blood poured from his mouth as he choked trying his damndest to hold on as life slipped away from him. He died staring at the Bush mask by his side, but not before letting off a rain of gunshots, going out in a blaze of glory.

Dougie snapped. He'd watched his cousin and best friend die. Even a high school drop-out such as himself could predict the outcome for him and Jason. But he swore on everything he loved that he would drop a few more pigs before he died. And he meant it with a passion. He raised up and let bullets fly like birds flying south. The volley temporarily pushed the police down for better cover. Though the police had been trained to deal with these kinds of situations, they also cared if they lived to see tomorrow. Dougie knew that this was his last day and acted as such as he let loose round after round.

But Dougie's camaraderie was his weakness, his emotions overrode his intellect and he made the mistake of checking on Bennie. Maybe he was still alive. He blasted his way to where Bennie lay. Gunned with one hand while checking Bennie's pulse with the other. "What the fuck you doing, Dougie?" Jason screamed knowing that it was a dumb move and could be detrimental to them.

"He's dead."

The reality of his man, cousin and best friend lying dead in front of him, literally fucked him up. His bold plan of attack, was no longer strategic, it had suddenly become emotional. Doug was pissed the fuck off. He rose up opened fire on everything in his line of fire. The different caliber of weapons sounded like a gun range with everyone firing simultaneously. The sound of bullets hitting metal, glass shattering, screeching tires, and police sirens flooded the air waves.

As Dougie looked up to hear what Jason was saying a chunk of his scalp got peeled back. The AR-15 fell from his hands as he flew backward, then a slug ripped through his head knocking a huge chunk out then another one and another. He hit the ground, sprawled out like a dead bird.

Jason ran to the van, by luck or the Grace of God, he managed to make it there. He tossed the deceased driver to the ground, climbed inside and put the vehicle in drive. He mashed the pedal all the way down to the floor. The van accelerated and sped toward the police vehicles. He rammed into them as they opened fired on the van. He ducked down and floored the gas pedal. He turned the corner and the engine died. He sniffed some coke, opened the door and hopped out, with his weapon in hand. Four bullets riddled his back, but they didn't stop him. He felt invincible like Scarface. He continued on, as two more slugs ripped through the back of his legs. He fell and quickly flipped onto his back, placed the gun to his head and pulled the trigger. His brains flew through the top of his head. His arms and weapons dropped at his side as he released his bowels and any life left in him. The police officers squatted down behind the parked vehicles as they slowly advanced toward the corpse. Once they saw that he was deceased they lowered their weapons.

What the fuck had just happened? Was the question everybody had on their minds.

3

"Doing it now, my nig. We ain't do too bad, either," Spoe said, with no emotion, into his phone in what seemed like a quick, one-way conversation. "Yo, I'm going to finish this shit up, take a shower. By the time you do what you need to do, come through and pick up your bread," he said and disconnected the phone and threw it in the mix of all the paper he was trying to sort out.

The goose down, crisp white comforter on the king size bed had quickly turned money green due to the bills of dead American presidents that covered the beautiful bed. While kneeling his sexy, muscular body down, on the side of the mattress, Spoe seemed to be quite exhausted as he sorted and stacked the Benjamins, Grants, Jacksons, Hamiliton, Lincolns, and Jeffersons into one thousand dollar piles. He had been counting and stacking the bread for more than an hour. The funny thing was that taking it had been an easier job than counting it. So far the count was better than half a million.

"The fruit from a long day of labor, baby?" Spoe's girlfriend, Bunny, came into the room and walked behind him. She kissed his neck and massaged his tensed shoulders. "That's a lot of money, daddy."

Any presence of her lit up the room and his face, "You know it." He spun around and gave her a long, wet tongue kiss. "All for us baby." And he meant every dimension of those words.

Spoe was old school in so many ways, especially when it came to his woman. As the man of the house, he felt it was his responsibility to be the sole provider. All Bunny needed to do was to look amazing, take care of his needs and make his house as comfortable for him as absolutely possible. She was great at both and that was something that Spoe never took for granted.

That's the reason why he spoiled her the way he did providing nothing but the best for them. Matching his and hers Porsche Panamera topped with the Cayenne for him and the 911 convertible for her. The cars were parked in a garage of an expensive condo that overlooked the James River; three huge bedrooms with high-end furniture and huge walk-in closets filled with the hottest trendy clothes and accessories. Spoe's and Bunny's elaborate lifestyle was made entirely possible by Spoe's shill thrill of relieving drug dealers of their proceeds — by any means necessary.

When it came to taking money, there was no denying Spoe was at the apex of his game. His peers either respected him, feared him or both. But the one thing that was a known fact about Spoe, was that nothing stood between him and his dead presidents, which was another thing he never took for granted. He knew, if he wasn't careful, he could get caught out just like that next man.

"How does that feel?" Bunny asked, continuing to massage his neck using her knuckles.

The only thing that he might've cared about more than his money, was the love of his life, Bunny. They had officially been together for five years not counting the two years that he chased her. Though he had more of his fair share of women running behind him, the only one he sprinted after was her. And once he got her, he vowed to never let her go. She was his queen, his prize, his trophy, his everything, and a blessing that he thanked God for every day. No woman had ever captivated him like she did, and he cherished her. He loved her more than he loved his own life. She was his fantasy. In an extremely lovingly borderline-smothering kind of way. There was no denying that Spoe was obsessed with Bunny and Bunny secretly liked it that way.

Though as handsome, charismatic and not to mention rich as he was, he could have anybody he wanted. There wasn't a day that hadn't gone by he didn't turn down women who threw themselves at him. He couldn't seem to see past Bunny. Rumor had it that Bunny, had put something in his food, or worked some kind of Haitian voodoo, to have him infatuated with her, but that was far from the truth.

The two had an agreement that they took seriously. It was simple: she had him and he had her. So she spent the majority of her time focusing on him and making him happy. In return, he gave his all to making her happy which as the man of the house, he went and got that bread and brought it back home.

The two were inseparable, spending damn near every waking moment together. Their chemistry, not to mention the sex, went together like music. Every move they made incorporated the other. Even when he went out on "jobs", she was always on call. Just in case something went wrong, she'd be the first one to know.

Bunny massaged his neck then leaned in and started blowing in his ears.

"Baby that feels good," she kept going until he said, "I could use your help to count this babe."

"No problem baby." She kissed his neck leaned in beside him and assisted him in the count process.

"How did it go?" she asked.

"It was like taking steak from a vegan. Easy. Shit went smooth," he paused for a minute, with a smile. "Too smooth. Shit was probably one of the easiest heists we ever did."

"That's 'cause you the best at doing what you do," she said, looking into his eyes then blessing him with a long intense Gone With the Wind kiss.

"With a cheerleader like you, I can't help but to win."

Making her heart smile, "You got that right." She looked up at him as her hands moved back in front letting the money shuffle from one hand to another. His bulging muscles and something about that black wife beater did something to her.

"Your hands feel wonderful," Spoe said. "But I need them fondling something else right now."

"Oh, really," said Bunny, eager to oblige.

"I need your help counting the money."

She cupped his balls. "Is counting money the only thing I can help with."

If anyone could take his mind off of business, it was Bunny. She was Beyoncé-fine, except cuter, if that was possible. Instantly, Spoe's dick grew two inches in the palm of her warm hand. He started to move the already counted money off the bed, leaving the rest where it was.

Bunny smiled knowing what was coming next, Spoe picked her up with ease, his muscles barely flexing with her weight.

Her legs wrapped around his waist. They kissed. It went on for a while. His cotton-soft, dark chocolate skin pressed against hers — the color of caramel — meshed like the perfect piece of candy. Spoe laid her on the huge king bed then peeled off his wife beater. Bunny caressed his bulging dick through his shorts with the toes of her foot.

For her, Spoe was definitely something to write home about. He was six foot two-inches of pure masculine perfection. Perfect skin. Perfect lips. Perfect body. And yes . . . perfect penis. Even his coal-black wavy ponytail, which hung past his shoulder, was perfect. Bunny couldn't decide which was sexier; her man or the fact that she was about to be made love to on a bed covered in money.

Letting no time pass, Spoe pulled her panties off, filled his hands with her forty-two-inch hips, and put his bust face forward.

Bunny's legs were spread apart like a wishbone, above her head. "Oh my God! Damn! Don't stop!" She cried and begged like a baby for more milk. And Spoe didn't disappoint, when the pleasure got to be too much, she tried to squirm away. Only to be pulled back in place by Spoe's strong hands.

He continued to go to work on her hot spot. When she was about to cum, and with those big doe gray eyes looking up at her he asked if she liked it, as if he couldn't tell by the way her ass had been bucking off the bed.

Every nerve in her body was so hyper-sensitive to his touch even the tones of his voice, deep and sexy gave her goose bumps. "If you don't know," she chimed, "maybe you need to keep trying."

"Be careful what you ask for," Spoe said with a mischievous grin. And the party was back on.

In the midst of writhing in ecstasy, she managed to get the begging words out,

"Please don't stop." She was at that cross road of lovemaking when she couldn't take any more, but yet didn't want it to end.

Bunny just couldn't help herself. When it came to their sexcapades, he always managed to take her to new places in the bedroom. He handled her sexually in the bedroom unlike any other, leaving her no choice, other than to concede to his every wish.

An hour later, high-pitched squeals of distress emerged from the box spring and mattress, and the faux marble headboard rhythmically drummed against their canary yellow accent wall. A half empty box of Magnum condoms lay on a night table next to the bed.

Bunny and Spoe were still on top of the king-sized bed engaged in fervent sex, lovemaking would come later. On her knees, hairdo — soaking wet — tapping morse code against the faux marble headboard, Bunny felt as if she was going to explode. Spoe kneeling behind her generous cabooz, he was hard at work from a southern vantage point, submerged balls deep into her plump apple-shaped ass with every forward stroke of his thick manhood. His fingertips sank into her pillow soft caramel flesh, as he held on to her hips, trying to control the pace.

"That's right," Bunny moaned. "Fuck da shit out dis pussy, baby!" She pushed her ass back at him, matching his thrusts as if it was an orchestrated dance.

Spoe welcomed the challenge, by upping the intensity. The two to them had been together for years and years of practice had made Spoe the perfect lover. He knew her every erogenous spot, and she knew his. Bunny thought to herself, no one had ever made her body perform the way Spoe made it feel.

Bunny's eyes were rolling in the back of her head, toes spread and curling, when the phone rang. By the sound of the ringtone, Spoe knew it was Tariq. He also knew that as much as he and Bunny were having, it was time to shut it down.

"Fuckkkkk! Baby! That's Tariq," he said and started stroking hard and intense. "Sorry baby."

Business was business and that was it.

Spoe needed to get the remainder of the now wet money counted and divided before his partner arrived.

Bunny understood that but right now there was no way she was going to let him go until she got hers. "Uah." Spoe tensed up when she stuck her finger in his butt, then relaxed. This wasn't his first rodeo and Bunny knew the pressure on his rectum would make him cum quicker, she was already there making the two unload in unison.

The doorbell rang as they were getting out of the shower. "Perfect timing." Spoe said, sarcastically, drying off quick, putting his towel around his neck and wrapped another around his waist exposing his hairy chest. He threw on a pair of basketball shorts and a T-shirt.

"Babe, I'ma grab this door, while you finish cutting the money for me. Cool?"

"I got this," she said in nothing but a sheer robe. The bell rang again, "Go let 'em in babe."

Spoe looked his woman over one quick time. Her nipples pointed out like cones, accented her small waist, hips and thighs. He licked his lips then shook his head. "You know we going for round two tonight right," he said as he kissed her before he walked off to answer the door.

Spoe headed to let Tariq in while Bunny began to count the money with only her robe on.

Tariq was their most frequent visitor as well as the only person, besides immediate family, that had ever come to their place. "What took you so long?" he asked, when Spoe finally sprung the locks on the door.

Spoe still had a few drops of water on him and his hair was wet from the shower. "What you think I was doing man?" he asked as he returned the two deadbolt locks into they cylinders.

Tariq shook his head. "That's all right, bro, I don't need to know the details of you and sis actions. All that y'all be doing, y'all need to have some lil Bunnies running around here." He shook his head with a smirk, and took a seat on the oversized sectional sofa, "You got that bread straight."

"Almost, Bunny's finishing up with it now."

"A'ight, that's what's up," Tariq trusted Bunny like a sister, so he didn't trip over her counting the money.

A few minutes later Bunny walked into the living room wearing leggings and a crop tank top. Her natural sexy strut should've been bottled up and sold or could've landed her on a high fashion runway. She handed the bag to Spoe with a heart shaped sticky note on it with the total written on it in red ink. He immediately placed it on the table.

Bunny greeted Tariq with a hug and a sisterly hug. "What's up T? You good?"

41

"Yeah, I can't complain, sis," he said.

After the small pleasantries, "The total on the money came up to $761 thousand, apiece. Yours all there, Reek."

"Not bad, huh?" Spoe said with a smile.

Tariq stuffed his half into a backpack. "More than I thought it would be. Life is pretty fucking awesome."

They went up in the stash house of some heroine dealers, expecting, maybe, half a mill at best. It was a pleasant surprise that they had exceeded their expectations. And nobody got hurt in the process. "Can't complain," he said.

The boys sat in the living room talking shop while Bunny fixed sandwiches in the kitchen. "You sure you don't want one, Tariq? I got the roast beef y'all like."

"Nah, man, I just ate."

"Huh?" both Bunny and Spoe questioned Tariq. He never turned down any of Bunny's food. "Had a little lunch date with a chick and shit."

"What chick?" Bunny asked being nosey.

"You don't know her," Tariq said nonchalantly.

"Oh okay, when will I get to meet her?" she asked getting excited at the thought of having a girl she could bond and shop with while their men got more money than they could spend.

"Chill Bunny, you're probably not gonna meet her." Tariq explained, "You know I don't keep girls around for too long." Tariq was like that. He was a shy, mild mannered kind of guy with a dry personality but oddly enough, he had a lot of heart and had no problem at all busting a cap in somebody's ass. When Bunny first met him, she thought of him as a weirdo. But after getting to know him, she learned to love him because he was Spoe's partner in crime.

Bunny laughed and ear hustled as she always did on the rest of the conversation.

Bunny fixed two sandwiches one for her and the other for Spoe and was sitting on the bar stool eating, when Tariq said to Spoe, "You heard bout them simple ass niggas, Mike and dem', from Jay-Dubb?"

Jay-Dubb was the hood's nickname for Jackson Ward, a famous area downtown Richmond, where wealthy blacks once socialized, owned businesses and allowed themselves to be entertained. An area where the legendary actor and dancer Bill Bo-Jangles Robinson, who called Richmond his home and Jackson Ward his playground, had been immortalized by a statue on the corner of Clay and Adams — his likeness suited and booted in the middle of an elaborate tap number for eternity. But now, though slowly being revitalized, Jackson Ward was mostly known for its infamous housing project, poverty, crime, murder, and most of all . . . drugs.

Spoe paused in thought. He knew a few Mikes, and Jay-Dubb wasn't known for producing the city's brightest cats. "Which Mike?" he asked after drawing a blank.

"Crackhead Mike that juked Rob."

Rob was a careless dope boy from the West End. That got caught with his pants down in his stash house with a stripper named Peaches. Peaches was Mike's cousin, and the brains behind the hit. Trusting his dick, a mistake on Rob's part, cost him thirty-two zones of coke and his life.

"What about him?" Spoe asked.

Tariq looked at Spoe unable to believe he hadn't heard. "It's been on the news all evening." Then it dawned on him, "Oh, but you and sis been in here on y'all baby making shit today."

Spoe shooed him off, "That's right tho'."

"On some fucking renegade shit. . . . Dude tried to knock off the Bank on Jefferson Avenue. And got smoked by five-oh in the process. Them niggas was battling with the police, in the middle of the street, in broad daylight, straight on some cold-blooded Wild Wild West shit."

Spoe, interest peaked but not surprised, asked, "Fuck outta here. Who was with him?"

Tariq shared what he knew from the news and what the streets were saying. "His cousin Bennie and two of his little homies. Five-oh sparked all of them." Tariq kept going not showing one bit of sympathy for the lives lost. "I heard them niggas jacked off too much time inside — all high on that coke and shit. Jakes were laying on them soon as they came out and it was on."

Spoe, bred to put in work, summed up Mike's flaws in one word: "Stupid," then asked Bunny to turn on the television, which she was already on it — channel surfing desperate to find the news breaking story.

A cat commercial was on NBC. Bunny tried the other three local networks, neither were showing the news at the time.

"Oh, shit!" A nervous Bunny thought out loud. "You said Jefferson Avenue right? It wasn't the Metro Bank was it?" she asked.

"Yes it was," Tariq said with nod.

Suddenly it dawned on Bunny that her oldest sister, Simone, was supposed to start working at that very bank today. Silently, she prayed, *"Lord, please don't have let*

45

anything bad possibly happen to Simone."

Then she asked Tariq, "Did anyone working at the bank get hurt?" Fingers crossed, hoping the answer was no.

That hope crashed and burned when Tariq said, "I think it was a security guard, and at least one employee, maybe two," he said. "But I'm not sure 'cause they say the details was sketchy, but heard that shit was a blood bath inside the bank and outside."

Bunny's blood froze as the chills went up her spine. She immediately reached for the phone.

She tried to call Simone, and the phone just rang and the voicemail came on. Then tried calling a few more times and still no response.

Though unlike most siblings, they didn't actually grow up their entire lives in the same house, they were still very close and kept in touch. Like all siblings, they had their differences and would bicker and argue, but make no mistake about it, that was still her big sister, whom she loved dearly and she'd go to war for.

Shit wasn't looking or sounding good at all . . . but what else could she do but try to keep hope alive?

4

Two hours later . . .

Bunny had stormed out of her apartment and rushed to her grandmother's house. When she arrived, Bunny and Simone's younger sisters, Tallhya and Ginger were already there.

Tallhya was twenty-five; two years younger than Bunny, and Ginger at age twenty-four was the baby of the bunch. As she took a seat on the living room couch, all three looked at each other but none of them spoke. There was an unspoken understanding between the sisters to just sit and wait for one of their phones to ring. After half an hour of sitting in silence, the only thing that could be heard were Bunny's tall thigh high Tom Ford boots' heels clacking back and forth when she stood up and began striding up and down.

"Can you stop pacing the damn floor please," Ginger their youngest sister said.

"Just sit your ass down. Everything's gonna be okay."

Bunny heard her youngest sister, but at the same time she couldn't help but worry about her older sister.

"God won't take her away from us like this," Tallhya the middle sister chimed in. Out of the four sisters, Tallhya was the soft-spoken one. The way she was, you would've thought she was the youngest of them all. She had this gullible innocence about her and because of it, her sisters were constantly trying to toughen her up.

"Yeah, because God forbid something happens, on everything I love, it ain't going to be nothing nice." She shook her head, "This is some bullshit, she don't deserve to be caught up in no shit like this." Bunny fumed.

Bunny decided to change her scenery and go to the kitchen to sit at her grandmother's kitchen table. She thought maybe if she sat at the table where she shared so many good memories with her sisters, it would help her feel a little better. Her foot was nervously bouncing off the floor. She'd dialed Simone's number for what felt like the fiftieth time. This time, instead of it ringing like all the other times she called, the call went straight to voicemail. And Simone's phone

48

never went to voicemail. She was always dependable and on point. Out of all of the four sisters, Simone was the oldest and the most responsible one.

"Look, if Miss-Goodie-Two-Shoes was okay, she would've made a way to call us by now. And she would've seen all our missed calls. She usually answers her phone or calls right back." Bunny made a good point. "Some shit musta gone down with her. Maybe we should call the hospital and see if she's there."

"Yeah, you right Buns. Her ole considerate-ass would've called us by now if she was all right," Ginger had to agree.

"Not the best sign," Tallhya added. "But there's probably a perfectly good explanation."

It didn't help that the police and the bank refused to disclose any information about the robbery, let alone about who'd been injured.

Bunny sucked her teeth. "The bank could at least have fucking common courtesy for their employees' families. And call and say look we can't give no details but your sister is okay."

"Maybe they're working on getting the employee emergency information," Tallhya said, trying to stay positive.

The vibe was glum.

The sisters' signature gray eyes that normally sparkled and lit up a room — were at half-mast.

The captivating gray eyes, high cheekbones, and deep dimples were gifts passed down from their mother, Deidra, who was a deadbeat mom who was usually nowhere to be found. Except with Deidra, being conspicuously absent was nothing new. All their lives, the only thing that was consistent with their mother was that Deidra only had time for Deidra. She had only given them two things: life and their enchantingly gorgeous looks.

The sisters were drop dead gorgeous, beauty queen beautiful. In fact, Simone had participated in pageants since she was about nine years old. As a young adult she had even won on a state level. She had that Vanessa Williams regal kind of beauty: sophisticated, well spoken, educated, and with a lot of book sense as well as common sense. Bunny on the other hand was a ghetto princess, Keisha from Belly kind of fine, she too had participated in church pageants when she was a little girl and had won Ms. Churchill, East End, and was also the Homecoming Queen. But she never competed in national beauty pageants.

Growing up and hanging out with the thugs in her school, she was rough around the edge. She had only attended one year of community college, but was very book smart and had more street smarts than any one female should have. She should've been the boy of the bunch, because she was bold, and had the heart of a lion. The girl overall was as sharp as the knife she kept on her at all times.

Bunny and her sisters were raised by their Me-Ma, Mildred Banks. Me-Ma was a strong, God fearing woman that had done the best job she could with her grand-daughters. Her daughter Deidra had dropped off all four of them when they were just days old and even though Me-Ma felt too old to raise kids again, she didn't have the heart to turn her back on them.

Bursting the bubble of silence, Ginger said what they all were thinking. "What if Simone got shot?" Bunny and Tallhya kept their heads down, each sulking in her own thoughts. Ginger continued, "What if she's —"

Bunny cut her off.

"Stop it right there, Ginger." She turned and hissed at her. "Just shut the fuck up. Don't even say that kind of shit." She'd had enough of the negative talking and thinking.

"We are not fittin' to sit here and talk no crazy shit like that into our reality. That's what we not gon' do," she said. "You hear me?"

Ginger rolled her eyes.

"It ain't like y'all wasn't thinking the same shit. I'm just the only one with the balls to say it," Ginger said, challenging her sister. Ginger was the baby, but she had always been the tough-ass of the four. She was outspoken and unapologetic about the things she said. She was also short-tempered and quick to get in somebody's face if they said or insinuated something she didn't like. She was a lot like Bunny except she could get a lot more ignorant. Whereas Bunny was the type to ask questions first, Ginger jumped to her own conclusions and acted on them with no hesitation. But the irony of all this was that Ginger was the most girly girl of the sisters. Always in heels, never in sneakers, Ginger was always dressed like she was about to walk the runway.

Bunny shot Ginger an intense look that Ginger knew all too well. Bunny started walking to get in Ginger's face when Tallhya busted out laughing.

Ginger turned her nose up and asked, "What the fuck is so funny? 'Cause it ain't a gotdamn thing funny about my sister dying."

Tallhya cut her eye at Bunny, laughed some more, then looked back at Ginger.

Ginger, sitting all proper in her tight jeans and studded stillettos was like, "What? What Bitch? What?"

Tallhya was by now in tears of laughter and couldn't even get her words out, she was laughing so hard.

Bunny not usually late to the draw, was now getting the joke, and cracked up laughing too.

That's when Tallhya, sharing the content of the joke, said, "You're the only one in here with balls — period!"

Ginger didn't like that at all. She huffed and puffed, "You fucking bitch! Your ass makes me fucking sick."

"It is what it is Gin. Don't get mad. You set yourself up for that one!" Bunny said in between chuckles, "Now act like you got some balls and take it like a man," Bunny exclaimed laughing even harder this time.

What could Ginger do? The truth was always in a joke, "You got me that time, Tale. I set myself up," Ginger admitted as she joined them in laughter.

All three of them cracked up laughing as if it was the funniest joke ever. Truth was,

Ginger did have balls — literally. Born one hundred percent boy, his mother named him Gene. But from the day that she started walking and talking, it was obvious that either God or one of HIS workers had made a mistake when it came to Ginger's gender. Ginger acted like a girl and always wanted to wear dresses. After a few years of fighting Me-Ma every morning when it was time to get dressed, Me-Ma gave in and let Gene wear what he wanted. And even though he was a boy, Gene had inherited the same high cheekbones and good looks from his mother which made him the epitome of a pretty boy so it was easy for him to pass himself off as a girl. All he had to do was let his curly hair grow out.

For this reason, Ginger had always been considered as just another one of those Banks girls. Sometimes they were compared to the Braxton sisters, except the Banks girls were prettier and neither of them could hold a note to save their collective lives.

"Fo' real tho', that shit was funny," Ginger exclaimed. She knew how to roll with the punches and she loved to laugh at a joke even though it was at her expense this time.

"Hell yea, that shit was funny," Bunny said still tearing and laughing.

Ginger rolled her eyes. The mesmerizing

gray eyes, along with a tight body, that had seduced many so-called straight men into her world of cross-dressing. She loved that empowering feeling she got when she slayed, conquered a straight man and dicked him down. Gene really wanted to get her boobs done but she never wanted to cut her penis off. She actually enjoyed using her "fun stick" as she called it.

"Will somebody share the joke with me? I could damn sure use a laugh." A visibly shaken Simone said as she stood in the front doorway. The sisters were so caught up in their conversation, they didn't hear when she unlocked or opened the door to let herself in.

Simone always made sure she looked presentable from head to toe and she always took the extra step to make sure she looked her best, but judging her appearance right now was a definite indication that she had had a rough day. Her cocoa brown smooth face had smudged eyeliner under her eyes, her makeup was smeared, and she had a small cut on her bottom lip. And her normally long bone, Pocohontas straight black hair needed a brush to it bad. Her black pencil skirt had dirt all over it, and her once crisp white Anne Fontaine shirt was wrinkled and possessed bloodstains, but what was she to do? Normally she would have never had a hair out of place, but at this very moment she was just happy to be alive. Simone stood there like a statue.

"Simone!" Tallhya was a thick girl. Not in a fat kind of way though. Even though she could fit some plus size clothes, she was thick in all the right places. She took more after her thick boned grandmother, but either way she was always light on her feet. She quickly jumped up and wrapped her arms around her sister so tight that she almost cut off her circulation.

"Oh my God! I'm so happy, you are okay!" she said. "We've been worried sick about you."

Simone shrugged. Okay? What did that really mean? Okay? How could she really ever be ok, the way her life seemed to have taken the wrong turn down a dark dead end alley, with one brick wall after another.

Her father, her biggest support system and benefactor, had died six months ago. She was now living back in the hood with Me-Ma because her father's wife, Marjorie, had thrown her out of her daddy's house before his body could even get cold. And today, she had had a gun pointed to her head, felt the feeling of somebody else's warm blood splatter on her and not to mention she had almost literally died . . . Hell no she wasn't okay.

Not to mention, the police were holding her favorite purse hostage. "I am living, so if that's what we are talking about, I guess I'm okay," she said. "It couldn't get much worse. So, it could only get much better . . . I hope . . . and pray!" she said trying not to let her tears out, then flashed a fake smile.

Ginger, quick to say the first thing on her mind said, "Girl, we thought yo' ass was dead." Bunny and Tallhya stared poisonous darts at Ginger, shut the fuck up sometime, the looks said. "Whatever," said Ginger, "Y'all bitches thought it, too."

"How come you didn't answer your phone?" asked Bunny, ignoring Ginger silly-ass. "Bitch, I was worried fucking sick about your ass. I drove over here like a bat out of hell trying to hurry up and get here because I was just to pieces when I heard." Bunny started going on a dramatic rant, back to her usual narcissistic self. "And the police probably be here at any time now to take my gotdamn driver's license from speeding."

"My apologies sister." Simone said as sympathetically as she knew how. "I didn't mean to make you do that."

"It's okay, Mona," Bunny said to her sister after making her feel even worse than she already was.

"But, my phone was highjacked during the robbery." Simone kicked off her heels and plopped down in one of the chairs at the table. "And not to mention my purse, the robbers took it, which is where my phone was. And the police were intensely interviewing us. And the worst part was I had the worst headache the entire time. It was all as if I was living in the Matrix or something."

"Sister, oh my God, that's the worst." Tallhya looked into her sister's eyes wishing that she could fix it.

"Not your Chanel Boy bag?" Bunny asked with a raised eyebrow trying to change the subject, all of the talk of the violence, and the fact that there was really nothing she could do to get it back, was making her mad.

Simone nodded feeling sick to her stomach as she thought about everything that happened to her today.

"That's why you should've let me borrow it, when I asked you for it," Ginger had to get her dig in.

Bunny scooped an unopened bottle of Cognac from her Celine purse. "You look like you could use a drink," she said.

Tallhya's eyes bucked like Bunny had pulled out a snake instead of a bottle. "You know damn well Me-Ma doesn't allow any alcohol in her house," she said as a reminder. "Why are you carrying liquor around in your pocketbook anyway?" She shook her head.

It was Bunny's turn to eye roll.

"Because I'm grown, bitch. Besides," she added, "I knew one way or another a bottle of liquor was gonna be needed and we all know you don't have none stashed in your room. Either to celebrate. Or . . ." Her voice trailed off. What the alternative could've been was best unsaid.

"I told you," Ginger blurted out. "She thought you were dead."

"Shut up, Ginger," Bunny snapped then told Tallhya, "get some glasses, please. No back talk and thank you very much."

Tallhya got four glasses from the cabinet. Simone who never drank anything stronger than a wine cooler, said, "Make mine a double."

Ginger squealed: "Dayum." Then said, "You sure you're a'ight?" as Bunny splashed a shot in each of the glasses.

The first sip went down as smooth as a ball of fire for Simone. She coughed. Better after that, the brown liquor was as soothing as a John Legend song.

"Have you ever seen anyone get shot in the face before?" Simone asked no one in particular. Tallhya and Ginger turned to Bunny.

Bunny downed a finger of the yak, "Fuck y'all look at me for?" she asked.

Ginger answered, "You the one always talkin' about how you 'bout that life. Bust a cap in a nigga's ass. Don't give a fuck . . . and all that ra-ra shit. So have you?"

Before Bunny could reply Simone said, "I never want to see anything like that again in my life. It was like. . . ." She couldn't think of any words that could adequately describe, "Goulish . . . like horrific."

According to the evening news, in all, thirteen people had died — a customer at the bank, two employees, six officers, and the four accomplices. It had been the most gruesome days in the new millennium of the history of Richmond City, a city that in the 90's was once called Murder Capital.

Ginger felt like she was going to throw up. "Ugh. Can we watch something more exciting or can we talk about something else?" she asked with a twisted face. "Dayum."

"No you didn't," Tallhya retorted, looking at Ginger skeptically. "You can be so inconsiderate sometimes."

"I just wish my dad was here," Simone dropped her head, "that's all."

"I know," Tallhya said, walking over to embrace her sister with a hug.

"But shytttt . . . don't we all. Don't we all wish our dads were here?" Ginger asked.

"Ginger you a shady bitch," Bunny shook her head and scolded Ginger with a punch in her shoulder, even though she knew the truth of the matter was that they all at some point or another wished they had a father like Simon, Simone's dad.

Bunny's dad was serving a life sentence somewhere in Colorado.

Tallhya's dad, according to Deidra, was a well known singer who was married, when he knocked Deidra up and two years after she was born died of a drug overdose. His manager found him dead inside a hotel room in St. Louis. And Ginger's dad, they were all still scratching their head trying to figure out who that was. The funny thing about that was that Deidra never offered any kind of story as to who or where he was.

When it came to dads, Simone had been the lucky one. Simone had a great relationship with him. She was the apple of his eye and she meant the world to him. In his eyes, nothing was too good for his princess.

Ginger said to Simone, "So . . . Ms. Touched-By-An-Angel," breaking Simone's brief moment of nostalgia, "you gotta go to work tomorrow? Or are they giving y'all time off?"

Some things can never be forgotten, Simone thought to herself.

"I'm never going back to that bank," Simone proclaimed for the first time, even to herself. "I may never step foot inside anybody's bank again. I'll do my banking online from now on. No thank you at all."

"Shit, I wouldn't either," Bunny agreed.

"And I don't blame you." Tallhya got up from the table and put up the ironing board and started to iron.

"Awww hell naw, you know the party is over now, this bitch about to start her wifely duties," Ginger said.

"And you know she don't play about that," Bunny chimed in. "And I thought I be on point with my man and his shit, but this chick right here," Bunny pointed to Tallhya, "she don't be playing."

Everybody knew all too well how Tallhya rolled when it came to her men. If Tallhya liked a guy, she not only gave them the world and everything in it, but she catered to them in every way. Though she was a little too needy sometimes, a man couldn't help but to love her.

That's exactly how precise she was about them. And Walter got the best part of the deal when he had married her. The only way Me-Ma would let him move in and stay at the house, so they could save money for the big wedding that Tallhya had always dreamed about was to make it official. So they went to the Justice of the Peace. Walker had been working extra long hours to make sure that Tallhya's big day was everything that her heart desired. Simone and Bunny didn't understand why they hadn't had a big wedding yet, because they — well not exactly *"they,"* but Tallhya — had won the Virginia State Lottery, for one million dollars. And after taxes, and fees, she opted for the yearly payout, so that she could get a check every month. After working her ass to the bone, she never wanted to work for anybody another day in her life. Mike had convinced her that they couldn't use their winnings toward their wedding, that that would have to be their nest egg. And she fully agreed, because that was her security. They both agreed that they'd invest their money in addition to him working to pay for the lavish wedding she'd always dreamed about.

"I wish I had a boo like you, sis," Ginger

said sarcastically.

"You make my Home and Gardens-ass look bad," Bunny had to admit to Tallhya.

"Look don't hate me because I'm wife material. All I want is for Walter to be happy."

"Leave her alone. Y'all stop messing with her! I respect that she's submissive," Simone said, wishing she had someone to be submissive to.

Just then Walter, Tallhya's husband, walked into the door, "Honey, I'm home." Tallhya ran to greet her man.

"Hey, Baby! How was your day?"

"It was great," he said, placing a peck of a kiss on her lips. "Just hungry as fuck. What's for dinner?"

"Good question," Simone said. "I was wondering the same thing, brother-in-law."

"Hey, y'all." Walter, a tall, dark and handsome man wearing gym clothes, had acknowledged his sisters-in-law. "What did Me-Ma cook? A nigga hungry as shit."

"Nothing."

"Nothing?" Both Simone and Walter sang in question in unison.

"She's been gone all day. As soon as she heard about the bank, she ran out here so fast she didn't do nothing. In fact, she barely had her wig on."

"Now that's a first," Ginger said. "She was on the move for sure."

Walter looked crazy, like he was about to snap. There was no denying that Me-Ma was the best cook in all of the southeastern part of the Unites States. If for nothing else, he came home every day just so that he could eat her home cooking and always took leftovers to work every day. A man never had to indulge in a restaurant when the kitchen where he resided served food and catered to him better than any restaurant he knew of. "Damn, so ain't shit cooked in here?"

Tallhya could see his frustrations on his face and she ran to his side to resolve the situation. "Don't worry baby. I will get you something to eat," she calmly said, aiming to please her man as her sisters sat and watched. "I'm about to run your shower water, and by the time you get done. I will have your food on the table, okay, baby."

"Okay. I'll settle for that." He nodded, not really happy, but he accepted it.

"You know this shit gets crazier by the day. Somebody better call Me-Ma before this man divorce her," Bunny joked.

"Shit is a crying fucking shame, if you ask me Ginger, that motherfucker need to cook his own gotdamn food or cook her some.

On some real G shit, he need to take you out at least one night a week on a date night."

"We saving for the wedding, you know that," Tallhya interrupted.

"That nigga makes me sick. He complains about every gotdamn thing. And I don't trust him," Ginger said.

"Yeah for Christ sake, call Me-Ma please somebody before we have to fuck him up," Bunny agreed.

Simone reached for the phone and asked, "It's kind of late for Me-Ma to be out isn't it. And you guys said she's been out all day too?"

Simone called and didn't get an answer and wondered indeed, *Where in the world was Me-Ma?*

5
YIELD NOT TO TEMPTATION

"The Bible says, if two or more come together, and pray then their wishes shall be granted, in the Name of Jesus," Pastor Cassius Street confidently said to the Members of The Faith And Hope Ministry as he led prayer. His straight-legged fitted jeans fit him to a T. The soft material of his designer jeans caressed the top of a pair of his ostrich cowboy boots, as he paced the pulpit. He beseeched in a strong deep voice, dripping with a perfect mixture of confidence and charm.

"I need all my prayer-warriors to get into the spirit. We must," he stressed the word must, "stand in the gap with a prayer of protection for the granddaughter of our own, mother Mildred Banks."

Sitting on the third row in her usual seat, only using her eyes Me-Ma, thanked the pastor in advance and a nod of encouragement and approval, then bowed her head down for the prayer.

"Lord we just honor and we just praise you in advance for all great things you will bestow upon our life. Lord, we ask you for the anointment and the protection for our sister, Simone. We praise you and we just magnify you. We just ask you to have your will done, to keep Sister Simone in your keeping care. We ask Lord, that not a hair be moved out of place, Lord Jesus we know you are a miracle working God."

"Yes, Lord," Me-Ma said aloud and raised her hand.

Me-Ma wasn't one of those so-called Christians, who only prayed in times of need. This woman prayed, every day . . . all day. She didn't even have to know the people and she prayed for them. And most of the time when she prayed, it was for other people, almost rarely for herself.

But Me-Ma's family was an entirely different story. She stayed on her knees for them. Especially, her daughter Deidra, she had always been a free spirited person. But when Me-Ma's husband Johnny, Deidra's father, died suddenly of a heart attack on top of his mistress of twenty years, their fifteen year old love child that lived one street over from them was revealed. Deidra was never the same and finding out that her loving, idol, role-model of a father was a two-timing womanizer, had damaged her deeply. If she couldn't trust her creator, her father, who could she trust?

From that moment on, Deidra could never connect with people wholeheartedly or truly deeply love. Neither would she commit to anything: a girlfriend, a job, a man, not even her own four beautiful children, who were the spitting mirror image of her. She picked up and disposed of people as if they were trash.

Me-Ma loved her daughter so much and was sure that Deidra's shortcomings were just a test of her faith. Me-Ma's faith was impeccable and knew that God may not have when she wanted him to but he would come in his time. And she believed that God was still working on Deidra and would deliver her from her demons one day and until then she would diligently watch over and pray for Deidra's children; her grandchildren.

Which was the one reason that she was always on her knees and in church now, with the prayer warriors praying for her granddaughter. Though all of the grand girls each had their own issues and could use God's grace and mercy. Tallhya had her battles with obesity and her self-esteem. While

Bunny, her ghetto princess of whom Me-Ma worried herself to death about. The child was so bold and defiant and besides God, that girl feared nothing. And Gene AKA Ginger, was an entirely different story, the poor thing had so many demons that all Me-Ma could do was plead the blood of Jesus on that child.

Oddly enough Simone didn't require a lot of her grandmother's prayers. Though Me-Ma would never admit it and would deny it to her grave, Simone was definitely her favorite. She loved them all immensely, but there was something about Simone, kind and gentle spirit that held a special place in her heart. The girl walked the straight and narrow and never got in much trouble. Simone was both spiritual and religious. She believed and loved the Lord without a shadow of a doubt. She was raised up in the First Zion Baptist Church and went every single Sunday with her grandmother even after she went to live with her dad when she was nine. Her dad would drop her off every Sunday so she could attend service with her Me-Ma. She sung on the choir and ushered on the usher board. But two years ago, when Pastor Jasper dropped dead of a heart attack on the pulpit, the church or Simone's feelings toward it were never the same. Simone hadn't stepped a foot in this church again. It was something about the man dying there that freaked her out.

Me-Ma looked up to God, begging for his mercy on Simone. In the midst, she saw Pastor Cassius' eyes open, as he was praying. Then saw Katrina making googly eyes with the pastor. Me-Ma shot her a look that only a mother could give her child. Cassius looked away quickly and closed his eyes and brought the prayer to a close.

Me-Ma honestly didn't think much of Katrina, coming onto the Reverend. It was no secret that damn near every woman at the church had fantasies of being the First Lady. The pastor confessed that he was waiting on God to send her to him. Meanwhile preaching on abstinence and waiting on the one God wanted for him. But his most important focus was building his ministry.

"How are you holding up?" Katrina approached and asked Me-Ma. "If I were you, I'd be all to pieces," she said. "But you look so calm. You don't show one ounce of weariness on your face."

Me-Ma was a genuine, kindhearted woman, but she didn't take mess from a soul. She had seen a lot of foolishness and

BS in her day. Me-Ma looked the young lady up and down, Keisha she thought her name was. Me-Ma had seen napkins with more material than the girl's skirt, leaving nothing to the imagination, except the price to further explore.

"Listen baby, I hear what they saying, but I know I got God on my side and God has the world in his hands including my granddaughter. And baby I got faith, and with God who am I afraid of?" she confidently asked.

Me-Ma knew the hot little heifer was only being nosey because the bank robbery was all everybody was talking about and the rumors were spreading faster than an STD in a whorehouse.

"It was an inside job. A million dollars was in the safe. . . . the bank robbers were Gangsta Disciples from Chicago . . . one of them got away, with the million dollars . . ."

But the one that bothered her the most, "Everyone inside the bank was killed, execution style. . . ."

The story snowballed one after another, each one wilder than the one preceding it. The church held night services three times a week but today's service it was a different kind of energy. As long as it didn't involve them personally, gratuitous violence compelled people to want to talk about it. It didn't matter if it was a bar, on a street corner, or inside a church — human nature was human nature . . . it didn't change.

Me-Ma took a seat on the pew along with a deep breath, and tried to control her mind from wandering to that place of what if?

"Devil get ye behind me." Me-Ma started to quietly say to God, "Lord if it was your will, to take her Lord, I just ask you to give me the strength, Lord Jesus."

Then she felt someone put their hands around her from the back. Me-Ma looked up and Simone was standing there and embraced her with a hug.

With the sight of Simone, Me-Ma, started screaming, "Thank! You! Jesus!" at the top of her lungs. "Thank you Jesus! Halllllleee-luujah!" she said four more times. "My God! My God!" She shook her head and tears began to form in her eyes.

This prompted all the prayer warriors to start shouting all around the church, Me-Ma fell to the ground and began crying, thanking God.

The Praise and Worship team surrounded and started singing the gospel hymn, "He has done great things for me . . . Greeaaaat thinggsss . . ."

The rest of the church members started

having a big Holy Ghost party while Bunny sat in the last pew of the church with eyes hidden behind her big Chloé sunglasses not affected by the way the Holy Ghost filled the place of worship.

The people shouted around the church and Simone wanted to join them but she felt weird singing with a church choir she hadn't sang with in so long. The only reason she was even there tonight was because she wanted to personally tell Me-Ma that she was okay. It was just something about the pastor that she couldn't put her finger on.

Pastor Cassius' church was filled with a diverse group of colorful characters, of all ages, nationalities, and from all walks of life. The people there were very radical and the fact that they were so dramatic in their acts of praising the Lord, and not to mention, Pastor Cassius, the leader and creator of the whole production, his animated over the top personality, it made Simone wonder if it could really be legit? Or was it a scam or a show?

Pastor Cassius was a whole other story, he was so flamboyant and in her eyes, everything about him screamed nothing short of a seasoned, homosexual pimp — pimping the pulpit.

He had mastered the Bible. He knew it, in

and out, and could recite it back and forth. His "game" and passion for the "Lord" was so airtight, that one couldn't help but to respect the self proclaimed "Man of God."

With the most beautiful cocoa skin that looked like it was softer than a baby's butt, he was definitely an attractive man, to the point that all of his "primping": the arching of the eyebrows, his big full lips permanently greased with ChapStick along with the pedicures and manicures twice a week, combined with his metrosexual tendencies turned his handsomeness into pretty.

Me-Ma, who was a wise woman, swore up and down that he was a good man that God himself rescued from the harsh world, and he was nothing short of a walking and living testament of what God can do. But Simone never trusted him, with a name like Cassius Street, who could blame her?

Though all these things were true and correct in Simone's eyes, she couldn't help herself, she had in fact, been blessed and God had spared her from wild bullets that had her name on them. The only explanation was, that it wasn't God who had jammed the gun of the robber when she thought she was breathing her last breath.

Because of God and Jesus Christ, she was

able to live on and see another day and that alone was enough reason to praise the Lord. So, she joined in and gave thanks to the Lord.

Pastor Cassius in his fitted straight leg jeans and cowboy boots stood before Simone, and said with the rest of the churchgoers watching and listening to every word about to proceed from his mouth, "My brothers and sisters, what we have just witnessed with our own eyes is nothing less than the work of the Most High. It's God's unchanging grace. It was only our prayers that led God to allow not one strand be removed from our sister Simone's head. In the midst of a war at her workplace, in the midst of the crossfires and gunshots and coworkers falling to her left," he dramatically shifted his weight to his left, "and to her right," then did the same thing with the right side of his body.

"Ain't God good?" The members started to clap and shout.

His words got the prayer service patrons even more riled up, the Holy Ghost took over, shouting, praising, and shouting took place for another forty-five minutes. Finally, resulting in a love offering of $212 taken up by Pastor Cassius for Simone.

After the big Holy Ghost party was over,

she stood at the door to give hugs and thanks to the church folks for praying for her. Then Me-Ma whispered, "Make sure you thank Pastor here, baby."

Simone shot a look at Bunny that said, "Rescue me," but Bunny with a smirk on her face, just dropped her head but not before giving her a look that said, "I can't help you with this big sister."

"Thank you Pastor for everything," Simone said. "I really appreciate your prayers and everything you did," she shook his hand, and before she knew it, he had taken her into his arms.

"We hug around here."

"Well, thank you so much for your prayers."

"It was most definitely my pleasure." He flashed his pearly whites at her.

"And I think Pastor has something for you," Me-Ma added.

"Oh yes," Me-Ma's voice prompted his memory, "Yes," he nodded. "Let's head to my study. Sister, we took a love offering for you and your family."

"Thank you." Simone was surprised at the thoughtfulness of the pastor. She'd always passionately thought he was a money hungry ex-pimp, drug dealer who was only into the ministry because of the lure of a greater hustle. She hated the fact that maybe she'd have to admit that pastor may actually be all right after all. Or maybe God was just dealing with him in his own way.

She had to admit, *Well, I guess if you think and speak something so long, you start to believe it yourself. Maybe God is really working on him,* she thought to herself as she followed him to his study.

"I think it's about $212 and of course you'd bless the church with half of that."

That's a new policy, Simone thought to herself, *they took up the love offering for me and my family and I have to let the church keep half. Well I guess half of something is better than nothing. But with this man right here, it's always something,* she thought, but instead just responded, "Yes, of course Pastor Cassius."

"You have to be strong and just have faith as you go through this. And know that all of the feelings you are having, God brought you through that ordeal today, he will bring you through feelings of any aftermath you may experience from here on out," he told her as he led her to his study.

"That's right Pastor, Amen." Me-Ma co-signed while Simone just listened as he continued.

"See you have to remember that the devil

doesn't show up in a red cape and horns. He comes in all kinds of disguises to distract you and throw you off course. You must not yield to temptation," he said as he opened the door to his office.

And they all got the surprise of their life.

"Oh, Jesus no," Pastor put his hand up and turned his back.

Katrina was in the pastor's study buck, naked, legs spread-eagled wide with a pair of red stilettos on her feet.

"Katrina!" Pastor Cassius yelled out. Katrina was so startled to suddenly find herself with an audience that she fell off the desk and crawled under it to shield her naked body.

"I am so sorry about that Me-Ma, I had no idea she was even in there," a startled Pastor Cassius tried to explain as he closed the door behind him.

"You should be ashamed of yourself," Me-Ma screamed through the closed door and finished with, "Devil I rebuke you in the name of Jesus." Simone couldn't contain herself and burst out into laughter, damn that was too funny and so wrong for church.

Me-Ma pleaded the blood of Jesus while Simone got her cash from the reverend and headed back home. She still had to prepare for the aftermath of the bank's bullshit in the morning. Even though she didn't plan on working there anymore, she still had to return tomorrow to finish the line of questioning and sign paperwork.

6
THE STEP MONSTER

Bunny took Simone back up to the bank the next morning, so she could get her car from up there. There was a big police crime command center on wheels still outside of the bank to try to collect evidence.

As soon as she got there she was whisked away inside, for the next two hours, they began to ask her pretty much the same questions they'd asked her the day before.

By the time the police were done interviewing all of the bank's employees, Simone was exhausted and beyond ready to go. She asked one of the men who seemed to be in charge, "How much longer do I have to be here?"

Agent Mark Dugan scrutinized Simone carefully with his hazel, quick eyes. "You're Ms. Banks, right? The twenty-nine-year old U of R graduate? And it was your first day at the bank?" He couldn't help but notice how beautiful she was and chastised himself

81

for being momentarily distracted by it.

"Correct. Correct. And correct," Simone said, a little nervous, but even more impressed. Dugan hadn't been the officer who'd questioned her earlier, yet he ran off her information without the aid of any notes. "I'm a suspect now?" she joked, but was serious.

Agent Dugan shoved his hands into the pockets of his slacks before saying, "It's my job to know who is who and what is what," he said with a corky smile. "Actually, we have everything we need from you. And to answer your question — No. You're not a suspect."

"Well, what about my pocketbook? One of the robbers had taken my purse and I haven't seen it since."

"Your pocketbook isn't a suspect either," the officer said with a smirk on his face.

Handsome and a sense of humor she thought to herself. "What I meant to say is, may I please have my purse back so I can go on with my life," Simone said in a serious tone. She refused to let the officer see that he was having an effect on her.

Agent Dungan, who resembled a younger Denzel Washington, was being a comedian, "I'm sorry. I was just trying to make light of the situation. . . ."

Simone had a feeling she wasn't going to like what he was going to say next.

"Your purse is evidence. Therefore, we're going to have to hold on to it for a while."

And she was right. She wasn't happy. She looked at him, and said as humble as she knew how. "Look I really need my stuff. My wallet, keys and cell phone. I can't drive my car without my keys."

After a few seconds of thought, Agent Dugan offered a compromise. "I can get your keys and your phone, but that's it."

"That would be greatly appreciated detective."

Simone went to tell Bunny, who had been waiting patiently, "He's going to get my keys and my phone, but that's all. Everything else is being held," she sighed, "for God knows how long."

"That's some bullshit," Bunny said exactly what Simone was thinking, but wouldn't say out loud.

"I agree, but this is the struggle."

"I know, sis. But it's going to be okay." Bunny tried to convince her sister, then asked, "You need money?"

"No, Buns, I'm good. I have that money the church gave me," she said, knowing she should have taken her sister up on the offer, but she didn't want to accept the dirty money.

"Girl, let me help you. After all that's what sisters are for."

"Bunny, I appreciate you, but I will make a way."

"How? You just said you're not going back to work again." She looked into her sister's eyes and saw how petrified she was at the sight of being back at the scene of yesterday's nightmare. "And I don't think your trust fund has magically reappeared yet. And even if you do get interviews, that whole thing is a process, it's not like you are going to be able to get paid right away. And honestly I don't know how far your check for one day at the bank will stretch. So let me help you."

Simone took into consideration what her sister was saying, and knew she was speaking the truth. As bad as she did need the help, she would feel like a hypocrite if she took the money knowing where it came from.

"I can't tell you how much I appreciate you offering me money, but really sis, I will be okay."

"I know you don't want to take it because you feel like it's blood money, but look money is money. Shit," Bunny sucked her teeth. "It all spends."

"You are right," Simone agreed, but still had to kindly decline her sister's offer, "and if I happen to change my mind, will the offer still stand?"

"And you know this, sis."

Simone looked at Bunny, "Thanks Buns. I love you." She leaned inside the car and gave her a hug.

"Ms. Banks," the detective called out to her.

Simone turned to look back to him, and he had her keys. She turned to Bunny told her that she would be okay, bye and had to go around the other side of the bank to get her car.

After finally getting her keys, Simone bailed out of the bank as fast as her Gucci sneakers would carry her. Outside, was a circus of news reporters and yellow tape separating the crime scene from a growing number of curious onlookers. She still felt like it was still the day before. She couldn't bear to look at the bank's surroundings. She couldn't get the scene from yesterday out of her mind. There were dead bodies under white sheets, pools of congealed blood, and bullet casings everywhere. The air smelled of death and anxiousness. Simone tried to block it all out, damn near running to her car like an immigrant escaping from a third-world country.

"Miss . . . Miss . . ." one reporter noticed her, prompting the rest of the media frenzy to go after her. It was a good thing that she had a great head start in front of them.

Once she made it to her car, a Mercedes C-350 convertible, she sped off. The Mercedes, as if on autopilot, navigated itself to her father's house. The house Simone had grown up in, the house that now legally, belonged to her stepmother, Marjorie.

Simone would've given anything to have been able to talk to her dad. He always knew exactly what to say to her, regardless of the situation. No problem was too big, or too small for daddy dearest. And on those rare occasions when Simon, her father, couldn't physically fix what was bothering her, he comforted her with the perfect words, hug, or ear to make her feel better.

But those moments were gone. . . . forever.

Simon was dead. He'd passed six months ago and that had to be the absolute worst day of her life. She took a deep breath as she parked in front of her father's mansion. She hadn't been there since the day of the burial when his wife basically packed all her stuff and kicked her out of the house. She hated having to humble herself to ask her stepmother for help but under the circumstances, she didn't have much of a choice.

Standing on the porch in a funk, Simone punched her key into the deadbolt lock and nothing happened. She wiggled it. Still nothing. *Odd,* she thought. This was the same exact key she'd been using since she was nine when her father and she first moved into the house. She removed the key from the lock, looked at it, then tried it again.

And at that moment, when the lock still refused to cooperate, reality plowed into her like a dump truck carrying a load of shit. And she didn't want to believe the ugly truth — the place where Simone had grown up in and had once called home no longer welcomed her.

Simone had been front and center at her father's funeral, burial, and wake but for some reason, the full reality hadn't hit her until right at this very moment where her key no longer worked in his house. Her dad was dead. Gone for good. And he wasn't coming back. Deep down, at that very moment, she felt a part of herself softly die.

She was on the brink of breaking down like a discarded, broken lawn chair when the front door flung open. Simone, reaching deep within herself, pulled herself together.

Even if it killed me, she thought, she wouldn't give Marjorie, the satisfaction of seeing her looking like a stray animal on the porch yearning to be rescued.

Marjorie stepped out onto the porch, the picture of smugness. "Simone darling," her exaggerated tone reminded Simone of the late Eartha Kitt. "The doorbell works just fine," she said, pushing the button with her pink and white French-manicured index finger to demonstrate, just in case Simone hadn't for some reason understood.

Simone stood in silence.

Filling the gap, Marjorie asked, in mock politeness, "Now what do I owe the pleasure?" Then the pretense of cordiality vanished as quick as it had appeared. Marjorie, as if just noticing Simone, balled her face up in disgust. "By, the way, you look a fucking mess. In fact you should be ashamed of yourself walking around here looking like who did it and why. You look despicable."

She had no makeup on her face and had on a velour Juicy Couture sweatsuit on. That morning she honestly just wanted to just stay in her Me-Ma's house under the covers, but she knew she had to go back to the bank to attempt to get her stuff.

Simone wanted to say, "And you always

look like the fake two-faced woman you've been since I met you," but instead she bit her tongue to avoid any more of a scene. She just said, "I had a rough twenty-four hours."

Reluctantly, Marjorie invited her in. "Make it quick, honey. I have things to do, people to see, and places to be."

Once inside, under the light, she was able to give Marjorie a once over look and it was official. It was rumored, by Ms. Godfrey, her neighbor next door, that Marjorie had been under the knife, getting all types of plastic surgery procedures. Once inside the house, under bright light, the rumors were confirmed. Marjorie's face was tight as fish pussy. She'd gotten a new nose, a facelift, and enough botox to fill the holes in the foundation of the Titantic. And if that wasn't enough, Simone couldn't help but notice, Marjorie had got permanent make-up tattoos in place of eyebrows and lip liner. *If her goal was to imitate a frozen clowns face, she'd succeeded with flying colors,* Simone thought.

Marjorie led Simone into the living room, which is off to the right of the grand foyer. "I see you've redecorated," she said checking out the room.

Marjorie's face wasn't the only thing that

had been drastically transformed into something almost unrecognizeable. The paint, the flooring, the furniture, the drapes, everything had been changed. Nothing was really wrong with the way it was before.

"The place needed it," Marjorie said with an edge. "It was a long time overdue."

"The Step Monster," the name Simone used for Marjorie, behind her back, had gone too far. The woman had done a master makeover on her outer person and the interior of the house, eradicating any and everything that could conjure memories of Simone's dad. Simone had always secretly disliked Marjorie, to be honest she hated the woman, but even she had no idea how much of a coldhearted bitch Marjorie truly was.

Her dad had been married to the woman for twelve years: filled with trips around the world, lavish gifts, romantic dinners and all the quality time Simon's company would allow him to be away. In return, Marjorie repaid her deceased husband by not even bothering to display a picture in which to honor his memory. Simone had heard of a new beginning, and Marjorie wasted no time starting one.

The house felt cold, devoid of love. "So," Marjorie said, "let's not play games, what is it that you want? I'm sure you're not here to give me any decoration tips." Marjorie tightened the belt on her white satin, fur-trimmed robe. Her breasts hanging under the flimsy material like two sacks of sand, which were surprising to Simone that she had not gotten them done. *I guess even the best surgeon couldn't help those saggy things,* she wondered.

Simone gave Marjorie the tea about the bank getting robbed, leaving out most of the details.

"I saw it on the news. But exactly what does that have to do with me?" Marjorie asked without any kind of sympathy at all. "You are not dead, so clearly that has nothing at all to do with me."

Simone took a deep breath, and let the comment roll off her back, like water, "One of the bank robbers took my Chanel Boy bag, with my money and ID — everything in it. I need my birth certificate that dad kept in his security box so that I'll be able to get a new ID."

Simone detested having to ask or to need Marjorie's help for anything. This was the same bitch that contested her father's will, and everything that Simon had left for her. Meanwhile, Marjorie was running through a life insurance policy she'd taken out on him. Simone would bet her life that her father was surely rolling over in his grave. His only child of twenty-nine years was broke, not a dollar in the bank. While his wife of twelve years was living the life of luxury in the fast lane with not one regard for her or care in the world.

"So, let me get this right," Marjorie said with a chuckle. "The bank robbers took the bank's money, your money, and your Chanel bag."

The old hag wasn't going to make this easy. Trying not to lose her cool, Simone politely said, "Yes, and my wallet. So I need my birth certificate so I can go to the DMV to get a new ID."

Marjorie's eyes turned dark and the horns went up on her head. "And since they took your wallet will you be asking me for some money, too? Is that what your real intentions are? You came to beg money from me?" She spat the words out like they left a bad taste in her mouth.

Simone hadn't considered asking her for money, but she thought, *Hell yes! Well, that would be the least you could do for me. You should have given me the money **my** dad left me. Instead, you manipulated my dad's will, put me out of his own house and changed the locks on the doors.*

If it wasn't for her mother's mother, Me-Ma, Simone would've been homeless.

Make no mistake about it, Simone loved and appreciated herself some Me-Ma. Growing up, Me-Ma was always generous, caring, and gracious. It was so sad, but true that Me-Ma was the closest thing to a mother figure Simone ever had. And besides a little more gray hair and a few more wrinkles, Me-Ma hadn't changed a bit. But Simone had. She was a mature, educated, grown woman whose father had worked hard so that she would always be taken care of, even after he was gone. And now her stepmother manipulated everything and left her with nothing.

It took every fiber of restraint and humility for Simone to answer Marjorie's question. She took a deep breath; slowly, inside inhaled counted to ten before exhaling.

At that point, she decided why not? What did she have to loose? It was simple, it was either yes or no.

Calmly, she said, "I wasn't here to ask for money but I could use some. I do need money right now. For the basics . . . gas and food. And I'm going to need to buy a new phone." Doing a few calculations in her head, she figured she needed about seven or eight hundred to get by, but settled for the bare minimum. "Do you think you can give me five hundred?"

The room, smelling like fresh paint and money, was a pin drop quiet for a few beats. Out of nowhere, Marjorie cackled like a witch with a black cat up her sleeve. The irritating bewitching laughter went on for a while. Finally, she stopped.

"So, you *need* me, huh," she said. "Where's your mother in your time of need?"

This was a low blow even for Marjorie, thought Simone, bringing up Deidra.

"Wait don't answer," she said, "let me guess. M-I-A as always." Marjorie added, "Besides pushing you out of her pussy that woman had never given you anything. It's just mighty funny how she's never around when you need her."

She was right. Deidra, Simone's mother, had never done a thing for Simone, except pass her beautiful looks on to her, which she was grateful for.

Simone bit her tongue, literally, ignoring Marjorie's childish attempt to make her loose her cool. Simone knew what Marjorie was trying to do. If Simone snapped on her, Marjorie would use it as an excuse not to give her the money. *Nice trick, but that won't work on me bitch,* Simone thought.

Marjorie, after not getting the results she'd hoped, scurried off toward the family room, the bottom of her robe including the fur trim flapping in the wind. Simone assumed Marjorie was going to get the money she'd asked for. A few seconds later, Simone heard voices coming from the room Marjorie had just gone into. She couldn't make out the words but recognized that the tone of it was Marjorie and Maria, the housekeeper, who had worked for her father for years.

Nevertheless, Simone couldn't make out what they were saying. Simone walked into the foyer taking a seat in a newly purchased high back chair, so that she was closer to the door.

Her thoughts drifted, off to a conversation she'd had with her father, in this very spot, when she was sixteen, about what time she was expected to be back home from her first real date. She'd made it home, thirty minutes before curfew.

The trip down memory lane ended as suddenly as it had had begun. "Here!" It was Marjorie, pushing a crumpled up piece of paper into her palm.

Twenty dollars.

No, that bitch didn't? The disrespect burned at the lining of Simone's stomach like a shot of cheap liquor. "What I'm supposed to do with this?" She held the twenty-dollar bill by two fingers as if it was a solid dagger. Now Marjorie was just toying with her. She had never felt so belittled in her life.

Marjorie, judging by the twisted smile and the spark of delight simmering in her eyes, made no effort to conceal the joy she felt at Simone's expense. "Darling . . ." she said, bubbling with self assertion, "you need to take that twenty and run along. I have a date" — making an exaggerated gesture of checking her watch — "and I've wasted enough time with the likes of you."

Simone and Marjorie had never really liked each other, they tolerated one another for the sake of Simon. Growing up, Simone had always given the respect she gave to all adults, like she was taught. But Simone quickly learned that respect wasn't something to be given, it had to be earned. And this trick hadn't earned a damn ounce of anything.

Simone decided to take Marjorie's advice, and get the fuck away from her. As she got up from the high back chair, Marjorie, adding insult to injury, said, "No more freebies here." And she didn't stop there. "You've freeloaded your whole life — Ohhh . . . daddy's little, precious girl. Well, that shit is over." She raised her voice, "Done! Finito! Your daddy's gone and that twenty dollars is the last thing you're ever going to get from me." The smile of glee was replaced by one of unadulterated hate. "You will never see another penny of your father's money. I'm gonna see to that little girl. And what are you gonna do about it? Nothing! That's what." Marjorie went on, "Because I have the best lawyer in the state and you don't have shit . . . not a gotdamn thing! Good luck with that in probate court. Now if you don't mind, get the fuck outta *my* house and try to figure out how you're going to feed your grown-ass self."

Simone seriously considered cracking Marjorie upside her poorly done surgically-enhanced joker face, but she wasn't a violent person. The last fight she'd been in was the third grade with a girl named Charlotte. Charlotte, a white girl, had told another girl that Simone's dad looked like the monkey Curious George from the book the class had to read. After Simone was done wearing Charlotte's butt out on the playground by the sandbox, Charlotte would never even say the word monkey again.

"How dare you," Simone said with disdain of her own. "You have the unmitigated gall to tell me, that I need to work while your selfish-ass is running around spreading my and my father's hard earned money like its going out of style.

"You mean my hard earned money," said Marjorie, hands on her wide hips. "You haven't the slightest clue to the shit I had to put up with."

Simone gave Marjorie a sideways look as if she was crazy.

Unapologetic, Marjorie said, "I not only had to play mother to your spoil-ass, acting like I actually give a fuck if you win this pageant or that you have the nicest dress for the many proms and homecomings. Chile please. If that wasn't enough, I also had to deal with your dear daddy's tiny-ass dick. That alone should be worth all the tea in China, having to fake orgasms and please myself for twelve, long years. That man's dick was smaller than a two year old baby's."

Before Simone had realized it, she'd smacked Marjorie so hard sparks came from her face. The skin — so tight from surgery — nearly ripped to pieces. Yet, the expression on her face never changed.

Simone had no idea what had come over her, but she wasted no time taking advantage of Marjorie's temporary shock. Simone cocked back as far as she could and blasted the witch one more time just because. It felt so good. One of Marjorie's fur slippers' heels wobbled, lost her balance, and busted her ass on the marble floor.

"You bitch." Marjorie threw the broken shoe at her. The shoe hit Simone on the arm, a nail, where the heel should've been, breaking the skin and drawing blood.

The site of the blood trickling from her forearm, coupled with everything else built up inside of her, was more than she could take. Besides, she thought, it was time to teach this hag a gotdamn lesson.

She had had enough.

Marjorie was trying to stand up on shaky legs when Simone caught her with a well-timed uppercut. The punch tagged Marjorie's chin like an unwanted tattoo. Marjorie fell back to the floor, kicking, and started squeezing. She wanted to choke some manners into Marjorie, and if Marjorie croaked in the process, so be it. Then maybe all her father's things would revert back to her anyway.

Marjorie's eyes looked for an escape. She made a funny noise — "Ooukkk-o-wokkk," that sounded like she was sucking a dick. In a morbid sort a way, it was noise to Simone's ears.

In third grade, when Simone was tearing a mud hole in Charlotte's little racist-ass, it had taken two teachers to get Simone off of her that was one of the reasons, Simone had avoided fighting from that point on, she'd nearly killed Charlotte.

It wasn't until Marjorie's face had turned a funny — not ha-ha funny, but oh my God funny — shade of purple before realizing what she was doing. Marjorie's eyes, where the irises had been, were now white.

Simone stopped squeezing, releasing the grip from Marjorie's neck.

Desperate for air, Marjorie inhaled — as hard as she could — before blowing out the lung-full of oxygen that kept her alive. With her hand around attack, she took a few more precious breaths.

The second Marjorie had a breath to spare, she said, "Get out, bitch! Get the fuck out of my house, before I call the police."

Simone knew Marjorie wasn't bluffing about the police, "I wouldn't expect your no class wannabe-ass to do anything else, but call the police." Simone lured her back, opened the front door, and walked out of her father's house feeling better than she'd felt in a few months. Whoever coined the phrase, "Violence never solved anything," was wrong. So, so wrong. . . .

Simone was about to get into her car when she realized it was gone. In the driveway, in the exact spot she'd parked, was a Dodge Neon.

Oh, this hag has really lost her mind!

Simone stormed back into the house like Hurricane Katrina, nearly knocking the door off of its hinges doing so.

Marjorie had somehow managed to pull herself off the floor and was sitting in the high back chair leaning most of her upper body up down on her legs. Her head jerked up as the door open. Her eyes, looking as if she wished she'd locked the door.

"Where in the hell is my car, bitch?"

Unable to look Simone in the face, Marjorie said, "Your car is outside."

She put her hand on her hip and said, "I drive a fucking Mercedes and the only thing in the driveway is a gotdamn Neon."

Marjorie clutched a lamp. Simone figured Marjorie intended to use the lamp for a weapon, if she needed it. "You don't own shit. The title to that car, registration, license tags, they were all in Simon's name, which means I own it now," she spoke in a tone a little above a whisper, "all mine."

Simone wished she'd choked the bitch out when she had the chance. She probably could've beat the case if she had: self defense, crime of passion or temporary insanity. She'd learned about the different criminology defenses.

Marjorie, holding the lamp with one hand and fixing her hair with the other, got bolder by the second. "I'm the spirit of fairness, the title and the keys to the Neon are in the glove box. You have about ten more days to get it registered. Be grateful."

"Grateful?" Simone questioned.

Simone had no clue where the phone in Marjorie's hand came from. *She must have pulled it from her ass,* thought Simone. Marjorie dialed 9-1-1. She told Simone, "Now get the hell out of my house." Then into the phone, "Hello, police. I have an intruder inside my home."

Simone walked closer, leaned down, got right up in her face, close enough to smell the scotch on Marjorie's breathe. "Listen to me," she said. "No more Mrs. Nice Girl. You hear me? You better make sure every I is dotted and every motherfucking T is crossed. That you're papered up with every document you can forge because I promise you on my daddy's grave." Then she coughed up a mouth full of saliva and spit right in Marjorie's face, just because and said, "I'm coming for you."

7

As soon as Bunny pulled off from dropping Simone at the bank, her phone rang. The sound of the phone made her heart smile. The ring tone alerted her it was Spoe, the love of her life, she answered right away.

"Hey baby," she said.

"Everything okay?" he asked, wanting to genuinely make sure that Simone was good.

"I honestly, don't know," she sighed, "I'm really worried about her. I just dropped her to her car and she was to pieces."

"Naw, man," he said with concern and disbelief.

"Yup, I'm leaving from over here by the bank and this place looks like Hurricane Katrina went through here. They got blocks blocked off from the chase. It just doesn't make any sense, the damage that was done."

"That bad, huh?"

"Yup. And I'm not even talking about the damage done to Mone."

"I thought she was good."

"I mean she good on the outside, but fucked up on the inside."

"What could we do to help, babe. Anything?"

"I offered her some bread."

"That's what's up, you know whatever we can do. We got her."

"Yeah, I know we do, but you know she was on that goody-two-shoes, I don't want to take no dirty money–type shit."

"Yeah, but shit if she need help. And if she not going back to the bank and her peoples cut her off. Fuck she gone do?" Spoe asked then gave his two cents. "Trust me that shit going to change real quick."

"I don't know," Bunny said, then changed the subject. "So what's up with you?"

"Everything good, I'm just making sure you and the fam okay that's it."

"Well, I'm about to swing by Me-Ma's and give this money to Tallhya and tell her to give it to Simone. She may take help from Tallhya rather than me."

"Good idea baby."

"Well, when you get done, let's go to that restaurant I told you about, and catch a movie or something."

"You know I'm always up for quality time with the love of my life," she said to him.

She could feel his blushing through the phone.

"I can't wait."

"Babe, that's right." She snapped her finger, just remembering what she needed to run by Spoe. "I keep forgetting to ask you, do you think we could hook Gina up with Tariq?"

Spoe sucked his teeth, "Baby, that's a negative. He's out there right now, doing him," he hesitated. Spoe wanted to make sure that he chose his words wisely, "And you know I don't really think that's wise for us to turn Gina onto him no way. Shit, that's a disaster waiting to happen."

"Damn baby, you act like my girl chopped liver or something."

"Come on now baby, I'm not saying that but, you already know. He's not ready. He's on a different time than I am. Maybe a couple years from now, he might be ready. But right now, he just having fun enjoying the single life."

"Maybe he needs to settle down," she snapped back, almost taking his analysis of Tariq personal. "Because that life he's living ain't really cool babes."

"By who standards tho'?" he asked, not being intimidated by her views, and then added, "Different strokes for different folks."

"You need to talk to your boy, before one of them chicks catch him slipping and next thing you know, he's in love with a stripper," she started harmonizing that song by T-Pain.

Spoe chuckled at Bunny. She was right, but it was still none of their business.

Tariq was his business partner and a hell of one, too. They went back a long way, he had principles, heart, and was trained to go at any time. But most importantly just like Spoe, he was about that money.

"You crazy babe, but I'm going to run Gina past him when I talked to him and see what he says," he said, just to shut Bunny up. He knew she'd keep going on and on like the Energizer Bunny.

"Can you call him now, please? Because I been told Gina I was going to see what's up."

"I'm waiting on him to call me back, I've been calling him all morning and he ain't hit me back yet."

"Sure you don't . . . the way y'all keep tabs on each other, I can't believe you don't know his exact location."

Spoe knew Tariq was probably up to his normal, but at the end of the day, that was his life and he was a grown man, free to do whatever it is he wanted. But still, Spoe needed him to call him back.

"It's almost noon, and I don't know where the hell that nigga at."

Tariq walked out of the bathroom in the nude, over to where his clothes lay. He had stayed far past his normal time, he thought as he picked up his Polo boxer shorts and slipped into them.

Damn, time flies, he thought to himself.

Tariq glanced over to the king-sized bed, where the gorgeous Tiffany Rolay laid on top of his white high thread count sheets. The sleeping beauty looked too peaceful to be awakened. Tariq took his time and lotion down his body, and then slipped into his clothes from the night before. As he bent over to tie his Air Jordan sneakers, the sun shined through the windows, which provided him the light he needed to tie his shoes.

Tariq walked over to the bed and sat down and ran his finger over Tiffany's soft succulent lips. Her eyes popped open immediately as if she had just dozed off and didn't know where she was. A smile appeared on her lips when she saw Tariq's face, "Good morning handsome! How long have you been up? And why you didn't wake me?" she asked.

"You were in here, knocked the fuck out." He rubbed his hands over her exposed nipple.

"A bitch was tired! Dealing wit ya ass, on your wanna fuck all night, shit. You beat this pussy up, boo-boo! I'm soooo sore down there," she said in a girlish giggle.

"You know how I get down, you knew what it was hitting for when you got up here last night." He smiled and stoked his own ego, "Major dick-slinging shorty. Now get dat ass up and let's figure out some breakfast."

"Waffle House?" she questioned.

He nodded with a smile. "That's cool."

"A'ight then give me a few minutes. I need to get in the shower and get myself together first."

"Well hurry up then, I ain't got all day, my stomach growlin' like a motherfucker."

"Damn! Okaaaa. Work with me, baby! Perfecting this beauty don't come in seconds, but I'm going to make it quick tho, just for you," she replied then flicked the sheet off her body and rolled out the bed.

Tiffany stood up and looked back at him, making eye contact with him placing a seductive smile on her face. She walked away swinging her hips, making her backside move like water.

He smiled at her.

Tiffany was a getting money kind of chick. Though Tariq met her when she first started working at Treats Gentleman's Club, in his mind she wasn't the average kind of stripper that he was used to. He couldn't put his finger on it, but it was just something different about Tiffany. Normally he didn't even try to rationalize why the dancers he usually hooked danced in the first place. But Tiffany . . . he couldn't figure out why a woman of her caliber would even let men play in her pussy for a few dollars.

Not only was she drop dead gorgeous; she was cultured. The beauty spoke fluent Spanish, French, and some Arabic. Taking away the fact that she took her clothes off for a living, Tiffany was definitely a classy chick, owning the best of everything.

Outside of the club, she wore only the best and latest of gear. Her purses were fierce, high fashion in the first degree, Hermes, Chanel, Louis, just to name a few. But her shoe game could give even Imelda Marcos a run for her money.

Tiffany drove a Mercedes SL-65, limited edition and had a plush condo. Tariq had only stopped by one time just to see how she was living, but it was against his princi-pals to stay or visit any chick. He would never get caught slipping at the hands of a female. It would be irony at its best.

Anytime that Tiffany had Tariq's attention for more than a few days, her swag and sex appeal had to be on point. And everything about her was everything that he liked . . . almost too good to be true.

Tiffany stopped at the bathroom door and bent over and touched the floor, then looked through both of her legs at him and started dancing as if she was in the club, giving him a show. That lasted for a couple of minutes and then she continued into the bathroom.

Tariq laid back and placed his hands behind his head, staring up at the ceiling.

Damn! Tiff bad as a muthafucker. She got that good ole snappa, too. I would hit that shit again, but naw I got shit to do in an hour. Matter of fact, fuck that breakfast, I'ma grab something on my way. Damn, this bitch stay soakin' the fuckin' sheets with that wet-ass pussy she got squirting everywhere. He thought to himself as he looked down at the wet spot in the middle of the bed.

Twenty-five minutes later, Tiffany walked back into the bedroom wrapped in a huge white towel and smiled at Tariq. "You want some more of this good, good?" she cooed.

"We gotta get outta here, Tiff, later on we could go at it. I got some shit to take care of."

"So, we going to spend some time again later on?" she coyly asked with a smile and a raised eyebrow. Tiffany was excited because she liked spending time with him.

He let out a smirk, "You sound surprised?" he teased knowing why, but wanted to hear her take on what was going on.

"Well, you know the word around the club is . . ." she said, wondering if she should tell him or not.

"I'm listening . . ." he shot back interested in hearing what the scoop was on the stripper-mill.

"You know me and you done got real cool, like real, real cool over the past couple of weeks."

"And we have," he had to agree.

"Well, the word is you kind of like variety. You are like a different woman literally every day kind of dude."

"Is that right?"

Tiffany gave him a playful hit, "You already know. The girls in the club like you because you got a big dick and you will give them a couple a dollars, but they know you not fucking the same chick two days in a row."

"That sounds about right."

"So the fact that we've been fucking, and chilling. Seems like I broke the record."

"You have," he couldn't deny it.

"I must be special," she got ahead of herself trying her hand.

"You are cool, mad cool. But I know your life, and your work, so I already know what it is."

"Meaning?" she asked.

"Meaning you got niggas and you do your thing, which I don't knock. After all I know where I met you at."

"I don't have to have them, like that. In fact, I like you. I really do." She looked in his face and said, "I really like you and I want us to be cooler than cool."

"Really?" he questioned.

"Seriously," Tiffany looked in his eyes.

"Time will tell, you just gotta prove it."

"And I will."

"Okay," he dryly said.

"Look, I know you think oh, I'm a dollar ho. About my money and all that."

"I do and I don't knock you for that."

"But, it's definitely more to me than meets the eye."

"I don't doubt that either."

112

She tried to pour her heart out to him. "It's more to me than just being on a pole and I hope you take the time to get to know me."

"Maybe I will. But for now, we are going to take it one day at a time. Every day seems like I learn something new about you, but no expectations okay."

"Okay, baby. I won't apply any pressure. But just know that I like you a lot and really feel like we could do anything."

"I feel ya," he said rubbing on her, then changing the subject. "Well, I gotta take a rain check on that breakfast," he said as her phone rang. "And seems like you need to get caught up on returning your calls, because they trying to catch up with you.... Duty calls."

Tiffany let out a laugh, "Rain check given! Just know I do collect on those." She smiled as she checked her phone.

"Oh, that's how it is, huh?" Tariq smirked.

"That's right boo. But in other news, I got some news that you could use...."

"Go ahead, shoot."

"Well, I know how you and ya man Spoe get down."

"What you talking about?" he asked as if he was surprised.

"Come on now, the whole Richmond

knows. . . ."

Prying into his business, immediately messed up his vibe, "You say that to say what?"

"Well, I know this nigga that's papered up like a muthafucker. Real flashy dude, not in the dope game, but got this other crazy scam going on. I been to his mini mansion before and it's nice as shit. . . . I mean really nice, no corners cut."

"Get to the point, Tiff!" Tariq sat up and looked into her eyes.

"Well, one day I was with him and he was talkin' all this big money shit. I'm like whatever nigga," she said to Tariq, " 'cause you know, working in the club, niggas always trying to impress you. So, you know I heard it all before though."

"Ummm-ha."

"So, I'm like bye boy! And was like I'm not fronting. Then he got up and walked out the room and came back seconds later with two big duffle bags. He dumped them out onto his bed."

Tariq didn't blink or utter a word. He just listened and she had his attention.

"Reek, my eyes got big as shit. I ain't never seen that much money in my life. Ole boy, looked at me and laughed, then he had the nerve to say. I bet you ain't never seen two million in cash before did you?"

"Had you?"

"I'd seen a lot of money. But I was lost for words because I wasn't expecting him to have two million. I thought he was all flash."

"Is that right?"

"Yes," she said making complete eye contact with him.

"He put the money back into the bags and took them back out the room, then came back like a minute later. I'm telling' you Reek, it's a sweet lick," she said with excitement.

"So he showed you two million in cash, huh? How you know it was two million?"

"Reek, listen to me Boo, it was definitely a couple of million, trust me . . ."

"Damn, a couple of mill, huh?"

"Yeah, it'll be like taking a bottle from a baby. I got everything mapped out, too."

"Who is this nigga?"

"His name is Marky, I think he's originally from New York somewhere though."

"So, this shit that sweet, huh," he said with a raised eyebrow.

"Hell yeah it's definitely sweet! I wouldn't bullshit Tariq. He got it like that! He probably has more than that where that comes from. I'ma be with him tonight, we suppose to be going to dinner then go somewhere else . . ."

"So, you got his address and everything?"

"Yes! He lives by himself, too. I'm telling you it'll be the sweetest lick you ever had!"

"How you know the bread still there, if it was in duffle bags. It's probably was being bagged up to go somewhere."

"No, he always got a bag of money laying around. Plus he had it in the car and was bringing it into the house. And I'm meeting up with him at the house tonight before we go out. I will lurk and see if the bag is still there."

"You say he going be wit you tonight, huh?"

"Yeah! Y'all could go take the money and meet me later with my cut . . . You know I'm about my money, too," she said jokingly, but was dead serious.

"So how much is ya cut suppose to be?"

"Two hundred and fifty thousand, that's all I want."

He smiled.

She quickly said, "You could always give me more if you want."

"A'ight, let me holla at my man. I'ma get back wit' you and let you know if we wit' it. Make sure you answer yo' phone when I call. This shit better be just how you said it was, don't waste my fucking time . . ."

"Cut it out Reek, its all good boo!" she said then straddled his lap. She kissed his neck deeply and moved her center in a circular motion. He pulled back and looked up in her eyes.

"Where is the money?"

She hesitated, "Now that I don't know for sure. I'm going to try to roam and see if it's in eyesight. If not, y'all are going to have to find it. I do know that it have to be upstairs somewhere judging by how fast he went and got it, then when he took it back."

"A'ight get dressed, I gotta go."

Tiffany climbed off his lap and picked her dress and six inch Chanel heels up off the floor. She slipped into her bodycon painted on dress then buckled the heels around her ankles. Tiffany picked up her Chanel bag, and headed for the door, tossing her red lace panties to him.

Tariq caught them and then placed them in her purse. He trailed a little behind her and watched her bottom bounce underneath the dress. Shaking his head, she had one of the sexiest walks he had ever seen. He got up and walked out the room behind her gripping two handfuls of her butt in the process.

Outside the sun greeted them with a warm kiss on her cheek. The smell of the fresh cut grass and clean air was pleasing to their nostrils. Tariq opened and closed the door to Tiffany's red coupe.

Tariq walked over to his four door Massareti and got inside. He pushed the button and started the engine, and watched as Tiffany drove away.

Biggie Smalls, "Ready to Die," blared through the speakers. Tariq bobbed his head and rapped along with the legend then drove away. The night with Tiffany was definitely memorable but it was now time for him to get back to his money. He turned the music down, leaned over and checked his phone. There were a few missed calls from Spoe. He and Spoe were supposed to be meeting, which was on point because he had an earful for him anyway.

"What it do my nigga?" Spoe answered. No hello. No hi. Just simply to the point.

"Mannnnn. . . . Got some shit for you."

"Where you at?" Spoe asked.

"We still meeting?"

"For sure. Just meet me at ya place now bro, I got some heavy, heavy news to drop on you my man!"

"Okay, that's cool. Be there in fifteen."

"I'm like a good forty-five minutes away, we need to really vibe on some real get money shit."

"Say no more . . ."

Tariq turned the music up and rolled his windows down, allowing the morning air to rush in. Tariq smiled like a snaggle-toothed child inside as he thought about the information that Tiff had given him.

Damn, a million dollars. . . . Two major licks in one month? Damn, life good. Shit, I hope that shit's there. I'm glad I started stickin' dick to Tiff. Who'd knew it would turn into a million dollar lick in the morning, damn, he thought.

The thought alone of the two million dollar lick had him on cloud nine as he pushed the pedal to the metal of his German Engineering to get to his destination to map out the plan. For the next forty minutes, all he could think of was his million-dollar cut and how Tiffany may have turned out to be an asset after all. She brought his two favorite things to the table; pussy and money. There was no doubt she was slowly becoming the woman of his dreams.

8

"Oh, Lord Jesus," Me-Ma screamed, "say it ain't so." Me-Ma sat at the kitchen table stunned. "This can't be right," she said, while reading the newspaper as she always did every single morning.

"What is it, Me-Ma?" Tallhya asked as she came running into the kitchen.

"Now, baby," she looked up. Giving Tallhya one eye and The Richmond Times Dispatch her other. "Walter don't have no kids do he, baby?"

"No," Tallhya said. "But in about two years we are planning on to have one."

"You sure about that?" Me-Ma asked, with a raised eyebrow.

"Yes. Why you ask Me-Ma? And you got that look on your face, like something smells fishy."

Me-Ma didn't respond, instead she started reading from the newspaper aloud.

Waltima Joy Ways-Walker graced the Earth for only 90 short days before she died in her parents' arms at The Memorial Regional Hospital, in Richmond, VA on September 16, 2014. After struggling with inoperable congenital heart disease, she passed gently into the arms of Jesus.

Waltima is the daughter of Walter Walker and Pamela Ways of College Place. She was the answer to their prayers, and they waited for her birth with joyful expectation of their first baby girl. During her brief visit on Earth, she enjoyed listening to music, cuddling with soft toys, and being held close by her parents and grandparents. She was loved by all who met her and will be greatly missed. Her presence on Earth will be missed.

A Memorial Service will be held Saturday, September 20, 2014 at 1:00 p.m. at Mimms Funeral Home, with a reception following at the Military Retirees Hall. Memorial contributions may be left at the Metropolitan Savings and Loan National Bank on behalf of: Memorial Fund of Waltima Joy Walker-Ways.

Waltima is survived by her loving parents Walter Walker and Pamela Ways of 1742 College Road, Henrico, VA and a host of other family and friends.

Tallhya was silent for a long minute. Then she said, "Read it again, please," and Me-Ma did.

"It has got to be another Walter Walker. This person can't be him, Walter Walker is such a common name," was her only explanation. "I mean surely if he had a child, he would've told me."

"You think so?"

"For sure, Me-Ma! I'm sure we would've been so deeply involved in that child's life. I know this isn't him," she confidently said.

"I would like to believe that but I don't put nothing past these men folks," Me-Ma said. "They will have a double life and not think nothing of it. They will act like it's no big deal. Trust me that's what Joe did to me."

"That was Grandpa, but that's not Walter!"

"That's what I thought. But that no-good-butt Joe was a good husband to me and a greater father to your mother, but still tipped off with the woman," she shook her head and continued, "with the woman down the street. Them sons of witches don't have no self control when it come to their peters." Me-Ma rolled her eyes and this whole thing was bringing back flashbacks of what happened with her husband. "Lord up in heaven, Jesus fix this. Just say it ain't so. I swear I don't want this for you. I want it to be a perfect explanation for this."

"Let me just call and get to the bottom of this."

Me-Ma took her reading glasses off.

"What can make my soul whole," she sung, because in the pit of her stomach, she knew that shit was about to hit the fan, "nothing but the blood of Jesus."

Tallhya reached for her phone and dialed Walter's number.

"Oh, Precious . . . is the flow. That can make me white as snow," Me-Ma sung. "No other fount I know . . . nothing, but the blood of Jeeeesus!"

"Hey," he answered in a voice over a whisper. No, hey you. No, hey baby. No, hey boo. No, hey beautiful. Just simple, hey . . . and before she could address him, he quickly shut her down, "I'm in this place handling some important arrangements. I will call you back in a few," before she could agree to anything, she heard the dial tone.

No, baby, are you all right? No, nothing. Tears came to her eyes.

"What happened, baby?" Me-Ma asked.

"Nothing," she took a deep breath. "He just said, he was about to make some arrangements, and he was going to call me back."

"I pray that there has to be a perfectly good explanation," Me-Ma said, shaking her head.

Tallhya was at a lost for words. She knew that there had to be a logical explanation, but then the, *what ifs* started to run through her mind. *What if it was true?*

Just when the tears started to form in her eyes, that's when she heard the door open and a loud voice call out. "Tallhya . . . Tallll-hya. Tallllhhhh . . ."

It was Bunny. She took in another deep breath, and she got herself together before answering her sister, "Yesssss. I'm in the kitchen."

"Chile, do you have to be so loud."

An energetic Bunny walked into the kitchen and gave Me-Ma a kiss on the cheek. "You look pretty as always Me-Ma."

"Thank you baby, and where you going looking like you about to work on Second Street?" she questioned Bunny's thigh high tall Tom Ford boots.

"Me-Ma these boots the style." It was the same answer she always gave to her grandmother. Me-Ma never approved of anything that Bunny wore.

"Says who?" Me-Ma asked.

Bunny didn't take her grandmother's comments to heart, it was normal for her to disapprove of the way she dressed. "All the fashion magazines, Me-Ma," she said with an easy smile.

"Well, they going to hell and you need to stop looking at those books getting ideas how you should dress. Didn't I teach all you girls to be individuals and be yourself. You don't have to follow the trends, baby."

"I know. I know, Me-Ma. I just look at them to give me some ideas."

"Lord have Mercy on you and those people," Me-Ma summed it all up.

"Well, I stopped by because we got a family crisis."

"You right about that." Me-Ma had to agree with Bunny and said, "My Lord, up in Heaven sure be on time."

"Me-Ma what you talking about?" Bunny put her hand on her hip waiting for the dig her grandmother was about to say.

"Bunny, Lord knows I'm glad to see you, and I know Tallhya is, too." She threw her hands up, "You know God navigated that hundred-thousand-dollar big car over here because He knew that your sister needed you."

"I know," she agreed. "That's why I came over here, because I wanted to give Tallhya this money," she went into her Louis bag, and pulled out a stack of cash wrapped in a rubber band, "to give to Simone. She's going to need it, but you know she's not going to take it from me."

"I'm not talking about that sister . . . I'm talking about this sister."

Bunny eyes shifted to Tallhya and asked, "T, what's going on?"

"Nothing . . ."

"Hog-mogg and bull crap! You a lie," Me-Ma put her two cents in it, and looked in the refrigerator and got a bottle of water out and handed it to her. "Chile, if I wasn't a saved woman, I would tell you go ahead and pull that bottle of liquor out of your purse, because your sister need a drink."

"Me-Ma what you talking about?" Bunny asked trying to conceal her grin.

"Chile, you know I know everything. I don't miss anything. But right now, you need to carry your sister up there to that Mimms Funeral Home and get to the bottom of this bull crap that's going on."

"Mimms? Who died?"

"I don't need to go up there," Tallhya said.

"And yes the heck you do," Me-Ma said as firm as she knew how.

"Can somebody tell me who died?" Bunny

asked again wanting to know what's going on.

"Your brother-in-law baby died."

"Huh?" Bunny turned up her face, confused.

"Walter got a baby, I saw it in the obituaries and it said devoted father."

"Oh hell, naw!"

"Watch yo' mouth," Me-Ma pointed to Bunny and then filled her in, "this chile don't believe do-do stink, even when it's in the middle of the floor."

"Girl, get your shoes, let's go up there and get down to the bottom of it."

"No, I'm going to wait until he get here. I know it's a perfectly good explanation, right?"

"Get your shoes now, and I'm not going to tell you no more," Bunny demanded. "If it's nothing to it, then it's nothing, but we going to see what's up," Bunny walked out of the kitchen.

"Baby, I know sometimes the truth hurts. Now we hope Walter would not have had a baby and didn't share that bundle of joy with us, but at the same time, if he did. You need to know."

"You are right Me-Ma. I do need to know. And even so, I need to pay my respects. Because any part of him, is a part of me."

Me-Ma thought how big of Tallhya that was, "You right, baby."

Tallhya got up and went and got her shoes and jacket.

Just then Bunny returned with a small Gucci overnight bag from the trunk of her car. She went into the bathroom and returned quickly transformed. She was wearing a Pink sweat suit and some Air Jordans to match. She put her Indique straight long hair into a tight neat ponytail and went into the front room. "Come on, I'm ready."

"We not going to start no trouble."

"No, we are going to get to the bottom of it."

"Then why you had to change?"

"Because I stay ready so I don't have to get ready. And no we not going to start nothing, but make no mistake about it, if a ho get out of pocket, I'm going to handle it."

"Come on Bunny, we not going for that," Tallhya said knowing how her sister will fight at the drop of a dime.

"Look Bunny, give him time to explain, let Tallhya deal with it, don't you go over there turning up. You hear me?"

"I'm not," Bunny said as innocent as she knew how. "We are good as long as they don't cause no static . . . it won't be none if they don't start none."

"Chile, Lord Mercy," Me-Ma said as she was reaching for the phone.

"Who are you calling?" Tallhya asked.

"Your brother, you need to carry him over there with y'all, too." Even though the sisters had all accepted Ginger's lifestyle, Me-Ma refused to acknowledge it and after all these years, still referred to Ginger as a boy. She loved him no matter what, but she prayed every day that God would "fix" her grandson.

"Me-Ma, please, don't call Ginger, I don't want her in my business."

"Chile please," Me-Ma looked Tallhya in the face. "If this man has lied to us, it's all of our business."

"No, we good. I got it handled. Remember we not going over there to start no commotion." Then as Tallhya walked out the door to head for the car, Bunny double backed to the kitchen and handed Me-Ma a stack of money. "In case you gotta bail us out," she said. Then burst out into laughter, even though she was dead serious, and headed out the door.

Another ring, Ginger answered.

"Hello, Gene. Meet yo' sisters over at the Mimms Funeral Home. It's a little situation that they are going to get to the bottom of.

And baby" — she paused — "don't wear none of them stilettos over there neither. If you catch my drift."

Me-Ma grabbed her Bible, and started to pray. Lord knows all parties involved was going to surely need it.

9

Lately, it's been hard times. I'm talking
about the financial side

Since the Neon that Marjorie had swapped
Simone's Benz out for didn't have a MP-3
jack, or even a CD player, Simone was
forced to listen to Anthony Hamilton la-
ment about his imaginary money problems
on the car's radio.

It's ruff out there, son
And they say when it rains it pours, (rain,
    rain)
Raining at my door . . .

Simone liked Anthony Hamilton and all,
God knows the brother could blow the soul
back into a corpse, but the song was killing
her vibe, which was already on life support
as it was. She turned the volume down on
the radio then switched lanes, getting off
Interstate 64 at the next exit.

She pulled into the parking lot of a place she knew all too well. Beyond the parking lot was three shiny silver stainless steel warehouses. Each 50,000 square foot structure filled with cow shit. The company, S&T Topsoil, belonged to her father, Simon and his best friend Tommy.

At the beginning of every summer, when Simone was growing up, Simon used to bring her to work with him every day, for the two weeks at the beginning of the summer before camp started and at the end of the summer when it had ended.

Simone hated it with a passion, but her father loved their time together. There was nothing Simon loved more than his only daughter and his company. Not even his wife, Marjorie, but he wouldn't ever admit that to her. Although their summers at S&T Top Soil ended years ago, Simone still used to drop by, from time to time, and bring her father lunch. But this was the first time she'd stepped foot at the grounds since he died six months ago.

It felt strange . . . really strange.

As she made her way to the main building, she remembered something that her father use to always say to her, "Inhale," he would say to her, and when she acted like she did, he would say, "deeper than that.

You have to really inhale." And then he would say, "You smell that? What does it smell like?"

Simone always responded the same way, "It smells like do-do."

Then Simon would always say the same thing, with the biggest smile, "Naw baby, that's what it smells like when you are stinking rich."

It was something about that smile and the man had the prettiest set of white teeth. When she got to be older and understood politics. She'd joke with her father about how he should've been a politician. Not only did he have a way with words, he could make anybody believe anything.

Back then she had taken those moments with her father for granted. Now, memories were all she had of him. And she couldn't get enough of them.

Simone made a right off "memory lane," and stepped into the main warehouse. The heels of her Giuseppe booties click clacked on the vinyl flooring as she made her way to a small, but efficient office off to the right.

The lady inside the office looked up from her computer and greeted Simone with a Queen-sized smile, waving her inside of the cramped office. "Girl," Beverly gushed, jumping up to hug Simone, "where have you been?"

The last time they'd seen each other was during Simon's funeral. Beverly stepped back and, with a pair of Never-Miss-A-Thing hazel eyes studied Simone from top to bottom. Then said, "What is it?"

Most women were born with a sixth sense, but when it came to reading people, Beverly's gift was extraterrestrial. "I'm fine," Simone lied, spun around so that Beverly could take a 360-degree of her outfit. Some jeans and fitted sweater and her gold Giuseppe ankle boots, "Don't I look it?"

Although she was like family, Simone didn't want to burden Beverly with her personal problems. But Beverly wasn't fooled. "You look like you could model in Vogue Magazine. You are damn sure prettier than all those makeup wearing skeletons in designer clothes, and ten times smarter," she said, changing the subject. If Simone wanted to confide in her about anything, she would do so when she was ready.

And Beverly wasn't just being nice with her compliments. Simone was fine by anybody's standards.

"I just hope my skin looks as good as yours does when I'm your age, girl."

Bev rolled her eyes, like she was offended

by the remark. "I know you didn't just call me old to my face?" At forty-nine, Beverly could still pass for a young thirty something. Simone said, "You are only as old as you feel."

"Then I feel like your slightly older sister."

A smiling Simone said, "Cool, I've always wanted an older sister."

"Slightly older," corrected Beverly.

"That's what I meant," Simone smiled at Beverly. Talking to her always warmed her heart, and she knew the woman was genuine, too.

After breezing through a couple prerequisite chit chatting, Simone asked if Tommy was in the building. "I need to speak with him if he's not too busy."

The inquiry took Beverly by surprise. She'd worked for the company for a long time. Simone's father had hired her, personally, two weeks after she had graduated from Reynolds Community College, twenty-two years ago. So, she felt qualified when she said, "Tommy's a damn fool." She looked off into space and then lightly shook her head before speaking. "As good of a man as your father was — may he rest in peace — but for the life of me, I could not figure out why he went into business with a scoundrel like Tommy. The man's a pompous pig, with the morals of a housefly."

Simone couldn't help but to burst out laughing. Beverly had definitely hit the hammer on the nail, but it had totally caught her off guard.

Beverly's face twisted into a frown, like she'd just tasted something bitter or spoiled and needed to spit it out right away. "Yeah, he's here," she finally said.

"Tell me how you really feel," Simone teased. Although she knew Beverly as the kind always spoke the gospel. Simone often wondered about the answer to the million-dollar question herself, what had her father seen in Tommy that no one else did?

Using the wireless intercom system, Beverly informed Tommy that he had a visitor.

Simone walked to the back of the warehouse, toward where the offices were located. Tommy's was next to her father's old office.

Seeing the door, with her father's name **SIMON GUNN** still stenciled on the outside, stirred up more memories for her. She tried to shove them away. It was hard, but she reminded herself that she needed to take care of what she'd come for before imploding to an emotional wreck.

"What can I do for you, Princess?" Tommy was standing in the doorway of his office grinning. "Come on in," he said.

Inside, Tommy's office was enormous; large enough to harbor a midsize aircraft. He hugged her, and whispered his condolences before offering her a seat.

The embrace was tighter and lasted longer than Simone thought was appropriate. Respectfully she pulled away.

"I need to talk to you about my daddy's will."

They took a seat on a coffee colored leather sofa. "Anything I can do for you Princess. You know good and well, all you have to do is ask? You know without a doubt, Uncle Tommy got ya!" He placed his hand on her leg and lightly squeezed her knee, pretending as if it was an act of comfort instead of perverted lust.

Since the day Simone had turned eighteen, whenever her father wasn't looking, Tommy gazed at her with lust in his eyes. Her skin felt the heat emanating from his touch. Simone could take care of herself then, and, as a grown woman she could take care of herself now. Simone casually brushed Tommy's hand from her knee, replacing it with her Louis tote bag. She took out a small notebook and pen.

"I would like to ask you a few questions," she said, looking him square in the eyes, "about my father's estate."

Tommy straightened up, putting his sleaze-ball tendencies in check, at least temporarily. "Me and Simon were business partners. Your father's estate . . . well, that's more like *personal* business. And your Simon's personal business was exactly that, as far as I was concerned."

If Tommy had been connected to a bullshit detector the meter would have put someone's eye out, Simone thought looking into his eyes.

"Give me break." Simone chided. "You and my father were friends since middle school. Five decades. I'm not asking you who he lost his virginity to, a question I'm somehow willing to bet that you could surely answer without much contemplation. I'm simply asking you about his will. Anything you can tell me would be helpful and appreciated."

Nothing!

Dead silence.

Tick-tock . . . Tick-tock . . .

The only sound in the room came from an antique Howard Miller Grandfather Clock.

"Tommy?" She urged, bordering on exasperation from his reluctance to help.

Tommy had a straight face and didn't say a word.

Simon once told his daughter that Tommy lost a ton of money playing poker because of a tell: he scratched the bridge of his nose every time he bluffed. "I don't know what you want me to say," Tommy was fidgeting. "If I knew anything about a will I would have let you know. Why wouldn't I?"

Good question, Simone thought to herself.

"I don't know anything," he rubbed his nose, and she knew he was lying. "But why are you so anxious about this will."

"Listen, I'm sure you've heard. Marjorie has everything and I have nothing. Not even a job anymore. The bank I started at yesterday was robbed."

"Not what I saw on the news?"

"Yes."

Hearing her problems somehow prompted him to spark up the conversation. "Did they offer y'all any kind of compensation?"

"No! Nothing! And Marjorie took my Benz from me under my nose."

"She did?" he questioned, not really seeming too surprised.

"Yes," Simone said, starting to feel the emotions coming.

"Well, you know that. You know she's going to milk the situation for everything she can get."

"I know."

"Now you know all the papers we had here, everything went to Marjorie by law."

"Yeah, I know."

"I wish it was different," he said, then dropped his head, "imp . . . imp . . . imp . . . it's a crying shame all the bad luck and the hard time you having."

"I will be okay," she said about to break down. "I know I will. I'm smart and strong. I will figure out something," she was trying to convince herself, but felt so weak. She couldn't stop the tears from coming.

Tommy took her in his arms and allowed her to let loose her tears. "It's going to be okay. Uncle Tommy got you."

"Thank you, I appreciate you," she managed to get out in between tears.

"I appreciate you, too. Don't worry I'm going to help you," he said then before she knew it, he had his hand in between her legs and started tongue kissing her.

She pulled away, "What are you doing?"

"What you mean? Just relax, I got you," he grabbed her and pushed her back on the couch.

"Stop! No! You fucking better not. Let me go," she screamed as she pounded on his chest.

He was still on top of her and his penis was hard as a rock.

Out of the corner of her eye, she saw a letter thick glass heavy frame on the table in front of the sofa. She reached for it and slugged it on top of his head.

"Oh, shit," he said, out loud and let loose of his tight grip he had on her. Simone was up and out heading for the door as fast as she could, when he grabbed her arm and looked her in the eyes, "Listen, as tough as things are for you," he said as sincere as he knew how. "You gone need a sugar daddy, if so, I will definitely take care of you. Will pick up where your father left off, if you wanna share some of that sweet, juicy pussy with me," he said then stuck out his tongue and made it motion as if he was pleasuring her vagina with his tongue.

Simone snatched her arm from him, "Go to hell. You disgusting pervert."

He palmed her butt with a smack and smiled, "This the real world baby. Real shit like that exists."

"Fuck you, Tommy," she stormed down the hall.

"If you ever need me, Uncle Tommy will be right here for you."

10

The loud pungent smell of weed assaulted his nose as soon as Tariq walked across the doorsill. He closed and locked the door behind him.

"Damn . . . my nigga, I got a contact and you ain't even took it out yet."

"This that shit . . . man this that shit."

"What's the heavy news you gotta lay on me man?"

"I just stumbled across a sting for two million dollars, nigga!"

"Foooo . . . real!" Spoe asked.

"Yeah, for real! When you known me to play fuckin' games about this paper?"

"Never." Spoe shook his head. "Run that shit down to me. Make that shit like music to my ears," Spoe put his hands up to his ears. "Two mill, huh? Who gave you the line on this hit?" Spoe needed details because he was the one that usually put the plans together, but he was happy that Tariq had come up with a job for them. He'd still have to check everything out though.

"Tiff did . . ." Tariq said with pride. Proud that he had a chick that could help them get money and not just spend it.

"Tiff? Who the fuck is Tiff?"

"You know the li'l bad bitch, drive the SL, I been fuckin' wit', Tiffany man."

"Oh, one of the ones from the strip club."

Tariq, nodded, "A'ight with that shit now." He laughed at himself. "You trying to say something 'cause all my joints come from the strip club."

"And the same strip club at that, but I won't even mention that shit tho."

Tariq laughed at himself. "I'm ridiculous, but the stripper hoes love me tho'."

"Naw, nigga don't get that shit twisted. They like that money. That's what their loyalty is to. Speaking of which, let's get back to it."

"And I don't never forget it . . . where their loyalty lie."

"Don't ever forget and when you get ready for a nice chick, Bunny got somebody for you."

"I bet sis do, and I'ma let you know the word."

"No doubt," Spoe said and then asked, "Yo, so is shorty official?"

"Yeah Spoe, I wouldn't be here right now if I felt for a second that she wasn't official. I been fuckin' wit' her for a couple of weeks now."

"That's a long time for you," Spoe had to admit.

Tariq smiled, "Real talk." He agreed and then got back to the topic at hand. "The bitch couldn't make no shit up like that. She knows how we get down Spoe! She got the address and everything. The nigga got a mini mansion, too."

"A'ight if you fuck with shawty and trust her word then lets move on it. We are going to have to leave that nigga in there stinking, too. Ain't much to it, we got to leave him, when its that much paper on the line, he won't take that shit sitting down, Reek."

"He ain't gone be in there and shawty want two-fifty for her cut, too."

Without hesitation, Spoe agreed. "She could get that! Shit, she putting us on to two free mill. Good job Reek, that's a nice sting sho-nuff," Spoe said, commending Tariq on bringing a lick to the table. Spoe was always the one who tended to stumble across their jobs. But all the excitement aside, Spoe had to ask. "But what the fuck you mean he ain't gone be there?"

"She going out with him and while she

144

out with him, we going to shoot to the crib and take care of what we got to do."

"My nigga, you know I'm not on that B&E type shit. Fuck all that sneaking around shit, Reek," Spoe said disappointed. "Man you know I like to be in control when we do shit this kind of shit, so it ain't no slip-ups."

"Man I know," Tariq agreed. "I just thought it was a good quick come up."

"But I'll go, my nigg," he said hesitantly, "for a million dollar profit, I'll go," he said again, more so trying to convince himself, of how he could sit back and chill, travel the world with Bunny. Then he spoke up again, this time more confidently, "A million fucking dollar, you got damn right I'm in. Then the two dapped and just like that. It was about to go down.

11

Bunny bent the corner almost on two wheels when she pulled up at the funeral home. Like a superhero she jumped out of the car, ready to solve her older sister's dilemma at hand.

"Bunny," Tallhya called out to her sister, who was hightailing it up the sidewalk of the funeral home. "Bunny! Hold on!" Tallhya hurried up and got out of the car to try to catch up with her sister. "Wait," she called out trailing behind Bunny.

Bunny finally got the hint, and decided to stop in her tracks. She huffed and looked at her overweight sister trying to move as fast as she could. "Well, hurry up then."

Tallhya had put a lot of pep in her step and finally caught up, "Look, we not here for you to act simple okay?" Tallhya had the most serious look on her face. She knew her sister all too well. What folks would never detect about Bunny, was that her looks were very deceiving. Behind every pair of mink eyelashes and red bottomed Christian Louboutin, there was more than meets the eye. In every Celine bags, Bunny packed a sharp blade and had no problem slicing someone up like a piece of deli meet or slapping the cowboy shit out of anybody she felt warranted it in regard to herself or anybody she loved.

"Well, they better not start none, it won't be none," Bunny said in a serious stance.

Tallhya grabbed her sister's arm and looked in her eyes, "As I said, before we left the house, and in the car on the way over here, we are not here to start nothing. I don't want to cause drama or be disrespectful in no kind of way. I only want to get to the bottom of this. That's it, that's all," she gave a hard, firm stare and made direct eye contact with her sister. "I'm not fucking bullshitting okay."

Bunny saw the passion mixed with the hurt in her sister's eyes, sucked her teeth and then nodded, "Look sis, I'm only here to support you nothing, else."

"I know, you are," Tallhya said, "and I'm glad you are here by my side."

"That's what sisters are for, right," Bunny reminded Tallhya.

"I know it sounds crazy, but if I see the

baby. I will know if it's his or not."

"Yeah, it does." Bunny put her arm around her sister and they walked side by side. "Sounds like some shit, that Me-Ma would say." She chuckled a bit, trying to shine a bring light onto the situation, "You know how them old folks are with babies." She transformed her voice into an old lady's, "Bring 'em here so I can see 'em," she tried to make jokes of the situation as they continued their stride to the entrance.

They entered into the quiet, morbid funeral home. "Yes, may I help you," the spooky looking man, dressed in all black startled them.

"Yes, we are here to see the baby," Bunny said making eye contact with him.

"Yes, this way."

The funeral director showed them into the viewing room, where the closed small casket rested on a pedestal. The whole ambience of the room was so gloomy. The second they saw the huge portrait on a tall gold easel of the innocent little baby girl in a beautiful white satin dress, the two were immediately sorrowful.

"This is so horrible," Bunny said, dropping her head. Just the sight of the picture of the little baby girl there with so much life in her eyes, made Bunny forget all about the intended turn-up and why she had come there in the first place. "It's just," she searched for the word, "it's just so, so, so tragic."

Tallhya couldn't help herself. She stared at the little girl with tears in her eyes, she was astonished at how she was looking at the spitting image of Walter. Even though Walter had a lot of explaining to do, he had stepped out on her and had a baby with another woman, and never uttered a word of the birth of such a little blessing to her. How could he keep such a thing from her? Indeed, it was a deep betrayal, but Tallhya still felt awful that Walter had lost his daughter. And in a strange way, at that very moment all Tallhya wanted to do was be there for Walter. Though she had not met her step-daughter, Waltima, she was sure that knowing her was an amazing experience and loosing the bundle of joy, a child had to be a heart wrenching pain.

Tears had also filled her eyes, and Bunny was at a loss for words. "Are you okay?" Bunny put her arm around Tallhya and nothing had to be spoken. The embrace simply said it all. "I'm here for you."

The two felt this chilling energy in the room, and on that note, "Not trying to be sympathetic, but this is so depressing. And can we just get the fuck outta here." Bunny had enough.

"Yes, I'm ready," Tallhya had agreed.

The funeral director, held a box of tissues in front of them and then Bunny asked, "Is it possible that I could have a card with the address, please I'd like to send some flowers," as she took a few tissues for herself and handed a couple to her sister.

"No problem," the well dressed man said, going into the inside of his pocket pulling out a metal card case and handing her what she asked for.

"Thank you. And you guys really did a good job," Bunny complimented.

"Thank you so much," he said with a smile. "This is our calling." Then he directed them to the hall, to the guest book, and instructed them, "Be sure to sign the book. I'm sure the family would like to know that you were here. That you came by and paid your respects."

"No thanks," Tallhya said.

Bunny interjected, "I think I will," and she did and proceeded to sign the guest book. The second Bunny had crossed her T's and put the pen down, that's when the door popped open. And two ladies entered.

"Yes, may I help you?" the one lady asked, as she looked the two sisters up and down.

"We came here to pay our respects, so sorry for your loss," Tallhya said as heartfelt as she could.

"And . . . who are you?" the woman asked, with a raised eyebrow.

A small chuckle came out, "Kimmy, calm down! I know who she is." A tall confident, slim lady with body to die for pointed to Tallhya, then came in closer and spoke up.

The beauty had taken on more curves than a racecar driver. Tallhya looked at her. She was drop dead gorgeous, in a rich kind of way. The woman was together in every sense of the word. Her long twenty-six-inch weave stopped at the small of her back and was straight like Pocahontas. "No worries, I know who she is," she pointed at Tallhya in a snobbish kind of way.

"Really?" Bunny questioned, returning the snooty look.

Tallhya only stared at the woman. She was stunned at how fabulous and gorgeous she was.

"That's Natalia . . . the mark," she boldly said, "you know the fat, pathetic, desperate, no self-esteem having, stupid bitch that Walter be juicing for all the money and shit. Remember, I told you all about her." She laughed as if it was the funniest thing she had ever thought about. "That's her," she

151

managed to get out somehow as hilarious as it was to her.

Bunny wasn't having it and had to bring the bewitching laughter to a halt. The cheap version of Pocahontas' laughs quickly turned to cries for help. Before anyone knew it, Bunny had hit her like Foreman hit Frazier, sent her straight to the floor and out cold immediately turning the lights out in Pocahontas' head.

"Guess that will teach a no-good, two bit ho to laugh at my motherfucking sister." Bunny was pissed and could not resist kicking her a few times the whole time, looking at Kimmy wishing to God Almighty that she would attempt to do anything. "Yes, I'm going to kick this bitch while she down," she boldly said.

The funeral director was in mere shock. All he kept saying was, "Oh, my! Oh, my!" He was reaching for the phone. Bunny saw him coming for the cordless phone resting on the charger. That was the only thing that made her stop kicking Pocahontas. She reached for the jack and tossed it across the room. "Oh, nigga you gone call the police on me? You bitch-ass nigga you?" She looked into his eyes and he thought he saw Lucifer himself in front of him.

"Just leave then, please just leave," he

cried out.

"Please sis, please let's leave," Tallhya said, knowing that Bunny would tear that place up. "Let's just go," Tallhya pleaded with tears in her eyes to her sister.

"Okay," she said, and followed after her. Before focusing her attention on Kimmy and with fury in her eyes, she said, "Tell that motherfucker Walter, he can get it, too. He's a real coward-ass nigga. And as for this bitch, right here," she pointed down at her. "Kindly let her know, I ain't finished with her. Let that ho know, that since she was down for the get down that every time I see her scheming-ass I'm going to wear her ass out."

Bunny kicked Pocahontas, who was still lying on the floor looking like she was a permanent resident of la-la land. Bunny added, "And that's a promise on her dead baby soul." She headed for the door.

The second Bunny's back was to Kimmy; she jumped on her back and started pulling her hair. This sent Bunny into a rage. Like she was a feather, Bunny swung her around and body slammed her.

Still unsure if the funeral director was trying to break up the fight or get a few licks in, but at this point nobody gave a damn. When Ginger slipped into the building and

153

all she saw was this man on her sister, she picked up a folding chair that was in the hallway, tucked away and busted him over his backside. "Fuck off my sister, nigga."

At that point, it was about to get popping, but Tallhya knew they needed to leave there. "Come on y'all. Let's get the fuck out of here."

And the siblings fled the scene like a shern-head jacked up off of embalming fluid.

12

Tears streamed down Simone's face as she drove the shitbox car from the company her dad once owned and not because she was sad. Nah, she had already been sad for way too long as far as she was concerned. The sadness she'd experienced after her father passed had threatened to swallow her whole, but she had gotten to the other side. She realized that instead of the full on pity party she had been throwing herself she needed to be grateful for the time she had with him, the one where all her needs were met and all the life lessons he had taught her. Hell, she knew up close and personal what it looked like not to have the kind of daddy that she had been blessed to have for twenty-nine years. Two of her three sisters both had trifling deadbeat good for nothing fathers while Ginger didn't have any idea which of too many to count sexual partners had deposited the lucky sperm into their mother that helped create her. Simone had a daddy, dedicated to her and able to express his love every single day so no matter what she would always have those memories to fall back on. And right now all she could wonder about is, *What would my daddy do?*

"Dammit," she spat out to no one in particular at all the emotions spilling over inside of her. So, no these were not tears of pity or sadness, these were the full expression of the rage bubbling up inside of her at the plain ole bullshit that had gone down today. If her father knew the dirty dog way Marjorie treated her after he was gone he would have thrown her out on her ass a long time ago. So come hell or high water Simone planned to make that happen, she didn't know when, but as long as her ass could breathe out a breath that conniving bitch would pay for the way she disrespected her father's wishes to have his only child taken care of. With God as her witness she swore the shit was going down.

And the way Tommy, that fake-ass buster had pretended to be her father's best friend all those years when in reality he was a disgusting predator waiting to pounce on her; his no good ass would get his too she thought as she sat there adding up the offenses. Before she could begin to formulate a plan Simone glanced down at her phone ringing and recognized the same number she'd seen earlier, but hadn't wanted to answer it. Of course the first thing that came to mind that is was one of her favorite stores calling to inform her of a sale or an item she had been waiting on. Being a spoiled daddy's girl, Simone had developed an over the top shopping addiction that had been funded by her daddy. Every high-end clothing store within driving distance of Richmond had her number on speed dial just in case any of her favorite designers' new lines came in. She ticked off her favorites; Louis, Celine, Balenciaga, Chloé, and Prada. Damn, she was missing her former life. She sure did her share of damage, but those days were gone and she wasn't in the mood to explain to the overeager sales woman on the other end why she hadn't seen her black card running through their credit machines lately.

I need to ignore that damn call, she thought, but since the person was being persistent she'd have to take out her frustration on them. Simone pulled her car over and answered the call. This no Bluetooth having bullshit was already wrecking her goddam nerves on top of everything else.

"Hello," she snapped into the receiver for once not using the perfect ladylike telephone manners her daddy had taught to her. The person on the other end of the phone took a deep breath before responding probably trying to figure out how to deal with the big no that they were guaranteed to hear.

"I'm looking for Simone Banks," the woman on the other end spoke. "Is this her?"

"Yes, this is her," Simone answered, desperate to get off the phone and back to her thoughts. She had a lot of things to figure out the first being how the hell she'd get another job which was only a close second to when would she put her whole entire foot up Marjorie's ass.

"This is Dr. Cohen's office. The doctor would like to see you at your earliest convenience, today if possible. It's about your test results." Upon hearing that Simone felt all the blood rush out of her body. That particular statement usually led to the person hearing it to begin playing out worst-case scenarios in their head except this wasn't the first time she'd experienced those words. Her father's doctor started with those words and just a short time later his daughter stood over his wet gravesite as his casket was lowered into the hole in the ground, as buckets of rain fell blending with the outpouring of Simone's own grief.

"I'm sorry what did you just say?" Simone's voice lost all the anger and attitude as she tried to process exactly what this woman was saying. By the time she hung up and redirected her car in the direction of the doctor's office downtown Simone had gone through an entirely different barrage of emotions. She had all but forgotten the mandatory physical she had recently taken that had been required for her new job at the bank. They'd done a battery of tests including taking blood samples, but nothing she'd given a second thought to especially since she was so young and healthy. Her immediate reaction was to reach for the phone to call her father and to have him meet her at the doctor's office, just a knee-jerk reaction before reality came flooding back knocking her into the present. She could have called Bunny, but as much as she loved her sister, the thought of her no-patience-ass in the doctor's office did not comfort her. Plus, all she had to do was call one sister to have them tell the other two and her grandmother. And the last thing she wanted was to worry her Me-Ma. Her grandmother would immediately remind her to pray and throw this whole medical thing up to God. Then, Me-Ma would insist on meeting her at the office with any available prayer warrior she could bring from church. So in the end she decided to go alone figuring how bad could it be? Just thinking about how her grandmother would handle the situation reminded her to pray. Her grandmother's feet didn't hit the floor in the morning without a prayer on her lips and of all her grandchildren Simone was the only one who maintained a close relationship to God. "Trust in the Lord for He knows your every need," Simone whispered to herself as she entered the office.

"The doctor will see you," the pert bottle blonde stood up and led her into one of the three patient waiting rooms. "You can put this on," she smiled as she handed over a paper hospital gown. Simone took it and had just tied the strings in the back when the door opened. Dr. Cohen, the internist entered in his white lab coat and carrying a clipboard like something out of a medical drama. Simone had been coming for her once a year checkup since she'd turned eighteen with another one of the doctors at the practice who had recently retired which is why she didn't really know this man about to deliver some hopefully not so bad news.

"Did you come alone?" his brow furrowed

as he approached staring from her to the papers attached to his clipboard.

"Uh, yeah. I was already in the car when I got the call. I figured how bad could it be?" Simone joked as she waited to see if the doctor would join in. He didn't. Now her ass was starting to really worry.

"I'm sorry to have to tell you this but your blood tests indicate an abnormality that points to ovarian cancer." He couldn't help but look glum giving this kind of diagnosis to someone so young.

Wait, what? Cancer? I have cancer? My father just died from cancer. These thoughts swirled in her head as she began to dry heave, her mouth feeling dry. She stood up pacing the room like a caged rat except it wasn't the room it had more to do with wanting to get out of her own skin.

"Ms. Banks, right now we need to administer a scan and some other tests to determine if you have cancer. But just know that with early treatment this form of cancer has an 80 percent chance of full recovery."

She didn't respond because Simone couldn't hear anything it all sounded like the Charlie Brown character, "waaa waaaaa waaaaa waaaa," his words were incoherent. Everything started to spin around her and she felt as if she were in some kind of tunnel. She could barely make out the nurse who rushed in helping the doctor pick her up and place her on the examining table. When Simone came to, the nurse was fanning her and rubbing ice on her face.

"What. . . . what happened?" she sputtered although to both the doctor and nurse it appeared obvious.

"You fainted." Both the doctor and the nurse answered. "We tried calling the name of next of kin on your contact forms and the number was disconnected." Simone sat there staring into space trying to connect when another woman entered with a glass of water and handed it to her. Simone began to drink, but what she really wanted to do was to throw the glass against a wall and smash it. She wanted to scream, but she couldn't. The doctor, nurse, and assistant fawned over her like a newborn baby. They checked her blood pressure, took her temperature and even offered to get her some food. Simone might have been hungry when she got there, but the news of her health crisis dissolved any hunger she may have had. All she wanted was to get home and to have Me-Ma tell her that God would take care of everything. That she would be all right.

"We need to schedule this surgery as soon

as possible," Dr. Cohen spoke in a calm manner.

"Surgery?"

"Yes, it's a standard laparoscopy so that I can take a look and find out what's going on. We will biopsy a small piece and that will tell us everything we need to know." He'd been doing this for a long time, but ever since the practice switched from regular to concierge medicine the care they showed was something out of the 50's. Hell, they even had an advertisement in the waiting room announcing that they now made house calls. Simone wished she were sitting in her Me-Ma's house with her family around her as she heard this news.

"Do you still have the same insurance? Blue Cross PPO?" the receptionist asked in a syrupy sweet way, same as the cashiers of all her favorite couture shops when they knew you were about to sign for some really expensive shit as Simone scheduled her laparoscopy. Simone didn't even have her wallet. The cop hadn't given it back yet and if it wasn't for the fact that bitch of a step monster had canceled all of her credit cards she might have insisted he release her wallet.

"Yes," she responded grateful that at least she could count on something in her life still working even if the reason sucked.

"Let me just get approval for the procedure," she smiled up at Simone, dialed a number and waited. The Bach piano concerto playing took Simone back to all the years of piano lessons that helped her to play this piece perfectly. She even played it at her first beauty competition and of course she won. Simon had been so proud, his attention lasered in on his baby girl up on that big stage making the other girls fade like background players next to her.

The receptionist had to call her name three times to get Simone's attention she had gotten so carried away with the memories of the music that for a moment she had forgotten where she was or why.

"Ms. Banks, the insurance company informed us that your policy is no longer current." The woman's thin lips pursed together, her eyes fixed on Simone as she moved her chair back. The receptionist had experienced the mercurial nature of patients and she didn't want to be caught off guard.

"I'm sorry, that's impossible," Simone sputtered and then had to listen as the woman patiently explained that because she was no longer an employee at her father's company they had canceled her coverage. With everything going on she hadn't bothered to check her medical insurance status. She hadn't held a real job at her father's company in years, but every two weeks he cut her a check that kept her flush, able to pursue her interests. And she had a three-month trial before she became permanent at the bank, which came with full benefits. But she hadn't planned to go back to the bank after the stick up.

By the time they hustled her out of there, she had received a list of free clinics mostly in neighborhoods that just a few months ago, she wouldn't have even dared to drive through. She couldn't bear to look directly into the doctor's face when she left. She felt so embarrassed that her insurance was no longer valid that she grabbed her keys, clutched the paperwork she had been given and walked back to her crappy car. She didn't know what the hell she was going to do, but she knew not to play around with her diagnosis. Her father had refused to go to the doctor for an annual check up no matter how much she prodded him over the years. Last year he began complaining of aches and pains and by the time Simone was able to convince him to see a doctor because he felt terrible, his prognosis was dire with doctors giving him less than a month to live.

"Seriously?" She fumed watching a meter maid affix a ticket on the windshield of her car. Simone picked up the ticket and threw it onto the ground giving the meter maid a hard stare just begging her to open her mouth because all of her manners were balled up in her fists ready to take someone down. But then she realized that the car wasn't in her name so she wouldn't get the ticket, the only silver lining in this shitshow of a day.

13

Me-Ma had too much energy to sit around waiting to hear what happened with her girls down at that funeral parlor so she did what she always did when worry got the best of her. She put on her blue dress with the white buttons that the girls had gotten, for Mother's Day, at some store called Anne Klein. As much as she liked to act like she didn't care about creature comforts, the soft silk and linen fabric against her skin made her feel like the Queen mother. The blue Taryn Rose shoes that Tallhya insisted she allow her to purchase with her "monthly lottery winnings" certainly made walking the six blocks to the church much easier. She would have been happy with the ortho-pedic shoes her doctor prescribed, but the girls took one look at the "prison warden" shoes and refused to allow her to wear them. Those damn shoes conveniently went missing and no matter how much she yelled they all feigned innocence. Because these were handmade by a doctor without looking like she was an old fart she gave in and let them purchase them for her.

"Save your money," her words fell on deaf ears as usual when one of her girls made up their mind to do anything same as it had been with their stubborn mother Deidra. She had to cover her eyes at the register as the saleswoman rang up the purchase. Me-Ma had lived her entire life being frugal, making the little she and her husband earned stretch to feed every mouth and she never compromised with the 10 percent she placed in the collection basket. She knew a lot of people called themselves children of the Lord except when it came to adding their weekly 10 percent. Then they were heathens and charlatans who pretended at serving God.

"Lord, I hope that wasn't Walter," Me-Ma talked to herself thinking about that newspaper lying on the kitchen table although she already knew in her heart that it was. She had a strong sense about things like this.

Tell the truth, shame the devil, tell a lie, shame yourself, she thought as she finished getting dressed for an impromptu visit with the pastor. Congregation enrollment dropped to their pre 1990's numbers down since the former pastor died and too many of the older members accused Pastor Street of appearing too secular to be a real man of God in his flashy clothes, but Me-Ma had taken the time and gotten to know him. She had been able to convince some of the old members to stay and to trust that the Lord had brought this man to serve them. Me-Ma had a lot of power in that church, and Cassius took full advantage of it by appointing himself as the son she never had. Oh, he certainly played on her need to be close to God, doting on her whenever she was around, making himself available whenever she needed him. But lately she was coming to the church a lot more often just to talk with him and that was getting in the way of his extracurriculars, but what could he do.

Unbeknownst to her, she helped raise money for all his pet projects shaming people into opening their pocketbooks and checkbooks for every little thing he swore would improve the church. Cassius even talked Me-Ma into helping to raise money so that they could televise their Sunday services on some second rate cable channel.

"If one person in pain or shame watches my sermon and because of it finds his way to the Lord then isn't that what God would want?" Me-Ma contributed generously and convinced the elders that the pastor needed to be given a clothing budget since he shouldn't be responsible for his television wardrobe. She cursed the small-minded people who talked about Pastor behind his back. She'd told many of the parishioners that she would pray for them, but coming from Me-Ma it sounded closer to a curse. She figured out that all the Reverend needed to solidify his image was to find himself a wife, settle down to stop the tongues from wagging on the fools running their mouths. She couldn't understand why her grandbaby Simone didn't return the pastor's interest.

"Hello Mrs. Banks," two young girls in those shamelessly tight fitting spandex pants that exposed all their business waved at her as she passed. Boy did she want to stop and tell those fast children to go put some loose clothes on and to start acting like they had some good sense. "Lord, give me strength," she said to herself realizing that they were barely out of diapers and here they were looking like straight up hootchies shaking their butts at grown-ass men as they passed.

"Girl, come on over here with alla that ass," one of the older boys shouted as the girls passed. And of course they stopped. Took everything Me-Ma had not to send those children back to their homes to put on something appropriate, but today, she had more pressing matters to take care of. Without meaning to she'd become the neighborhood matriarch, and as much as she protested she wound up accepting the position since very few adults had the good sense to "pick up after their dogs" as was the old school expression. These were lay down with dogs and get up with fleas kinds of people and Me-Ma hated it. Any good therapist would say that her incessant need to help others stemmed from her inability to aid her own child, but she didn't come from that self-help generation where therapy was even an option so for her she was simply being a good neighbor.

Things had gotten so confusing the past few days that Me-Ma needed to make sure she had her house in order and not just her religious one. First this thing with Simone, nearly getting killed at the bank and now this thing with Walter reminded her of the need to get her affairs in order and what better person to help her to do that than her pastor. She took all her legal paperwork out of the safe box in the closet her husband had purchased all those years ago when their daughter was still a little girl and stuffed them in her purse.

"We've come this far by faith, leaning on the Lord . . ." one of her favorite hymns played over the speaker system in the church as she entered. The calming music immediately put Me-Ma at peace.

"Trusting in His Holy Word, he never failed me yet . . ." she found herself getting carried by the spiritual singing along at the top of her voice. God didn't care that she couldn't carry a tune a half a block all he knew was her heart was pure. Clapping hands interrupted her singing and Me-Ma turned to see Pastor Cassius Street coming down the aisle of the sanctuary. He was the kind of man who dressed to impress so unless his look was a hundred percent together, he didn't leave his house. His flamboyant purple suit shimmered as he moved up the aisle toward her, the off white collar shirt, pastel yellow, cream and purple lace tie, and ivory snakeskin shoes had taken him hours of careful planning to match so perfectly, but he would have never admitted to that.

"Pastor, you look so handsome," Me-Ma gushed at how put together he was, not like these other men his age who still had their asses hanging out their pants. He reminded her of the way men got all decked out in the 70's. He threw his arms around her hugging her tightly. This little lady may have gotten on his nerves with all of her suggestions and demands, but she sure did help to keep the coffers filled. Cassius had never met a compliment that he didn't like so he made a point to give Mrs. Banks extra attention for hers.

"I love that dress. Designer?" he asked staring at her appreciatively. The whole point of him being a clothes whore had to do with the way people responded to his efforts, the more effusive they were the higher up on the patron food chain they went. Well, that and the size and frequency of their donations also contributed to the kinds of time he allocated for them on his schedule. She also had that fine as wine granddaughter who would give the right look as First Lady.

"How is my favorite member? And how is your granddaughter recovering after yesterday's ordeal?" he reached for her hand and held onto it as he stared into her eyes, all sincerity. Cassius made sure to come off as a concerned pastor. He knew better than to let her know that he had a more personal interest in her granddaughter. He fashioned himself a religious Kanye West in need of a woman of equal measure to help raise his profile and Simone was fine enough and educated enough to do just that and she had that big ole hump on her backside which would even make the men jealous and the women envious.

"Pastor I need help with some important legal matters."

"Absolutely Mrs. Banks. Anything for you."

"I don't have an updated will that includes my granddaughters. Who knows how long the good Lord will see fit to keep me here on earth?" The walk over to the church had worn down her body. The pastor led her over to a pew and the two sat down.

"I am here for you. How can I help you?"

"Will you be my witness?" She leaned close to him. "There are so many things I need to address. I figured if I ran them past you maybe you'd help me come to terms with what I need to do." Cassius nodded his head up and down a little too eagerly, but Me-Ma had been so busy thinking about the heaviness of her decisions that she hadn't been paying attention.

"Absolutely, but first let us pray," the pastor bowed his head and started to preach the gospel. Me-Ma lowered her head, her thoughts traveling to gratitude at having formed such a close bond with this man of God.

". . . Humble yourselves therefore under the mighty hand of God, that he may exalt you in due time." By the time Cassius released Me-Ma's hand she had gotten real clarity on what to do next.

"Now you know I love all my granddaughters equally, but the one that I trust the most to handle my business is Simone. She's levelheaded and fair enough to look after the others and she's also the oldest and most educated so I trust she will handle the legal matters and paperwork more appropriately than my other granddaughters.

"What about your daughter?"

"There is no way I could leave anything to her. Those girls would be homeless and hungry if she got her hands on my property or what little insurance money I have. Lord forgive me for saying this, but my daughter is the reason I need to put things in writing. My husband and I drew up these papers so long ago that Deidra is still the sole heir to everything and that would be a disaster . . ." Just as Me-Ma started to finish the door burst open and standing there owning a pissed off expression wrapped in a fuchsia colored dress a good size too small with all her woman parts bursting out stood Katrina. The pastor's face clouded over as she strutted to where they were sitting, only to be replaced by a blank smile giving nothing away.

"Pastor, may I speak to you?" she said through clenched teeth her anger so strong she didn't use the good sense God had given her to have manners and acknowledge his visitor.

"Why hello Katrina," Me-Ma jumped in thinking that if this hot-n-tot thought she could be rude on her watch she had mistaken kindness for weakness and was about to get herself old schooled. The arch of Katrina's right eyebrow raised up 'cause this wasn't a sister used to dealing with other women in any capacity. In fact she usually dismissed females in the most rude and arrogant way. She had a body and an attitude made for men and men only so to have to give some ole biddy her attention fueled her annoyance at the pastor.

"Ms. Banks," she responded painting on a faux smile. Now Katrina's legendary bad attitude and temper weren't exactly wiped away, but she realized she needed to play her position if her goal was to become Mrs. Street and First Lady of the church and she couldn't have anything getting in the way of that. Her current position as part-time church bookkeeper made it so she didn't have much interaction with the members, but in her new role she'd have to at least pretend to like these people. Cassius stood up, always a gentleman and turned to face his visitor.

"Katrina, I am in the middle of something. I can call you later if you need to discuss the books," he offered trying to maintain professionalism, but she had an agenda and would not be deterred from it and she sure as hell wasn't playing second to this old biddy.

"Well, Pastor, excuse my interruption, but I needed to stop by and make sure that you were okay? When you failed to show up to the elaborate dinner I had prepared in your honor, the one you had confirmed earlier in the day I got worried." Her words may have been polite, but this bitch was two seconds from blowing. Well before Cassius could respond Me-Ma had grown too tired of this hussy's interruption to put up with another moment of her foolishness and responded for him.

"Ms. Katrina, our pastor was simply being too polite to tell you that he's not interested in whatever you are serving up tonight. Now, you need to get on out of here in that dress you done grown too big to wear and stop embarrassing yourself," Me-Ma said to a stunned Katrina. At first the fullness of what had just happened didn't register fully to her so she glanced from Cassius to Me-Ma before she had recovered enough to go ham about to pummel a senior citizen.

"He can tell me himself," she growled her right eye twitching that this old woman had the nerve to be all up in her business. Katrina assumed that it had probably been too long since she remembered what a good dick felt like, but this old lady needed to stop cock blocking and get her ass to stepping. Katrina had no plans to go anywhere until she got exactly what she had come for. Now the pastor cursed himself for mixing business with pleasure because this hothead knew entirely too much about him.

"Please I need a moment," he asked Mrs. Banks as he jumped up and hustled ole girl out of the sanctuary and into the hallway where they could have some privacy. Even from inside the office where she sat, Me-Ma, could hear the litany of curse words streaming out of Katrina's mouth and rolled her eyes at the foolishness. Lord she wished these girls could have just a little dignity which made her think about her daughter, Deidra who had called the other day to announce she had taken up with some new underachiever and was living not too far.

Pretty is as pretty does, which was damn ugly as far as Me-Ma could see when it came to her only child. If that girl hadn't been so beautiful she might have had to develop other qualities like humility and kindness, none of which were evident in her. No matter how many times she had prayed up that child Deidra, being Deidra, consistently proved to be an utter disappointment to both God and to her mother.

"Sorry for that," Cassius announced as he hurried back to rejoin her. After his "conversation" with Katrina in the hallway, Cassius was anxious to wrap up with Me-Ma. Secretly he was hoping Mrs. Banks wouldn't notice his rush to get her out of there. Katrina had been gracious, well maybe that wasn't the right word, desperate enough to offer him a nooner.

"No problem. It gave me time to sit with the Lord."

"I need to say that as much as I appreciate your desire to add a religious component to this I really think that what you need is a good attorney."

"When my husband and I prepared this last paperwork Pastor Jasper helped us and then we got a notary to sign it. Gale who used to be a member here."

"And I would be honored to do that, but

these days there are so many stipulations and loopholes that unless you have a law degree you can't figure it out. Not to mention you need to make sure that your document is airtight from what you told me about your daughter. Do you know our member, Sister Lauryn Shelton? She's incredible and I have had the good fortune of sending some of our other parishioners to her and they all raved about her." He tried not to focus on his watch, but the blowjob he had been promised made it difficult to think about wills and deeds and whatever else Me-Ma wanted him to look at.

"I know that chile. Her grandmother was a good friend of mine before she passed."

"Great. Why don't you call her office and her secretary will be able to make an appointment for you." No sooner had the pastor finished with Me-Ma then he found himself with his pants down around his ankles and getting properly serviced by Katrina. There were two kinds of women who could be depended on to give the best blowjobs. Either big girls or ugly girls, it was almost like they had something to prove but whatever the case they made a lot of men happy. *Hell,* Cassius thought with a smirk they were the very reason somebody had coined the term, 'booty-call' in the first place 'cause a man of his stature couldn't be seen publicly with them.

The pastor couldn't help but to be grateful about the perks of the job, he had them coming and going and they were more concerned about protecting his reputation so he rarely had to worry about things getting out. Katrina on the other hand was the exception and she was already starting to be a problem. He was a little sad that he'd have to end things with her after he shot his load into her mouth. Damn. He loved anyone who could swallow like a professional.

14

"Thank you for shopping at Nordstrom's," said James, the cashier, a third year sophomore at VCU, who was working part-time for a few extra dollars to party and buy weed. But at that very moment, he would have traded a pound of the most exotic marijuana, for a taste of this exotic flower — gray eyes, long bone straight hair, stopping at the small of the back, right where the tightest designer Robin jeans in six inch Gucci stilettos standing at his register. Nordstrom's policy on pushing up on customers was clear; get caught, get fired.

But pussy trumped policy.

The cashier returned the credit card to the hottie along with two white shopping bags and a receipt for the purchase. "If you need any help with anyyyy . . . thing else, Ms. Green, I put my name and number on the back," James said, gesturing toward the receipt.

You bold, Ginger thought, of the cashier and then snickered to herself . . . *and cute.* But he also wasn't in her league and was clueless. Clueless about her name; the cloned credit card she'd used was in the name of Rebecca Green, and clueless about her sex. Or was he?

Ginger put the plastic away, next to the other four in her cross body Louis bag, and returned the cashier a beautiful smile. "I doubt if you'd be able to handle me," she said, with a raised eyebrow before stepping away toward the store's exit.

Ginger handed both of the bags to Deidra, who was waiting outside.

"Is everything in there?" she asked Ginger, who was the youngest of her children. She'd always been the one who'd tried the hardest to please their mother, even when Deidra didn't deserve a damn thing, which was most of the times, never. The woman was possibly one of the most selfish women on the planet. All she cared about was herself, and what was best for her; no one else, not her children, not her mother, just herself, Deidra.

Up until this afternoon, as usual, Ginger's plans had been to do her thing solo, especially when she tightened plastic. When doing dirt, she always preferred to do it alone.

This was her preference and her motto. Just in case, if something went wrong it was no one else to blame, just herself. And she didn't have to break bread with anyone, unless she chose to. But the main reason Ginger preferred to work "dolo," instead of with an accomplice it eliminated the stress of worrying about that person, down the line, ratting her out in order to get themselves out of a jam.

A crease wrinkled her plans after she got a call from her mother before leaving the house. For ten minutes Deidra prattled her way about a two-week vacation to the Caribbean, she and her "friend" were taking. Ginger hadn't bothered asking if her "friend" was a man or not, because Deidra only had male friends.

Before she knew it, Ginger had been persuaded into agreeing to not only get her some things, but to let Deidra accompany her to the mall.

Of all the siblings, Ginger was the one who yearned for Deidra's approval and jumped through hoops to get it. Deidra took advantage of it every chance that she got.

Ginger racked up more than twelve grand in charges on designer clothes, shoes and accessories, for Deidra to take on her trip — not including the two shopping bags from Nordstrom's — to five separate, bogus credit cards. "You going to be the best dressed bitch your age on the cruise," she said to her mother.

Just as Deidra was fixing to say something, a tall black man with chocolate complexion, walked by. Ginger thought he resembled Morris Chestnut. His chocolate drop eyes thoroughly inspected Ginger and Deidra's assets. And before keeping it moving, a smile creased his face, like a dog trespassing on a truck, with racks of prime cut filet mignon.

"Ahmen." Deidra cleared her throat, as if the way her dress clung to her bubble butt and toned legs. "Thanks for the compliment," she said to Ginger, referring to being the flyest bitch her age, on the trip. "But make no mistake about it," Deidra added, "Deidra Banks look good for *any* age."

Good genes ran in the Banks family: and Deidra was blessed with a closet full of them, enough to pass down to her four children, and plenty left over for herself. Something she proudly passed on to each of her children.

As they were leaving the outdoor style mall, Ginger put a little extra in the sway of her hips, matching Deidra's high-heeled strut bounce for bounce. Strangers mistook the two for sisters, clueless to just how clue-less they were.

"Where do you want to do lunch?" Ginger asked, enjoying their time together, some-thing that rarely, if ever happened when she was a child. "It's on me."

"Oh! My! God!" Deidra's heels anchored into the linoleum stopping her strut. Ginger followed the path of Deidra's eyes, which were locked on the bag in the window of the Louis Vuitton store. "Damn," said Deidra obsessing over the design of the purse. "That thing right there would look so good on my arm," she said.

Ginger looked at the small rectangle card, connected to a string, from the inside pocket of the purse, $3,200.

Which was a problem, five thousand was the limit on each of her cloned credit cards and she had already run through half of her limit on all of them. It was only one way to cop the bag that her mother wanted. She would have to use two cards, and even then, she would be well over the amount that she usually charged on any piece of stolen plas-tic.

It was no need in pushing her luck any-more today, "How about if I get it for you next week, Ma?"

"That's cool," Deidra said, sucking her

teeth, before pouring a cold glass of guilt. "Too bad the trip isn't next week, huh? I guess I could carry it when I get back from the trip, huh?"

Ginger had to fight to keep from laughing at her mother's shameless attempt to con her. When Ginger was young, the rare times Deidra was around, Ginger would do anything to make her happy and proud of her to make her want to spend more time with her. Back then, nothing Ginger did ever worked, but to this day, she never quit trying.

"Let me go in, and check the temperature." Meaning she wanted to get a feeling for the vibe inside the store. "If it looks right, I will swing it for you. No promises."

"Are you sure that's what you want to do?" Deidra asked as if it was all Ginger's idea. "Because I have no problem waiting."

"Is that right?" Ginger began walking away. "Then we can fall back and go get lunch then. I'm starving," she put her hand on her stomach.

"But since we are already here," Deidra said reaching out grabbing Ginger's arm, before she could take another step. "You might as well . . . aha . . . go ahead and check the temperature."

"Wait here." Ginger flipped her weave and

went inside the store.

In her mind, she swore that Deidra was the only person that Ginger ever cared about getting approval from. But it wasn't true. Ginger aspired to be rich. To look rich and be respected as a rich woman, everywhere she went. This was the reason why she hustled and played with the credit cards the way she did. Not because she needed to, but because she liked the feeling of compliments and the attention she got when she put on the clothes. Unlike Tallhya she didn't need a man to validate her. Her beautiful, extravagant "things" never failed her.

The scent of the new Louis was intoxicating upon entrance to the store. The smell of richness was the aroma of the place. It reminded her of that new car smell, not that fake shit, the "car-scent" they try to peddle in the auto stores. This smell triggered something in Ginger's head, that made her remember how bad she wanted that new convertible Lexus in her life.

One day soon.

"May I help you with something?" The saleslady was an anorexic-looking chick with shockingly bright blond hair, which the roots let on, was so not her real color.

Besides Ginger, there were two other customers in the store, a couple who were being stalked by the only other salesperson looking for a sure commission.

Ginger instincts told her to fall back, and she'd planned to listen. So that she wouldn't look too crazy, before leaving, she asked to see one of the purses from behind the counter.

It was the same model as the one displayed in the store's window. The one her mother almost broke a heel and her neck trying to stop to get a better look at.

Olive Oyl flipped her neon hair over her shoulder as if she had better things to do than her job.

This bitch is tripping, Ginger thought. Reluctantly, Olive Oyl fetched the bag, but not before bluntly informing Ginger of a small detail, "It's $4,100, and we don't have layaway and we never have sales or markdowns."

Ginger exhaled and thought to herself. *Girl, don't even let this definitely in need of a French-fry heifer fade you. Thank the bitch for her help and keep it moving.* But emotions got the better of her. "I'll take the matching wallet also," she firmly said. Then plucked two credit cards from her own Louis wallet. "I'm trying to earn frequent flyer miles so divide the total."

Ginger's eyes were glued on Olive Oyl as

eyes were fixed on the two credit cards in her hand as she was trying hard not to shit a brick. "I'm going to have to see some identification, 'Mrs.,' " another quick glance at the plastic then back to Ginger, "Rebecca Paige."

She smirked then added, "Not mine, but it's the store's policy."

I'm sure it is, Ginger thought. Since the surge of online shopping, stores rarely asked for ID anymore to confirm credit card purposes. All that was needed was the card number, which Ginger had memorized.

Olive Oyl was being a smart alek, and hating, either that, or was hipped to game. *All in all, she better be happy that she's getting this damn commission.*

Negative thoughts was a cancer, Ginger shook the negativity out of her space and into space. She dug into her wallet and found the ID that matched the fake card. The same dude that had hooked her up with the plastic, one of her friends with benefits, had supplied her with a complimentary ID. Doug told her, better to have it and not need it then to need it and not have it.

She smiled, thinking of Doug's words in her ears. That's why she fucked with Doug; he was smart and great in bed. Ginger passed Olive Oyl the fake driver's license that Doug insisted that she take with her. Olive Oyl checked the creds. After seeing the headshot of Ginger smiling for the camera above the name Rebecca Paige, she reluctantly swiped the Visa and American Express, splitting the price of the purchase, on the two cards just as Ginger had asked.

"Thank you Darling." Bag in hand, Ginger showed the raggedy bitch her back and sashayed out of the store.

Without breaking stride, she nodded a quote, "lets go," to Deidra. It wasn't until she was inside of Ginger's six year-old Honda, with engine running, did Ginger start to relax. Even then, she still felt a little uneasy, which was odd for her. Usually it was an adrenaline rush, but not today.

"Lets go to Ruth Chris," oblivious to Ginger's anxiety, "I got a taste for one of their juicy tender steaks."

The mall was behind them. The Honda headed east on 64. On the radio August Alsina's, "If I Make it Home," played.

Ginger turned up the volume. Being as if they were at the club, three strobes of light bounced off the dashboard. "What the fuc—"

Woop! Woop!

Police.

■ ■ ■ ■

9:00 p.m.

"Ringgggg . . ." Spoe and Bunny's house phone rung, which was a surprise because it almost never did.

The two old friends sat on the couch looking at each other knowing damn well that it couldn't possibly be the call that they were waiting for, but nevertheless Spoe got up to answer it. He looked at the caller ID and it read: UNKNOWN.

"Hello," he said into the receiver.

The automated recording immediately, starting talking, "You have a prepaid call from," there was a brief pause and then Ginger spoke her name, prompting Spoe to call out Bunny's name, "Ayo Bunny! Babe!"

Then the recording sprung back into action, "From the Henrico County Jail. Please hang up to decline, or press zero to accept."

Spoe couldn't press the zero quick enough to accept the call.

"Hello," Ginger, said.

"Yo," Spoe said, "the fuck?"

"They knocked me off coming out of the Louis store." Ginger was about to give Spoe the details, when Spoe cut her off.

192

"How much the bail?" Spoe asked as Bunny walked up and he said, "It's Ginger, she down Henrico."

"The magistrate ain't give me no bail," Ginger informed Spoe.

"Don't worry, the judge gone give you one in the morning. Hold your head and Bunny gone be there to get you," Spoe promised then handed Bunny the phone.

Bunny took the phone out of Spoe's hand, "Bitch, what the hell happened?"

Spoe corrected Bunny quick, "Don't ask her that on 'em phones. You know 'em people listening right?"

Bunny nodded to Spoe, agreeing and then she spoke into the phone to Ginger, "I'm going to be there in the a.m. to get you. Okay. So hang in there," and in Me-Ma's voice, "joy going to come in the morning."

Bunny could tell that her last comment marking their grandmother managed to put a slight smile on Ginger's face.

The rest of the evening went by at a snail's pace for Bunny thinking about Ginger as well as Spoe and Tariq waiting for Tiffany to finally call.

"Man this shit is whack, you know we not use this. Waiting around for a call to move," Spoe was right. He was one of those people that he like ritual, he was organic and believed that's how things should be. Not forced but should come when he felt it in his gut. With his balls and heart out of the equation, that was a lot of the reason he was so successful at what he did, he always trusted his instinct.

"Man she going to call soon," Tariq trying to assure his friend since third grade as he was a little concerned about the awkward silence between the two of them.

Spoe began to think to himself, how he hated breaking his routine of doing things, but then he thought about his cut of the million dollars that could be in his safe tomorrow.

Just then the phone rung, a smile covered a relieved Tariq's face, as he answered quickly the second he saw the caller ID revealing Tiffany's number.

"Yeah, beautiful," he said as he winked and smiled at Spoe. There was no doubt that he was trying to convince his childhood friend that he really wasn't sprung out on Tiffany as he was. Tariq put the call on speakerphone so Spoe could be privy to the info she had. She let out the address and that was the green light to proceed with their plan.

Spoe went into the bedroom for a quick change into his work clothes, and went over to the bed where Bunny was stretched out watching television, and laid on top of her.

He blessed her with a long passionate kiss, "We just got the call."

"You sure this Tiffany bitch is okay?" she questioned.

"Yes, I guess, Tariq said he bet his life on it," Spoe said.

"He better and hers, too. Hope that bitch value hers cause if she ain't on the up and up, I'm going to deal with her myself," Bunny promised.

Spoe knew that Bunny meant business. His wifey was extremely territorial. He knew that she didn't like the fact that he had to depend on any other woman besides her, for anything. Spoe wasn't going to even entertain the treacherous thoughts of what Bunny would do to Tiffany if the information she gave wasn't on the up and up.

"Well, that girl is all about her money, and she want her cut."

"Seems like it," Bunny agreed.

"Why you say that?" Spoe questioned Bunny as if she knew something that he didn't.

"I looked at her Instagram page and I saw her."

Spoe kissed his wifey-boo again. "You something else," he said not even surprised that Bunny knew everything, including the girl last eye exam, there was to know about Tiffany.

"Hand me that phone on the night table," she said to him. He did and she started showing Spoe Tiffany's pictures she had posted on her page.

"You don't be playing do you?"

"Nope not when it comes to my man, I don't. Nope not about mines."

He kissed her again, "I love you woman, and you know that!"

"Yes! And know that I love you more," she kissed him back and embraced him tight. Then asked, "I just wish you could stay here in my arms all night."

"Me too baby, but duty calls. Gotta go get the bacon."

Bunny sighed and for a couple beats there was silence between the two. Then she jumped into character, "What you need me to do to help you get ready."

"Nothing I'm good babe, I got it covered."

"You sure?" she questioned as Spoe got up and slipped into his all black gear. She tried to do any little thing to help him as if he was her son. He didn't mind. He gave her a long hug.

"Go and get that money baby and bring it back to Momma," she kissed him and smiled at him.

"You better believe it baby," he said as he headed for the door. "Come lock the door, babe."

Bunny walked behind him and he turned back around and spoke to her.

"And if Ginger call back, let 'em know, not to panic. We got 'em as soon as they give a bail."

Once she shut the door and watched them get into their work van and pull off, she wondered exactly how Ginger was holding up.

15

"Bail denied!"

The decision not to grant Ginger a bond came from behind a bulletproof glass by an overworked magistrate. A deputy grabbed her arm and began to usher her away before a stunned Ginger could respond.

Ginger jerked her arm away. "Hold the fuck up! I didn't even get a chance to speak. Y'all acting like I done killed somebody or something. Damn, even the Briley Brothers got a damn bond."

Deputy Foster allowed Ginger to vent, as long as she didn't get too out of pocket, she was cool. He'd been doing his job, escorting detainees through Henrico Jail for better than fifteen years. Some of them were innocent, but most were as guilty as charged. Their crimes were none of his business; he just did his job.

"Are we in America or North-fucking Korea?" Ginger huffed. "Credit card fraud and grand larceny, that's all I'm charged with and I can't get no gotdamn bond? Fuck!"

Actually Ginger had twelve counts of fraud, and eight counts of grand larceny and a list of other white-collar charges.

Tightening his grip this time, Deputy Foster directed her back toward post processing, a room where they changed the detainees out of their street clothes and into prison beige stock jail uniforms.

"I'm willing to bet the reason the Magistrate refused to give you bond," he informed Ginger, "is because you don't have a valid ID. You could be a serial killer for all we know. For all you know they could be a terrorist . . . you got four IDs and none of them are you. The Boston Bombers didn't have IDs as intricate as yours. So you can't really blame them for taking those precautions." Deputy Foster got to a door and handed Ginger off to a female officer to get changed out.

"Jane Doe, no bond," he told his colleague and looked to Ginger. "Behave."

The female's badge read Duncan. Deputy Duncan was short, with chocolate skin, and a military fit body. She sized Ginger up with a pair of hazel eyes. "Small," she was referring to Ginger's size, and it came more off like a statement then a question.

What size smock she took was the least of Ginger's concerns, she had much bigger fish to fry, which was a lot harder to do being that she was the one in the hot pan of grease. It turned out that Olive Oyl, the anorexic white chick from the Louis store, had called five-oh, with the omnipresence of surveillance cameras, it had been easy to go back, to pick up Ginger's movements after leaving Louis Vuitton, she and Deidra leaving the mall, putting the bags in the car and the license plates of her Honda as they rode off.

"Take all your clothes off and put them in this." Deputy Duncan handed her a small metal basket, "And hurry up. We don't have all day honey."

Chile please. Bitch you much be crazy . . . like you really think I'm going to hurry up to get locked down? Think again, Ginger thought as she unbuttoned her blouse slowly.

Two buttons . . . Deputy Duncan rolled her eyes. "Get a move on it," she tried to rush Ginger, but Ginger wasn't having it.

She rolled them right back like, *whatever.* The blouse finally unbuttoned, Ginger took off the blouse, folded it up neatly and then placed it into the metal basket. Thanks to all the hormone pills she had taken since age eighteen, a killer pair of C-cup breasts filled the cup of the Victoria's Secret royal blue lace bra.

Deputy Duncan walked her eyes down to Ginger's ironing board flat stomach and then slowly back up to her breasts with the healthy appetite and appreciation of an admiring lesbian.

"Good," said Deputy Duncan with no shame in her tone. "Jeans and shoes."

Ginger saw the lust written all across Duncan's face, and she milked it, taking her time. Deputy Duncan deaded her fake hurry, enjoying the striptease that Ginger was putting on, while it lasted. Ginger wished she'd worn more clothes.

And finally in nothing, but matching lace panties and bra, she struck a pose. Then gestured for the prison rags to replace the garments she'd disrobed.

Ginger's heart skipped when Deputy Duncan said, ". . . everything."

With a lot to conceal and nowhere to conceal it, Ginger sighed at the perplexity of her situation.

"You sure about that," Ginger said in her sexiest voice. "This may be too much for you," she licked her lips and batted her long mink eyelash extensions, in a seductive way.

"Trust me, I can handle what . . . ever you got." Duncan shot back. "Now strip."

"Okay, have it your way," she moaned in a way that she knew turned on Duncan, as she unsnapped her bra, freeing a set of perfectly round mounds of soft flesh, sitting at attention like two puppies awaiting a treat. A nod at the panties from Deputy Duncan, trying to conceal a smile, but Ginger had other things that needed to be concealed.

They were at ground zero when Deputy Duncan unleashed a wild scream. "Package!"

Thinking that Deputy Duncan had discovered drugs on the Jane Doe's person and by the sound of her shriek, was engaged in a physical confrontation, Deputy Foster ran to assist his colleague.

Confused, Deputy Duncan stammered, "S-she'sss a dude," pointing at the seven inches of proof, strapped between Ginger's legs and ass cheeks.

"What the fuckkkk?" Foster was shocked, too.

16

Under the pale light of a full moon, Spoe and Tariq stepped from the cover of a thick patch of wood, about half a football field from a white plantation style mansion.

In what little time they did have to prepare, they'd done their homework. It was a Thursday, every Thursday around 11:00 p.m., the Bloody Lion Crew left the house together, usually for a couple of hours, but never more than three or less than one. So, Spoe and Tariq figured they had at least an hour to find the bread and get ghost, but had decided to only allot themselves thirty minutes to make it happen.

The crib — 7,200 square foot, on three acres of rural property belonged to a dread called Dino. Dino was the head of a crew from New York, called the Bloody Lions Posse, who was heavily into distribution of cocaine and Ecstasy. But even after doing their due diligence, Spoe still couldn't help his feeling of uneasiness combined with a bad vibe.

"That bitch Tiffany, is sure she seen a mil-ticket?" Spoe had to make sure.

Tariq eyes still on the empty house, "She's never steered me wrong before and I'm sure she's not going to start now." Tariq looked his man in his eyes, "She said it was *at least* two million dollars."

"In a suitcase with a gold lion head?" Spoe questioned, then added, "It sounds like some shit you'd see in a movie?"

Tariq hunched his shoulders, he had to agree, "True dat. But you know like I know, real life can be crazier than fiction. Take this house for example. You wouldn't think a black person would be living in it, unless they were the help. The shit looks exactly like Candy Land, the house Jamie Foxx blew up in the movie Django."

The sound of barking dogs rang out.

Woof! Woof! Woof! Woof!

The barking originated from two silver back pit bulls. Together the dogs weighed more than 200 pounds, and had heads the size of watermelons.

Spoe gripped the handle of the sub-machine gun hanging from the strap around his neck. Busting a cap in the dog to keep from becoming a Scooby snack wouldn't be a problem. Fortunately for all parties involved the pits were chained and caged in a 12×12 pen.

"Nah, man, let them live." Tariq suggested. "Let's focus on this bread."

"Tonight is their lucky night," Spoe said, as he looked at the trained attack dogs.

Focused back on the house, Tariq said, "We keep to the script." According to Tiffany, she was upstairs when she'd seen the suitcase. So, she had no idea where Dino kept it. "We toss the house for no more than twenty minutes and then we out with or without."

Spoe didn't like scavenger hunts. His preferred method was to snatch somebody up. It never mattered if it was the actual victim, victim's ole girl or ole lady. He'd torture them until he got what they needed.

Tariq could see his friend's apprehensiveness, but he said, "Spoe yours is normally riskier than this."

"Yeah, it's always produced results for us. Big results."

The problem: these dreads originated in Miami and had no family in Virginia and to top things off, their entire crew was treacherous to the core. These were the kind of gangstas that would rather die a violent death than bow down to cowards to torture.

"A'ight man. It's your play?" Spoe said as they crept through the darkness wearing all black. "We'll do it your way." He had no reason not to trust Tariq's judgment, after all the two had been in business together in some sort of way for over fifteen years.

The house was wired with an alarm system from one of the companies that put their signs in the yard as a warning for casual trespassers and kids. For anyone with even average knowledge of how the system worked, the alarm was as usual as the caged guard dog.

Tariq was far from average when it came to disengaging alarm systems, he was a pro. A good alarm took him three minutes to disarm. In sixty seconds give or take they had bypassed the crap system and were standing inside the kitchen. The fridge, stove, and dishwasher were all high-end stainless steel appliances. The island's black marble top matched the onyx-colored floor. The kitchen opened up into an extravagant styled living room, a seventy-inch TV mounted over an enormous granite style fireplace. Gold tables, white Italian leather sofas, and Arabian silk high back chairs. Everything was spotless, and not to mention the place looked like a museum.

"Are these cats really drug dealers or does

Martha Stewart live here?" Spoe half joked with a raised eyebrow.

"Shit is unbelievable right?" Tariq impressed by the one and only lick that he had ever brought to the table.

"It is but we don't have no time for a tour, we need to get to this money."

"Let's start upstairs," Tariq said, for the first time taking the lead. "Come on."

Spoe followed as Tariq lead the way. They turned left, bypassing the grandiose living room, through an archway and up an oversized spiral staircase, which was also marble and wider than two driving lanes of I-95.

At the top, was a loft with more rooms going in either direction, "Man I know this is yo' show, but in all this house and the time we on, there's no time for roaming. I think its best for us to split up. You take the rooms to left and I will hit the right, then look for the master bedroom."

Tariq agreed with the plan, adding, "Good idea. We start at the furthest point and work our way back to the loft. Either of us find the loot we holla and we out."

Spoe, taking the responsibility for tossing all the rooms east of the loft; Tariq all the rooms west of the loft.

"Sounds Gucci to me."

Then they parted like two determined

prizefighters, after bumping gloves in the middle of the ring to their respective corners, except they were retreating to their separate corners of the house, not a ring. And before a purse would be divided, they would have to find it first!

Tariq opened the door of what seemed to be a mini theatre, he didn't think it was a likely place to hide the bread, but one would never know if they didn't look. The walls were textured and red. Thick leather, reclining chairs with cup holders the same oxblood red as the walls faced the 120 foot white screen. It was improbable that a suitcase would be able to fit inside or under the recliners, but he lifted the seat cushions and felt under each one anyway. The only money he found was $3.17 worth of loose change. He ripped the screen off the wall, checking behind it. Nothing there.

Something caught his attention on the wall near the front to the left of the screen. It was a barely noticeable vertical seam. A door; a door with no discernable latch.

The only purpose for having a hidden door would be to conceal something. The question was, what was being concealed? One thing for sure, two things for certain, he'd find out soon enough.

Tariq tried pushing at the door; first in

the center, then on each corner, hoping it was one of those pressured-spring latches.

Negative.

The seam was too narrow to slip anything between it, so prying it open wasn't an option.

He was wasting time. *Get the fuckin' door open Tariq. Come on man this is yo' shit. This the shit you do,* his self-conscious was talking to him.

Touching the wall, to the right of the seam, he ran his fingers from top to bottom. Nothing. He went out a little wider with his hands, repeating the process.

Bingo!

Camouflaged in the textured soundproofing material was a small button. He pressed the button and the door slid open, on a recessed, mechanical track. Inside the space, were racks of electronic material. A sub woofer, DVD player, tuner, hard drive, amp, etc. . . .

No money.

Who the fuck goes to this length of secrecy to conceal a stereo? Tariq thought. The answer was no one.

The longer Tariq looked at the audio and video equipment the more he sensed something was definitely offbeat.

What was it? He was wrecking his brain

trying to figure it out, but knew he didn't have but so much time to jerk off in there.

The minute he was about to give up, and then it hit *him.* He hit himself with the heel of his hand for not pinning it off top. It was the subwoofer. Toshiba made all of the equipment inside of the closet, except for the subwoofer. It was also at least a couple of years older than the other stuff.

After closer scrutiny, Tariq was on to the charade. The subwoofer was one of those "in your face," stash boxes. Like the fake rock people hid the spare door key in and left in the front yard. Inside the sham sub woofer were eight neatly wrapped bricks of coke.

It wasn't the million dollars that they were looking for, but it was a heck of a bonus to a great start. Tariq stacked the bricks inside of the duffle bag before moving on to the next room, one room down, and four to go.

Meanwhile, Spoe was ready to toss the third room on his end. The first two, besides a couple pieces of jewelry, were a bust. Before he was about to go to work, he took a deep breath to clear his head.

When Spoe was thirteen and was running wild, an OG name Butter took him under his wing and blessed him with some food for thought.

"Productivity," Butter said, "comes to the brotha that most persistent *and* patient. Remember that young blood." Spoe swallowed the gem whole and kept it down. He'd been shining every since.

Spoe took a deep breath to clear his head, before he got back to work. Though the master bedroom was bigger than the entire apartment of some projects he'd been in, he didn't get discouraged. If the money was truly there he'd find it. He flipped the mattress on a king-sized bed, and found a 22-shot Glock. He put the pistol in his waist, got on his knees and looked underneath the box spring.

Nothing at all, but a few specks of dust was all that he found.

He pulled the bag from behind the wall and checked behind the headboard. Nothing. He didn't stop there, he continued to look, underneath and behind the oak dresser, chest, and the two night tables, still came up with still nothing. One by one he removed a collection of paintings from the wall, looking for hidden safes. The room had a fireplace almost as big as the one they had passed downstairs. He searched inside the fireplace and around the hearth, for loose bricks, concealing stash spots. He continued from the floor to ceiling, book shelves, bathroom, and a sitting area framed by a bay window and an antique armoire, where he found nothing besides a collection of high-end watches bammered in a wooden box inside of the armoire.

As he made his way toward a closet, he hoped Tariq was having better luck. And quickly let the random thought go. If Tariq had found the money they wouldn't still be inside the house searching. They'd be in the truck celebrating, but that wasn't the case at all.

Spoe opened the door to the walk-in closet, which was the size of a two-car garage. Just like the rest of the crib, the design and organization could have been overseen by Martha Stewart herself. Clothes were coordinated by colors and seasons. To Spoe, except for the guns, it seemed like something more suitable for a cat like Nick Cannon than a drug-dealing cat like Dino.

Dudes were seriously strapped. Hanging from a customized pegboard, were two AKs, a M-14, a Heckler & Koch UMP, and an array of semi-automatic pistols. Spoe took notice that a few spots on the wall were currently unoccupied, letting him know that Dino and crew were strapped.

Then he noticed something else. On the floor, beneath the guns, was a suitcase.

Brown. And embossed in its leather was a lion's head.

Bingo!

God was good! They'd finally found what they'd come for and more than they'd expected.

Motivated by the ease of the score, Tariq wanted to keep searching. "This spot is a fucking gold mine." He said to Spoe, adjusting the strap on the duffle bag, weighed down with coke, over his shoulder. "No telling what else we might find."

"Yeah. Like a hot ball and a cold casket," Spoe nodded toward the suitcase in his hand. "I'm Gucci with this."

On their way down the steps, Tariq asked his friend since third grade, "So, when did you start letting the possibility of death hold sway over how you live life?"

Good question, Spoe thought. He was contemplating an answer when the gunshots rang out.

"Bbbrrat! Bbbrrat!" The barrage of 9 mm hollow points from the MP-5 hit home. Boring through the flesh of its targets. Blood poured through their fingers as they clutched at the fatal holes.

From the elevated position on the stairs, Spoe had a better fight line. He'd spotted the dreads creeping before they spotted him and squeezed off the first shot, dropping two of Dino's men.

Dino watched his two soldiers' chests open up right in front of him. The severity of the wounds, they'd bleed out in a matter of minutes. It was nothing he could do for them, but see to it that their killer would die, and hard. The remainder of Dino's crew sparked back, sending the sound of gunfire echoing through the house.

"Boom, boom, boom, boom . . ." Spoe shoved Tariq down. "Back upstairs." The odds weren't in their favor going down. "We've got to find another way out."

Bullets slammed into the steps, all around them, kicking up chunks of marble as Spoe and Tariq army crawled on their stomachs back to the top of the stairs. Attempting to slow down the pursuit, even if only for a second, Tariq fired blindly over his shoulder.

"Bbbrrat! Bbbratt!" A lucky shot winged one of the dreads in the arm. Tariq caught one in the shoulder and two slugs would've split Spoe's dome if he hadn't moved his head just in time.

When they made it to the loft, Spoe saw that Tariq was bleeding. "You okay?" He asked, and then fired off a few more shots. "Bbbrrat! Bbbratt!"

"Boom, boom, boom, boom!"

Spoe ducked his head. Tariq fired back. "Bbbrat! Bbbratt!"

"Yeah" — Bbratt-Bbratt — "it's only a scratch."

Suddenly the shooting stopped. Dino announced, "No way you make it out alive, Sty." His accent was so strong that his words were hard to make out. But their meaning was crystal clear.

Spoe retorted by bucking back, squeezing the trigger. "Bbbratt!"

"You need to worry about your own mortality."

"Bbrratt! Bbratt!"

"Besides I've decided not to let the possibility of death, get in the way of living," Spoe said confidently.

"Then have it your way, Sty."

"Boom! Boom! Boom! Boom. . . ."

A downpour of hot lead stung the loft like a swarm of killer bees. They took cover behind the leather sofa, which ate the brunt of the damage. But the longer they stayed still. The more their chances of getting away lessened. Tariq looked to Spoe. "What's the plan?"

"Boom! Boom! Boom!"

"Bbbratt!"

"Down the hall," Spoe said. "It's a bedroom facing the way we came in. We hit the window and run for it."

Tariq did the quick math, "That's a thirty foot drop minimum." The house had vaulted ceilings.

"Got a better idea."

"Boom! Boom!"

"Bbbratt! Bbbratt!"

"Any plan beats no plan when facing a life or death situation."

"Lead the way."

They eased from behind the sofa, racing down the hall toward the bedroom Spoe had peeped earlier. Dino and his crew didn't see them dip. Tariq and Spoe hoped to get a sixty second head start before Dino and assassins realized that no one was shooting back. Spoe kicked the window out and the sound of the breaking glass was drowned out by the echo of gunshots. Using the suitcase, he knocked away shards of glass that were sticking out from the frame. Then he threw the suitcase out of the window. Fifteen seconds after abandoning the sofa in the loft the suitcase landed calmly, with a *thump* in the backyard. But lucky for it, it didn't have bones to break, but it was a whole other story for a person.

The impact alone from a bad landing, could jam their thighbones pass their pelvic and into their stomach. No walking away from that. Spoe took a quick glance at the door. Then turned to Tariq and said, "See you at the bottom."

Spoe hit the ground hard, but the tuck-and-roll, maneuver he used, absorbed most of the impact. Besides the tweak in his ankle, he was Gucci. The duffle bag tumbled from the window next, with Tariq right behind it. He nailed the tuck-and-roll landing, like he'd been on a mission with Field Team 6 and was on his feet.

Boom! Boom! Boom! Boom! The shots came from the window Spoe and Tariq had just jumped from. Bullets kicked up dirt near where they lie.

"Oh, shit!" They didn't expect it to come so soon, but they took off running.

"They in d'back yard headin' for d'woods." It was Dino, he ordered his crew to get down there. "And let Brutus and Cleopatra out of their cages."

After hearing their master's voice. The two silver back pit bulls bit the chain on the cage, trying to eat the lock off, to get in on the action.

Slugs followed Tariq and Spoe into the woods. The van they had driven was on the other side, half a mile away.

Spoe's ankle was worse off than he thought. He was having trouble walking, let alone running. And the suitcase, which weighted more than thirty pounds with the money, was wearing him down.

"Let's split up." It was a decision that would later haunt Spoe. "Take the suitcase, I can move faster without it."

Tariq didn't like the idea of splitting up, but with gun toting Jamaicans and two bloodthirsty pit bulls in hot pursuit, there was no time to debate it.

Reluctantly, he said, "I'll meet you at the car."

Spoe's ankle was throbbing, and he didn't want to slow his partner down. "If I'm not there five minutes after you, I'll see you at the crib."

They split up for the second time tonight the first time was when they searched for the money. Spoe hoped that bitch Lady Luck was in a good mood and would continue to ride with him. He got his answer soon enough.

Spoe's calf felt like it was on fire. Blood poured from down his leg. He tried to keep it moving, but his leg called it quits. He'd been shot.

"What I told ya, Sty?" It was Dino, with dogs barking in background.

"Dead-mon walkin', Sty."

Spoe aimed his gun in the direction of the

voice and pulled the trigger, but the MP-5 didn't bark; its clip was empty.

Fuck!

Dino's turn . . . he pointed the gun at Spoe's head.

Dead-mon walkin'.

Spoe's last thought was of Bunny. Her birthday was next Friday and he was going to surprise her with a trip to St. Thomas. Even the thoughts of the love of his life, wouldn't allow him to go out like a sucker. He would never beg for his life from a motherfucker. Instead he looked that nigga in his eyes and waited. Dino pulled the trigger, making good on his promise . . .

Dead-mon walkin'.

The bullet penetrated the skull Spoe's right ear and sliced through his brain as if it was kosher deli meat.

"No, mo' walkin'," Dino said, after spitting on Spoe's body. "Just dead-mon."

He made sure that his crew dumped the body so that if it was ever found, it could never be traced back to him.

Lights out! Everything went black.

17

"This is just bullshit!" she screamed pounding the steering wheel of the car taking out all of her frustration and anger at this piece of shit she was now forced to drive. How could she pray to a God that had taken everything she had been given away including the only man she had truly ever loved. Everything had been taken away; her father, her sense of safety, her car, credit cards, medical insurance, and now her health. What the fuck? Was this some cosmic joke played out for God knows what reason? Life just wasn't making sense to Simone anymore. And just as luck would have it, at a time when she just wanted to be alone to collect her thoughts, her phone wouldn't stop ringing. Her phone was blowing the hell up, but after that last phone call from the doctor she wasn't in any rush to answer an unfamiliar telephone number again. She couldn't bear to get any more bad news today. But then it dawned on her that maybe it was one of her sisters calling because something had happened to Me-Ma.

"Hello?" Simone's soft voice gave no indication that this could be the same person who moments earlier had been screaming at the top of her lungs in a rage.

"This is Detective Mark Dugan, do you have a moment Ms. Banks? I need to ask you some questions?" Of course the detective sounded polite enough but after the day Simone had been having she couldn't bring herself to respond like a normal human being.

"What do you want?" she snapped at him, her voice came out sharper than she expected but she didn't care enough to apologize.

"I just need you to come in and take a second look at your original testimony. There is a possibility that you may have left something out yesterday. You've gone through a very traumatic experience and often victims subconsciously block out some things that resurface when they go over their statement."

"Detective, I told you everything that I saw happen. There is no way I would or could ever forget any of what I saw yesterday."

"I understand, but you would be doing us a great service if you could come down to the station. Oh, and we're ready for you to reclaim your belongings. They have been photographed and logged in and we won't be needing them. Because the suspects are dead there won't be a trial."

"Fine. I'm on my way." When Simone hung up all her thoughts went to her Chanel bag and the possibility of having order restored at least in one small area. It was a small yes in the victory column, but she'd take it. Luckily she wasn't that far from the station so she took the back roads and made it there within ten minutes. When she entered the station she immediately started to feel nervous. Something about being around all those uniforms and guns made her feel very uneasy. Even though she had never committed a crime in her life Simone could not shake her feeling of discomfort.

You would have thought a purple spotted giraffe or some other creature had entered the room from the amount of interest Simone's appearance had generated. Officer Johnson, a tall, good looking man in his thirties who had never met a woman he didn't find fuckable, motioned to his partner, Darby Cole, a seasoned veteran in his forties with a wife and three kids he magically forgot about on Tuesdays when he visited his mistress. The officers were just about to make a wager on the hottest woman they'd seen in ages without the distance of a television or movie screen between them. This was their thing, betting to see who could date attractive women, usually damsels in distress who came into the station alone. Their coworkers were busying themselves suddenly finding things to do in Simone's general area so they could at least get a good look at her ass.

"May I help you," a young white officer Peterson, jumped the line and rushed over to help Simone.

"Dammit," Johnson and Cole couldn't believe they had been beaten to the punch by one of the rookies who had as much chance of hitting that as Manson did at being granted his freedom.

Officer Peterson didn't bother to disguise his interest in helping Simone in other ways, too.

"I'm Simone Banks, here to see Detective Dugan," she answered glancing around for him.

"Damn, he always gets the fine honeys," another dejected officer across the room joked with his buddy as if Simone would have been interested in either of them. Like all the other grey-eyed Banks girls Simone had grown so used to men making fools of themselves for her benefit that it almost didn't phase her. At an early age Simone's father realized that his daughter would have men after her, strictly based on her appearance so he'd made her work hard on her academics, wanting her to have something other than beauty as currency.

"Right this way," the officer led her through the station hoping to use the opportunity to work up his nerve to ask her out on a date. Black women intimidated the hell out of him with their brazen confidence, but he had always been attracted to their beauty. Even though he came from a very old fashioned Italian background where his parents expected him to date "his own kind", all his girlfriends had always been Black. "So are you friends with Detective Dugan?" he asked hoping like hell that this was some business call and he could have his shot at her. Simone pierced him with her eyes, this sister was not in the mood to be his first foray into the dark and lovely club and that was putting it nicely.

"No, I'm a suspect in a crime," she informed him certain he would lose interest. But if the officer was deterred he certainly didn't show it. Actually he took that whole innocent until proven guilty thing seriously, but it would be another two years before he flipped that script and began to see all suspects as guilty.

"What did you do? Steal a man's heart?" Officer Peterson tried, desperate to see more of this gorgeous creature. Her look cut him down and quickly neutered all thoughts of them together just as they arrived at the doorway of the detective's office. Spotting Simone and the young officer he had to stop himself from chuckling as the cop stared lustfully after her. Detective Dugan had to admit that her beauty put most women to shame, but for him this was strictly business he reminded himself.

"Ms. Banks," he greeted her only to be met with the coldest stare he'd encountered in recent memory. This version was decidedly different than the one he'd experienced the first two times he saw her.

"So, can I have my purse and get out of here?" she asked as she took a seat in one of the chairs directly in front of the officer's desk.

"Police stations make you nervous, huh?" he asked. His job had taught him to read people quickly and her aversion to the precinct was only one of the things he had assessed in that moment.

"Don't they make everybody nervous?"

"Mostly the guilty ones," he laughed attempting to put her at ease. In his experience if he could get a person to let their guard down by some friendly bantering it usually helped him to learn what he needed to know about a person.

"I'm here for my bag," she told him standing there stiffly. Without meaning to he found himself staring at her. The detective couldn't help, but wonder what happened since the last time he had seen her. She had been upset, but under the circumstances that made sense but this version of Simone, he couldn't quite reconcile with, she acted kind of nasty which surprised him.

"Yes, and I will give it to you, but first I have a few questions I need to ask you." As soon as she heard that Simone's arms folded across her chest as an icy cold frost set in. The detective told Simone, "I didn't realize a woman's purse could cost that much money?"

"Then you haven't shopped at Hermes before," she quipped not giving a shit if she sounded rude. What was really rude was him dragging her in here to pick up belongings the police should have never taken. And she really missed her purse. Foolish as that might sound, Simone always cherished her purses and treated them as if they were their own entities. This particular purse was dear to her because it was the last purse she had purchased with her father.

"Excuse me for saying it, but isn't it a bit excessive for a person with your revenue stream?"

"You mean how the hell does a lowly bank teller afford a purse that costs more then my yearly salary? Is that what you want to know?"

"Well, frankly yes. And it's not like the rest of your wardrobe is off the racks from Kmart or nothing. You have very expensive taste." And what he didn't say was very tasteful it was, too. Most of the women tromping through here made damn sure you knew that they were flossing expensive shit. They strolled through the doors with their labels on full display to prove they could afford some classy shit, but unless you knew quality Simone's high-end designer clothing slipped under the radar. That quality alone interested the detective because he wasn't used to people like Ms. Banks.

"You think that if I can afford to shop in high-end shops then I must be doing something illegal? Is that what it is? I'm a kept woman or a booster? That I lie, cheat, and steal for a living? If I were a white woman I doubt you would be so quick to quantify my belongings." She sat back shooting poisonous looks at him.

"Did I say that?" the detective hated that she had busted him for putting her in a pile with the rest of the people he met in his line of work. If only she knew that he didn't think of her like that. That it was just one of the pitfalls of the job to categorize the people that you met, good, bad, pimp, hooker, thief, victim. He did not want to admit his prejudices out loud.

"You didn't have to say it. I saw it all over you."

"Fine. You're probably right, but your situation does not add up. You don't have a work history so it's more than a little suspicious that it's your first official day working at the bank, and that very same morning, the bank gets robbed. You wouldn't find that the least bit suspicious yourself? Come on? You seem like a very intelligent woman, be honest with me."

Now Simone had just gone from riches to rags but she also wasn't going to admit that the detective had a valid point.

"Whatever! But let me tell you that if I were dumb enough to rob a bank I'd be smart enough not to waste six whole minutes threatening a teller and taking her purse to give to my ghetto fabulous wanna-be girlfriend. Do you feel me? Any girl in the hood with that person would have to flash it and then that woulda led you right to her boyfriend so the whole thing is just plain stupid if you ask me." She rolled her eyes at him.

"Okay. So you don't know any of the perps?"

"I cannot answer that question truthfully because they were wearing masks so I did not get to see their faces. Therefore, I cannot wholeheartedly say that I did not know them. I lived in this neighborhood with my grandmother in my childhood years and then I went to live with my father. Now, I've been living with my grandmother for a few months so it could be that I've seen them around the way if I knew what they looked like. But like I said, I did not get to see their faces so again, I can not efficiently answer your question." Simone smugly sat in her seat. She was not going to be tricked into answering certain questions in order for the prosecutor to try to turn her words around later and try to implicate her. She was too smart and educated to fall for that, "But I will say this," Simone concluded, "it is highly unlikely that I would have known the robbers."

"Can you at least look at their photos? Maybe they will jar your memory?" he said before he pushed a set of mug shots at her. He watched her closely to see what her reaction to them would be. The slightest reaction and he would know that she was in on the heist. Simone didn't bother to hide her surprise from the detective. She shoved the photos back toward him. "So, do you recognize any of them?"

"Yes. I recognize all of them. They were just kids from the neighborhood. Jason Kill? He dated my sister Tallhya about five years ago. She fell hard for his swagged out bad boy behavior. He put her through it having so many baby mamas and boy was he mad that she wouldn't give up her birth control to become the next one. Told her that if she loved him then she would have his baby. Me and my other sister, Bunny, told her that if she ever became pregnant by that thug she better keep it moving. We were not going to be related to anybody that stupid. I think it scared her enough not to give up her pills. But she wouldn't give him up because he was her first love. One night she was supposed to go out with him, but our grandmother said she wasn't feeling well. She's actually kind of psychic and something told her to keep Tallhya at home so she didn't go and he wound up getting shot trying to stick somebody up at a convenience store. Thank God Tallhya listened to our grandmother that night because he made his side chic go with him to drive the getaway car and she was arrested and charged along with him. My sister told me he and the girl were sentenced for a few years. I thought he had a longer bid and was still locked up, but when I moved in with my grandmother, I saw him around the neighborhood. The rest of the guys, I can't tell you much of. I've seen them around with Jason, but I didn't know any of their names." Detective Dugan kept watching Simone. He hadn't expected her to admit that she knew the guys even after it showed up on her face that she did.

"So you're admitting you knew the ringleader. The one who set up the robbery and got the others to go along. That's interesting." Detective Dugan stared

"The only thing me and those thugs have in common is the color of our skin and the neighborhood I happen to reside in at the moment. We are nothing alike and if you try to connect us you will be sorely disappointed. Our social circles couldn't be more different."

"So is there anything about that day that

struck you as odd?"

"You mean other than winding up with a gun to my head because a group of thugs decided to rob the bank that morning? Or having these young kids kill the person standing next to me while I feared for my life? Or having a gun pressed against my head? Or watching a man get his head blown off for moving his hands? You mean aside from those events did I find anything odd about what happened yesterday? No, nothing else out of the ordinary officer."

"Okay, Ms. Banks. Look, I'm going to get your belongings." He stood up and left the room, pretending not to pay close attention to her every movement. In his line of work, he didn't come across many sisters like this one. Fine. Educated. And classy. He didn't know her entire story, but based on what he had learned so far, things weren't adding up. She still hadn't explained her high-end taste or where she got the money to satisfy it and he guessed that she wouldn't. When he returned and handed her the bag enclosed in a plastic evidence bag, numbered and logged out, she took it and stood up to leave.

"Don't you want to check the contents, make sure all your stuff is still there?" he asked, used to people wanting to blame cops for any and every thing.

"The bag is worth more than anything in it," she said, removing the plastic bag and leaving it on the desk.

"And if I need to get in touch with you?" he questioned, for some reason he was in no rush to see her leave.

"Oh, is this an indirect 'don't leave town because I plan to catch you lying' threat?"

"Somebody has watched their fair share of cop shows on television," he smiled enjoying the chance to end their meeting on a more civil note. "I know you're not leaving so I'm not worried."

"Really? Because I might sell this bag and skip town," she joked, but what Simone failed to tell him was that as soon as the words were out of her mouth she wished that her words were a real possibility. She knew better than to try to sell her bag though. The bag had cost her father a grip and the resale price wouldn't even be close to half of the original cost. The resale would probably only get her a weekend visit to Atlanta and that wasn't nearly far enough. Not far enough at all from this nightmare.

18

"Tiffany!"

"Yes, baby," she said calmly.

"Shit, just got crazy! Real fucking crazy," Tariq said from the other end of the phone after he'd been waiting for Spoe for the past three hours and he hadn't answered.

"You get the bread?"

"I did, but shit went bad." He sounded worried, "My boy's fucked up," he stuttered. "I think he might even be dead."

"You sure about that?"

"Yeah, I'm sure."

Tiffany took a deep breathe, "Man come over to my house. You can take a shower and get you some rest. Shit, going to be okay. Spoe going to call."

"No! You don't understand. They hunted him down and killed him. I know they did."

"Just calm down, baby. It will be okay. Just come over and let's put our heads together."

"Bet!"

Tariq thought for a second about calling Bunny and filling her in, but he wanted to keep hope alive. He prayed to God, Allah, and everybody else that his soldier was being a warrior and could endure. Besides he didn't have the heart to break any kind of news to Bunny.

Tariq pulled up to Tiffany's house and seeing her house, from the road, gave him solace. Maybe she was right, he did need a shower to clear his head and think.

As he made his way to the front door, he started to think how Tiffany could possibly be "the one." He thought about the years of joking Spoe on being in love and now he himself was falling.

Before he knocked on the door, Tiffany opened the door with a smile on her face which once inside of her house, quickly turned to a frown.

"What the fuc—" He was caught off guard.

"Glad you could make it!" the olive skinned Italian dude holding the shotgun waved them into the room as two other well armed men kept their pieces trained on a shocked Tariq. "So we meet again. Didn't I tell you that it was a small world?"

Well right there in the mix wearing the brand new body hugging Herve dress and

Balenciaga leather wedge booties she had suckered Reek into buying just the other day after performing some exceptional deep throat action stood Tiffany.

"What the fuck, Tiff?" Tariq made the motion to reach for her, but the man who had waved them in turned his gun on him.

"Move and I will blow your motherfucking brains out," he promised and so Tariq backed off of Tiffany, but the look he gave her, promised that he'd kill her with his bare hands.

The treacherous woman didn't bother to look remorseful as she held out her hand to the guy, flat palm facing up to the guy who had to be the one Tiffany called Marky all the while throwing shade at him.

"Told you he'd come," she bragged as the guy laid a thick ass stack of hundred dollar bills on her.

"And you were right. Good job, baby!" he commended her as he laid a juicy deep tongue kiss on her.

"I'ma go into the bedroom, but don't take too long. This gangsta shit gets my juices flowing." He smacked her on her butt as she walked off.

"Bitch, you set me up!" Tariq reached out to grab her before she could leave, but the click of a gun being activated stopped him.

236

He was all fucked and it was all his fault for believing a skanky-ass stripper bitch who made a living fucking random niggas for cash would play fair with a real nigga. He looked at her in disgust.

"Hell, it aint like you my man or nothing so there is no need for me to stress myself protecting you. Ain't that what you said?" she laughed as she delivered the gut-wrenching blow that had been a direct quote when he had all the power just a few hours ago. "Well, get back to me when you decide if taking me seriously is an option. Oops! I understand now why that might not be happening," she swung her hips a little extra as she sashayed out of there shooting him a dirty look over her shoulder 'cause this shit was now his problem. Tariq had always been told that his love of new pussy would one day be his downfall and he hated to think that this might be that day, but it looked that way.

"Look man, no disrespect, but I'd been set up. We didn't know nothing 'bout you or your house."

"Yeah," he answered making Tariq think that he was leaning in their direction. To be fair, it wasn't like he couldn't recognize the validity of his statement if that was all there was to it.

"While you make a very valid point there is something important that neither of you factored in when you decided to rob me a other night."

Shit! Tariq thought, *This isn't for the robbery at Dino's this is from the other night. Damn!*

"You see I'm incredibly, how shall I say this? I'm protective about my shit. I work real hard at what I do so when someone or people, like you believe that you don't have to work because you can just take mine it pissed me off. You motherfuckers are under the illusion that it's your right to steal from me? Why? Because you grew up piss poor and no one gave a shit about you? Well boo-fuckin-hoo for your non-existent father and your whore of a mother who didn't make sure that the guy she was fucking gave a shit?"

"No disrespect. It's the nature of the beast. I'm sorry man. I'll give you your money back." Tariq thought about all the years of he and Spoe's careful hits he had and now he was caught out there like an amateur.

"Are you sorry or sorry you got caught?" He smiled at the man he had at his mercy sadistically enjoying his fear, at how the tables had turned. "It ain't fun when the rabbit got the gun, huh?"

"Nope."

"Great," he continued, a huge smile of forgiveness plastered on his face as he extended his hand to Tariq who was filled with a feeling of relief when he saw Marky smile. The expression on his face turned sour when he felt his arm being twisted straight out of the socket. "Do I look like a fuckin' idiot to you? You motherfuckers stole from me time, and time again and neither of you had the good sense to hide it. No, you took my money and spent it like it was water and you bitches were Niagara Fall and the shit would never stop flowing." The realization that this was the owner of the majority of stash houses they had robbed rocked him to his core.

"You might know me by my other name." He leaned forward and slowly and methodically unbuttoned his shirt showing hints of the full body tattoo inscribed with the name he figured out moments earlier.

"I want my motherfucking money!" Ghostman's gravelly voice raised sounding like a wild beast hungry for revenge. To say Tariq was shaking in his boots as he began to circle him was an understatement. Considering the crimes they had brazenly committed against him, he knew he wanted payback and the way things were going he was afraid he'd end up forced to pay with his life.

"I can give you everything we have," he figured that if he offered to pay the guy back he would have a better chance at leniency, knowing good and damn well that there was no way his ass was willing to go straight back to ghetto poor which happened to be a few levels under the poverty line. These were levels so low no one ever talked about them, but they all existed in the lower socio-economic areas.

"And you think what? That it will be repayment for the pain and suffering you caused me?" Ghostman screamed causing the heathen in front of him to start praying for God's mercy and grace.

"I think you should let me use this." One of the men held up an Uzi and pointed it at him.

"Which one of you was the mastermind? You or your boy?" Ghostman got right up in his face as if daring him to lie.

"Me. I'm the one that made all the plans. I found the dope houses, cased them, and made all the plans on how it was gonna go down. My boy just came along to help me. It wasn't his fault, it was all mine." Since

Spoe was dead and dead because of him, it was the least he could do. He had not expected Ghostman's reaction.

"So you were the mastermind?"

"I said it because I'm the one that got us into this messing 'round with that bitch ho, Tiffany." Whap! Whap! The butt of Ghostman's gun whacked Reek across the temple collapsing him to the floor in a heap.

"Where my money at? I mean the rest that you haven't blown on bitches, cars, and dumb shit."

"At our stash house," Tariq admitted, but then he started to hope like hell that Bunny was with her sisters and not laid up waiting for Spoe.

"Look, man you not going to be able to get it without me. Let me go get it. You can send Tiffany with me."

"That would mean I trust you two to leave this room." His muscle men started to laugh at the idea that Ghostman would do anything that stupid.

"We wouldn't run. We'll just go and get your money and bring it back." Reek nodded to Ghostman with a faint smile on his face like he had just figured out the key to saving his ass.

Tiffany came back into the room and

made a suggestion. "Have Spoe's bitch bring the money."

19

"Bitchesssss I'm free! The things we take for granted."

"Not quite! You gotta abide by your house arrest rules. Only church outings and that's it."

"You know I'm going to get me some passes to the doctor and some more shit. But bitch I'm free. I will figure out the rest!"

"You gotta stop fucking with Deidra, you know that right?"

"I know I can't believe that, bitch left me high and dry!"

"I don't know why, the bitch been leaving us all for dead since she gave birth to us."

"Damn, I'm hungry as hell," Ginger's words elevated competing with music, singing and cell phone pinging messages in the car. "Something about almost cutting a niggas balls off always makes me wanna eat some down South food like barbecue hot links, chicken gizzards, and fried fish with some baked mac and cheese and collard greens."

"Nuh-uh Gin, that all sounds good except for the chicken gizzards part. That shit sounds nasty. Who the hell eats chicken gizzards?" Bunny exclaimed.

"Bitch, I know you not tryin'a get all uppity on me? Don't act like you ain't had nastier shit in your mouth!" Ginger began making sucking noises while she pretended to be sucking on a lollipop.

"Yeah, I suck dick and what? And I bet you my man's dick taste better then some nasty-ass chicken gizzards." Bunny nudged her sister playfully. There was never a dull moment when her and Ginger got together, "I'm driving and since I'm also the one paying I say we hit up Mama J's kitchen. All this talk about food got me fienin' fo some fried catfish, collard greens and potato salad," Bunny said starting to salivate thinking about how good that food would be.

"Me-Ma can cook you that shit at home, besides why you wanna drive this nice-ass car up into that hood. We don't need to test our luck to see if we can get outta another place alive in one day," Ginger shrieked ready to make her case until both of them were interrupted by their sister's screams.

"Oh, Lord! Oh, Lord!" Tallhya cried from

the back seat. Her body wracked with sobs as she screamed out in pain like a damn lamb brought to slaughter. Bunny and Ginger jumped in their seats. They had completely forgotten that Tallhya was sitting in the back seat. She hadn't said a word since they got in the car after they left the funeral home. This whole time she had been in a zombie-like state. Now it was as if she was coming out of her trance and finally reacting to what had happened.

"No, Lord, no!" she hollered. A look passed between Bunny and Ginger as they drew visual straws to choose which one would be the first to deliver the 'shut the fuck up' sermon to their bereaved sibling.

"Ain't like that nigga died or nothing," it was Ginger that started first. "Hell, I never liked his selfish-ass no way. None of us did." She sure wasn't lying but Tallhya was way beyond the point of being able to be reasoned with especially about the trifling piece a shit she called a husband. All her screaming and hollering had begun to grate on her sisters' nerves and Bunny was a second away from completely losing her shit.

"Tale? Babe, you're gonna be all right." Bunny spoke in the sweetest tone. It was a tone she usually reserved for her man and not one of her siblings, but as bad as Tallhya was right now, she needed to calm her sister down. It was hard for Bunny to sympathize with Tallhya though. Bunny didn't play that victim role and had no time for crying over no man, especially not one who had the bad taste to cheat with someone else and act like it wasn't his fault. Walter would have been buried alive if it were up to Bunny.

"Hell no, I'm not gonna be all right," Tallhya finally answered back flinging her tears and sadness all over the car interior. All this emotional drama had started to affect Ginger's attitude. "How could he do that to me?" Tallhya's voice wailed on.

"That motherfucker ain't thought about nobody 'cept his self. Shit, I bet he ain't never even gone down on you." Ginger snapped her fingers as she rolled her eyes upwards at the very idea that any man would get the chance to leave her unsatisfied. Ginger loved her sister, but saw this whole episode as plain ole stupidity and had to stop herself from saying as much. "You need to go home and burn all this nigga shit. Make a great big bonfire in the front yard on some Waiting-to-Exhale-type level. I promise you, seeing that shit go up in flames, would make you feel better."

"He's my everything and now what is my life without him?" Tallhya squealed and kept at it, digging the hole of self-pity a little bit deeper with every sob.

"And that big ole butt girl he had all over him? Did you see that heifer?"

"Yes, I saw her, and the truth of the matter is, she was pretty and way better looking than me."

"No the hell she wasn't," Ginger said. "That bitch was plastic as these damn tities I bought. That ho bought all that shit."

"Yes, probably with my money."

"That's why you gotta look out for yourself. Stop giving them niggas yo' money. They don't deserve shit."

"And if a ho stand by and let a man take money from another woman. That ho got a whole other set of issues. I don't care how much of a bad bitch she may appear to be on the outside, but she got low self-esteem to accept that kind of shit."

"You right about that." Tallhya had to agree, "And besides her breath was stinking, talking about she's Walter's fiancé."

Ginger laughed at Tallhya's weak attempt at bad-mouthing Walter's mistress. Tallhya had always been the softest out of the four sisters. Before Simone went to live with her father Bunny had to stick up for her sister in school because she was always being taken advantage of by the other kids. She never cursed or talked bad about anyone so to hear her try to badmouth someone was almost comical.

Ginger busted out laughing again, giving Bunny a high five.

"I'm glad you two find my tragedy so amusing," Tallhya said.

"Oh, Tale," Bunny laughed. "Please don't play the woe is me card. This is not a tragedy. You were too good for Walter and you know it. That no good, cheating liar don't deserve you. I know you love him and you're hurting right now, but you are better off without him," Bunny said reaching in the back to grab her heartbroken sister's hand.

"Amen to that!" Ginger exclaimed, "Now can I get Hallelujah?" she went on in her best preacher impersonation as she raised her hands as if she was praising in a church. She looked over at Bunny, but she was giving her the "time to get serious" look. "Okay, for real though. Walter was selfish and his ass was basically broke so I don't get it."

"I love him," Tallhya screeched throwing herself on the mercy of the seat, bucking back and forth, cradling her sides as she droned on.

"Look sis, when you done with all this crying and carrying on you need to figure out a way to make his ass pay for betraying you," Bunny said starting to lose patience for Tallhya's victim bullshit. She couldn't imagine loving a man who treated her the way that she had observed Walter treating her sister. As much as she didn't believe in the whole modern day self-esteem crisis the girl needed some serious charge by the hour help. She thought about how lucky she had been to find a man like Spoe who committed himself on the same deep level to Bunny as she did to him. But not to get it twisted Bunny saw herself as wholly incapable of putting up with any bullshit from anybody, dick or no dick including Spoe and he didn't expect her to deal with bullshit from him either. "You hear me Tal? This feeling sorry for choosing a looser bullshit has to stop."

She admonished her little sister, but what Bunny didn't get was how much she sounded like Deidra who had no patience when it came to tears or neediness. Bunny wished that Simone was with them because of the four sisters, she was the only one who possessed real compassion and understanding in emotional situations like this one. Right now with Tallhya looking and acting so vulnerable she knew Simone would know how to handle it. It seemed that what her sister needed was to be able to break down and let it all out without being chastised for it, but Ginger and Bunny weren't built for that sentimental stuff. They weren't kum-baya hug it out kind of girls. They had tough skin and even tougher hearts. Bunny thought about calling Me-Ma and filling her in on everything that had happened. She decided against it because as sweet as her grandmother was, she was very protective of her granddaughters and Bunny was almost positive if she called Me-Ma, she would go Government grade A Ham on Walter and even the good Lord couldn't save him.

"You don't understand. I'm not lucky like you are when it comes to men. I have to take what I can get and Walter is the best I ever had," their jilted sister swore through the tears sounding like a crazy bitch.

"Don't you ever get tired of accepting so little from the men in your life? For a big girl you almost as pretty as my fine-ass and if you thought a little more of yourself you'd bring the men running." Ginger, like Si-mone and Bunny didn't understand why Tallhya allowed a steady stream of losers into her life. Me-Ma used to say that she had a magnet attraction to Mr. Wrong. She'd even thought that demanding Walter commit to her before marriage would guarantee her loser streak would come to an end, but clearly it didn't.

"Look honestly, if you feel that way, because you are fat, then loose some weight. Carry your ass to the gym. Watch what you eat. Go to see a nutritionist and push away from the table." Ginger knew it hurt, but hell the truth hurts. And some things need to be said.

Bunny hit Ginger, "Now that wasn't nice you fucking trannie! But for real Tallhya, you are pretty and if you don't like what you see in the mirror. You can do something about it."

Just at this moment the phone rang and Bunny's phone blew up over the bluetooth. She switched it to her headpiece when she saw that it was her man Spoe calling from Tariq's phone. Her sisters were so nosey, but Bunny would not allow them to live vicariously through tales of her good fortune. "Y'all need to shut the hell up so I can hear my bae," and Lord why did she say that? All it did was to remind Tallhya of her new single reality and the boo-hooing escalated to a whole other level.

"Bitch, shut up," Bunny snapped at her sister who was too far gone to listen.

"Lord why you have to say that to her?"

251

Ginger whispered at Bunny and then whipped her head around at the hot mess her sister had collapsed into. Bunny hit the button on her earpiece and tried to make sense of what Tariq was saying. She couldn't really understand what he was saying because his voice was cutting in and out but from what she could hear, him speaking fast, and she could hear the panic in his voice.

"Shut the fuck up!" Bunny screamed her emotions coming apart at the seams throwing her sisters off. She had gone from normal to apoplectic, her tone strong enough to quiet Tallhya's wailing.

"Tariq, what did you say?" Bunny said into the phone as she grew intensely focused trying to listen to her man's homeboy. But Tariq's frazzled tone triggered an alarm bell deep inside of her that damn near rocked her to the core. See Bunny could tell that something was off. He didn't sound like the man she had watched leave her house to head off to work with her boo. He sounded spooked giving her an eerie premonition that she tried to shake off as she struggled to hear what he needed from her. She pulled into a parking lot and was finally able to hear him clearly, but what he kept saying wasn't making much sense.

20

Me-Ma rode the elevator to the third floor just like it had been explained to her on the telephone. When she got off she stood facing the glass and marble entryway of the law office of Callahan, Crosby and White. The senior Mrs. Banks didn't normally find herself in places like this and she had to admit, she felt a bit out of place. Me-Ma's first thought was if she had dressed nicely enough for the meeting, but her second and the most important was how much would this whole thing cost?

"May I help you ma'am?" a red headed receptionist seated behind the desk looked up to greet her before fielding more phone calls.

"Yes, I'm here to see a Lauryn Shelton," Me-Ma informed the young woman, "I have an appointment"

"Certainly ma'am. Can I have your name please?" the friendly receptionist asked.

"Mrs. Banks" Me-ma replied.

"Hello, Mrs. Banks. Miss Shelton will be with you in a moment. In the meantime, can I get you some coffee, tea or another beverage while you wait?" the woman asked and though she was actually thirsty Mrs. Banks didn't want to waste time sipping on a drink when she came to handle important business. Not to mention that this woman charged by the hour and how was she to know that an hour didn't officially begin until she saw that lawyer.

"No. I would like to see Miss Shelton. I don't have time to waste in here and I am certainly not going to be getting any younger the longer this takes." Me-Ma planted herself at that desk her expression told the woman everything she needed to know so as she called Lauryn and also sent her a quick e-mail to let her know that keeping this particular person waiting didn't seem like the best idea. And just as Me-Ma had made up her mind to go off on a tangent the door flung open and there stood Lauryn Shelton, looking just like her mother and grandmother. *Poor thing,* thought Me-Ma.

"Mrs. Banks, Reverend Street told me to take very good care of you." Lauryn grinned up at Me-Ma who couldn't help wishing that God had been a little kinder to that young lady when it came time to hand out the looks, particularly when it came to that man size nose fighting for space on her tiny face. Oh well, at least she was smart enough to have focused on the things she could do something about like her career.

Miss Shelton wasn't completely unattractive it's just that her eyes were set too close together and not to sharp on her nose, but the size and shape appeared better suited to a more masculine profile, but she seemed nice and that went a long way in life, at least that's how Me-Ma thought. By the time she left that office having handled all her legal issues Mrs. Banks felt relieved that her daughter and all four of her granddaughters would be provided for exactly as she wanted after she shuffled off the mortal coil. "Mama," Deidra stood up from her perch on the porch as her mother stepped out of a freshly painted Lincoln town car. Miss Shelton had insisted on having the company driver bring Me-Ma home after they finished with her appointment. Me-Ma had originally planned on taking the bus back, but darkness had fallen by the time they finished with all the paperwork. It had taken a lot longer than she expected to cover all the things she needed to in her will.

Normally these things were handled in stages, but Me-Ma let Lauryn Shelton know that she didn't plan on wasting any more time coming back and forth for that hourly wage and that she wanted to take care of everything in one day. Considering how dark it was when they finished, Me-Ma agreed to the ride home after Miss Shelton reassured her that she wouldn't be billed for it.

"Where you coming from?" her daughter questioned as if their roles were reversed and it was Deidra and not Me-Ma who was the mother. Her daughter grew immediately suspicious especially because everybody knew that Mrs. Banks would never spring for the luxury of a car service.

"Oh, nothing. I was just visiting one of the gals from church and she sent me home in that thing. Her mother waved it off as if it was nothing. Me-Ma didn't feel guilty about her little fib. After all it wasn't exactly a lie and it was closer to the truth than a lot of other things she could have said. Besides, Mrs. Banks didn't see how it would be any of Deidra's business for her to have to explain her whereabouts to her daughter.

"Uh-hum," she muttered not that great at pretending to feign interest in the affairs of others even her own mother or children.

"I wish I knew you were coming. I would have cooked a big meal and I would have told the girls. Right now I have no idea where they are for me to tell them you're out here." Me-Ma unlocked the door to let her only daughter inside. "If you're hungry I can fix you something quick to eat. It won't take too long and from the way you're looking you need to eat something."

"I wish mama, but I can't stay too long. Lenny is waiting for me," Deidra insisted. This Lenny happened to be the new guy, Me-Ma wasn't sure he'd last with her daughter long enough for them to meet. Her daughter never seemed to have a shortage of suitors, but sometimes the rotation happened so close together that she didn't have much time to get comfortable with the last person.

"This Lenny? Is he a good man? Is he nice to you? Treat you good?" Her mother hovered and couldn't help but ask twenty questions still trying to form a stronger bond than the one that broke all those years ago.

"He's great. But he's having a hard time lately. The economy in this climate is hard on Black men," Deidra sounded like she was reading off of a political cheat sheet. She followed her mother into the kitchen and watched as she began to remove pots from the refrigerator and place them on the stove.

"Mama! What are you doing? I told you I can't stay and eat!" Deidra interrupted her mother as she excitedly began to prepare a meal to feed her daughter.

"Yes, baby girl," Me-Ma used the pet name her husband had coined shortly after Deidra had come home from the hospital. "I'ma have this food on the table before you know it." Her mother jumped the gun, fighting to keep her daughter there at least until her grandkids returned. If she had been right about Tallhya's Walter being the same one from the newspaper, Tallhya would surely need her mother and it would be nice if for once it could be the one who brought her into this world.

"I don't have time to eat. I got to go and meet Len," Deidra insisted becoming anxious as she paced the length of the kitchen floor. "See, we were trying to get enough money together to turn our luck around." Her mother froze in her spot as she realized that this visit mirrored all the others and nothing about it was personal. Deidra only showed up when she needed something and no matter how much Me-Ma wanted to think otherwise it always proved to be the cause. She needed to borrow money; money that she would never pay back even though she insisted that it was just a loan. Deidra was always full of empty promises. Once again, money proved to be the only reason her daughter ever bothered to show up.

"The girls are doing good by the way," Me-Ma said, ignoring Deidra's request for money. "Well, not really actually. They all going through stuff — heavy stuff. They sure could use a bit more of your time Dee, especially Simone. Don't know if you heard, but she had just gotten a job working at the bank when it got robbed the other day. Scared the poor girl half to death. She ain't been back to work since and I'm not so sure she should go back." The whole time Me-Ma talked Deidra began to pace, if not pacing she was fidgeting with her hands. She wasn't about the pressure to be nothing to nobody and her mother trying to make her feel guilty had actually started to annoy the fuck out of her. *See,* she thought, *that's why I don't come up in here people always wanting something from me.* Course the irony of her being there skipped right over her head.

"I don't see how Miss Priss has any choice." Deidra sucked her teeth just thinking about her oldest daughter who ain't never had to do nothing she didn't want to thanks to that father of hers.

"Please won't you wait and talk to her," Me-Ma kept trying to get her hard-hearted daughter to spend more time with her own girls. She knew that they were all grown, but she knew that they still needed a mother, even one as selfish and narcissistic as Deidra.

"Humh! She better keep that job so she can meet a rich man, whose gonna take care of her. That's what's wrong with that girl. Sisi ain't thinking about that. She already hit the lottery with Simon for a father. Hell, if his ass had been as generous to me as he was with her I woulda stayed with him." Deidra thought about Simon always coming home from his grass fertilizer business with dirt under his nails. She liked her men pretty decked out in fine clothes and she liked them to take her places and all he could talk about was building his business. Those suckers always talk about getting that money and she didn't have any reason to believe he'd strike it rich any more than the others who talked a big game to get into her pants.

"He really did love that girl. Shame he's gone." Me-Ma shook her head.

"I woulda thought she'd hit the jackpot when he died, but I guess he wasn't as in love with his child as we all thought."

Deidra laughed real nasty and petty. You could feel the jealousy shooting out of her. "Didn't leave his only child one damn iron dime now she back sucking on your tit just another mouth to feed." Deidra shook her head at the pure disappointment of her daughter's situation. When she heard that Simon passed she had expected to get in on some of Simone's inheritance, but that proved to be one more damn disappointment. She had always warned these girls that you can't trust none of these men, but they all had rocks between their ears.

"No, he loved that girl. It was that wife who stole that chile's money."

"Whatever." Deidra snapped she had lost all interest in talking about this nonsense. She had to address her own needs and get moving. She went over to her mother and snuggled her head into the crook of her neck the way she'd done since she was little. "Mama, I need you to loan me some money? Just 'til I can get on my feet?" Me-Ma smiled like the thought of giving her child and some anonymous man money one more time didn't break her heart. That smile had to be the only thing standing between her and tears streaming down her face. But just 'cause she always said yes didn't mean she wasn't planning on getting something out of it for herself.

"Baby girl, you wanna go with us to church this Sunday? It would mean so much to me. I can give you some money today and more after the service. That way I'd have time to get to the bank," Me-Ma knew that her daughter's Achilles Heel was money. She didn't care what it took, but she had been praying that one visit with the Lord would turn her daughter's life around. She'd seen God work plenty of miracles and as long as she lived she would always pray for the deliverance of her only child.

"Sure mama, I will go with you to church. Maybe I can get Len to come with me. You'd really like him." Deidra's lie swelled up her mother's hope but in actuality all she wanted was to get that money and get her ass up out of there. Being in that house riled up feelings of discomfort and sadness, emotions Deidra spent her life running from man to man to avoid. Before her father's death her entire identity had been being her daddy's girl. The moment she discovered her father had another daughter it smashed her world into tiny pieces and left her on the search that would prove elusive. All she wanted was a man she could both love and trust.

"Let me go and get you that." Me-Ma

stopped with the pots and went into the bedroom where she stashed her envelope of cash. Simone was the only one who knew exactly where she kept it, tucked right there in the family Bible, not the one she read everyday, that one never left her side, but this one had all the names and birthdays of family members written in it. Me-Ma clutched the envelope to her chest as she placed the Bible back on the shelf, but when she turned there was Deidra standing in the doorway watching her.

"Mommy, I really appreciate your help. You know I wouldn't bother you if I didn't need it. Like I said, it's just 'til we can get on our feet." Whether she realized it or not Deidra said the same exact thing every time she came begging for money, the last time was less than a month ago. But poor Me-Ma was always just happy to see her daughter that it almost didn't matter to her that the visit was financially motivated.

She opened the envelope stuffed with cash and counted out five hundred-dollar bills and handed them to her daughter who balled them up and stuffed them in her purse, course she kept her eyes on that envelope as her mother returned it to its place in the Bible noticing how stuffed it was with cash. She couldn't believe how cheap her mother was being when she had all that money on her. "I know you got to go, but I really wish you could stay and visit to see your girls?" Now a second ago she might have been planning to run out that door once that money hit her hot little hands, but now it seemed her daughter had another plan.

"You know what, that sounds good." Deidra led her mother back into the kitchen. "You want me to help you with anything? Why don't you take those shoes off and go put on your house slippers. Make yourself comfortable momma." The syrupy thickness she put on display for her mother should have made her suspicious, but Me-Ma like a lot of parents of failure-to-launch children chose to be blind to most of her daughter's faults. She still blamed all Deidra's problems on her husband's duplicity, but never ever did she put the fault squarely where it belonged.

"Soon as I get back I'ma cook you those turkey legs you like so much," her mother offered, feeling full of love as she went into her bedroom to change into her housecoat and slippers.

No sooner had she left than Deidra flew into the bedroom to retrieve the rest of her mother's money. Course she hadn't expected the door to fling open and for her two youngest daughters to interrupt her plan.

"Mommy!" Tallhya shrieked, dried mascara streaked tearstains running down her face. At the unexpected sight of her mostly absentee parent Tallhya went flying toward her. She missed the look of annoyance on Deidra's face, but had she seen it in her current state it wouldn't have stopped her daughter from throwing her arms around her mother's neck and holding on for dear life, the sobs coming back in full force.

"Girl, you 'bout to knock me down with all that. Ain't like you skinny like your brother." She rolled her eyes at Ginger making a mental note to keep him away from Len. *You just never know with these men,* is how she always thought.

"But you don't know what just happened," Tallhya tried to explain. "Walter used me, mama. He has another woman," the blubbering and waterworks caused their mother to take a step backward. She was already upset that their presence had thwarted her plan and now all this crying and touching her. She wasn't about that at all cause unless she and the other person were fuckin' she didn't see any point in any kind of physical connection.

265

"And unless you're blind and didn't notice the Dolce skirt and red bottoms pumps and this fabulous long weave honey, then you on something else 'cause ain't no kind a man here." Ginger ran her hands up and down her body to punctuate her point, "This is all woman all the time 'cause I am strictly dickly." She poked out her lips and swiveled her hips in front of her mother rolling her eyes up toward the sky.

"Look Miss Thang, I didn't give birth to no fourth girl. You have a penis and that's to remind you that you are not female so if you wanna be a little sissy that's on you and not nothing I did so don't go blaming me."

"Course it ain't. You would have had to be here raising me like a mother to know what the hell I am." Ginger's words stung Deidra, but she was too proud and stubborn to let anyone know it let alone show it.

"You need to respect me. I gave your ass life instead of getting you scraped out of me like I started to do. Don't make me sorry that I didn't." Deidra's harsh words did exactly what she intended, they caused Ginger immediate and irreparable emotional damage. If you caused Deidra the slightest pain, she would maim you permanently if she could, her Scorpio stinger always ready to strike.

Ginger looked from Deidra to Tallhya whose reaction to her mother's viciousness was to comfort her little sister. A full two years older than Ginger, Tallhya had more time to grow used to the vicious tornado that was their mother.

"She didn't mean it," Tallhya tried to make an excuse for Deidra, but the damage was already done as Ginger took off for her bedroom with her sister on her heels. Finally left alone in the living room, Deidra hurriedly grabbed the envelope and ran out of the house. All Deidra cared about as she stepped outside had to do with the loot she had shoved into her purse. Len would be so happy when she showed him what she had gotten.

Me-Ma entered the living room excited to talk a little more with her daughter, but instead she found herself standing alone. Her eyes immediately went from the space where she kept the Bible to the table where it sat now empty and open.

"I can do all things through Christ, which strengthen me. I can do all things through Christ, which strengthen me. Yes, Jesus, yes. And though I walk through the valley of the shadow of death, I shall fear no evil for thou art with me."

"Me-Ma," Simone entered a short time later, assessed the situation and helped her grandmother up from her knees where she had been praying. "You all right?"

"Your mother just left," Me-Ma threw her arms around Simone before she could finish, but they both knew exactly what that meant.

21

"Everything?" Bunny said wanting to phone Tariq back and confirm the words that had just been spoken because this shit sounded crazy. But nothing about his tone or words led her to believe he was in the right circumstance to answer her call.

The words kept ringing on out, on and on in her head. *They got us, bring all the cash, everything, or they going to kill us.*

The thought of something happening to Spoe would literally kill her. He was everything, her heart beat because of him.

She ripped through their apartment locating the piles of money in all his hiding places. When she was done she had at least a million dollars in cash, money neither of them ever thought they'd have to part with. The memory of the sound of her man's voice scared her so shitless she would gladly hand all this cash over and more just to have him safe at home. In the kitchen she located the extra set of keys to Tariq's pad, a place she'd actually found for him on the other side of town. Just as she was leaving Tariq's place and wiping out his stash her phone rang.

"Hello," Tariq's number came up on her Bluetooth and she felt relieved to see him calling her back.

"Bunny? Or is it Bunny rabbit? The unfamiliar voice on the other end of the phone snickered to himself or whoever thought that shit was funny on the other end. "Tick-fuckin'-tock you wanna see your man any time soon?" he warned her, full of bravado. Whoever this person was who had her man she already hated him, but if she possessed anything it was street smarts.

"My friends and family call me Bunny," she snapped having no interest in pretending to be nice. She figured that she would give this guy the money and then she Spoe and Tariq would be on their way.

"Wow! So it's like that? Well, I just have one question for you little Bunny rabbit. Where the fuck are you with my goddam money?" he hollered into the phone, the sheer magnitude of his anger came over loud and clear and threw the normally composed Bunny into a new level of panic.

"I'm on my way. First I had to drop my

sisters off and then I had to go to two places on the opposite side of town," she explained.

"You want to see your friend, bae, man, daddy whatever the fuck you people call each other, again I suggest you get your ass here right now! You hear me bitch?" He had Bunny all twisted until the moment he called her a bitch. Unlike a lot of women who had been worn down by the overuse of the word in rap songs and popular culture and found it acceptable she didn't play with any form of being called out of her name.

"I ain't no female dog so don't call me one," she shot out getting ready to go ham on him for that shit. But instead of Ghost-man coming for her he actually found her rage funny and burst out into hysterical laughter.

"I'm glad you find me so funny," Bunny stated dryly.

But he wasn't laughing at what she said. What he found so hilarious had more to do with how most people treated him, since his name alone instilled fear everywhere he went, people normally kissed his ass and knew to be afraid when they saw him. To hear her talk to him like that was pretty funny to him.

"Guess I needed a good laugh. I'm giving you twenty minutes to get your ass over here." Bunny glanced down at the Waze app on her phone and saw that her estimated arrival time was less than ten minutes.

"See you then," she said and then hung up noticing her hands were shaking like she had Parkinson's disease or something. She had to slap the steering wheel real hard to stop them from moving like that. Her thoughts drifted back to Spoe, and hoped he wouldn't be upset with her for going against his wishes. He always told her that if he got caught she was supposed to take the money and run as far away as possible. Take that passport and leave the country, but she couldn't. She had to try and rescue him even if it meant walking into a dangerous situation without knowing if either of them would make it out alive.

"I'm Bunny," she told the high class thot who answered the door. Yeah, she had a full head of natural hair that cascaded down her back and her eyebrows were on fleek, but since she was here it meant they were enemies.

"Umph!" She ran her eyes over Bunny's velour sweat suit and her Louis handbag then snarled at her, but smiled at the duffle bag she was carrying.

"Then you better run your ass upstairs 'cause Ghostman don't like to be kept waiting. Bunny swore that she saw that girl coming outta Tariq's apartment building a few weeks ago, but maybe she was wrong. She'd have to ask him she thought as she raced up the stairs. As she stepped inside three armed men were passing a joint between them.

"No!" Bunny dropped the bags loaded down with money onto the floor. Her eyes laid on Tariq in the corner tied up. He had a look of desperation in it.

"Where is Spoe?"

"Aw, she came for her man. Ain't black love beautiful," Ghostman joked.

"You got your money, where's Spoe?"

Ghostman laughed. "I'm sorry sis," Tariq said with tears in his eyes. He started to try to fill Bunny in, but Ghostman shut him up by turning his gun and shooting Reek in the chest, killing him with one shot blood splattering all over the room.

Bunny screamed, "Noooooo!" as her heart dropped into her stomach as she stumbled about to pass out from the shock at witnessing the murder of her husband's best friend.

"Why did you have to kill Reek?" she screamed at Ghostman. "And where is Spoe?"

"This motherfucker stole from me and for all I know you could be the ring leader and your ass could get the next bullet out of this piece." He waved his gun at her making the other two men laugh.

"Damn," one of his goons interjected, "that looks like some good pussy she hiding under those baggy ass pants." Bunny turned and gave him the finger not caring one fuck that he held a weapon capable of taking her out in one shot. These weren't those normal everyday niggas she was used to dealing with, the ones who talked a good game, these guys didn't care one bit that she looked fuckable. They would just as soon shoot her without hesitating.

Ghostman motioned to one of his men to pick up the bag Bunny had dropped on the floor and to bring it to him. He opened it up and checked the stacks. He had to play along.

"And why should I let him live?" Ghostman's sadistic tendencies were fully exposed.

"Please, please don't hurt him! Where is Spoe?" she screamed.

"He's already dead."

Bunny dropped to the floor her tears came like a gusher. "You fucking monster! You had your money. You had your money," her words rang out falling onto ears that didn't give two shits. Ghostman was a business-man and killing of the man that stole from him was business.

"This man stole from me! You think he should have lived to what? Steal from me again? You think I'm fucking stupid?"

"Fuck you! Fuck all of you!" she screamed. "How could you?"

"Fuck me? Fuck me?" He reached over and snatched Bunny up off the floor. "If I wanted, I could bend you ass over that table and fuck the shit out of you then pass you over to these two. They don't get that much pussy so you can see how that would appeal to them?"

"Yeah, I want some of that," the most vocal of the gunmen chimed in, thoughts of a naked Bunny fighting struggling while he fucked her was giving him a hard on.

It wasn't fear that kept her from telling him off, her eyes blazed at him, but Bunny didn't speak. She couldn't. Her grief had taken absolute and total control rendering her momentarily mute. There was no telling what she would do or say now that he had destroyed her life.

"I may let you off this time, but that would mean you never mutter my name or tell anyone what went down in this room. If you do, you should know that I will find you and let these men do whatever they want to you and that hot little body before they kill you. Do you understand?" A look passed between Ghostman and Bunny.

"Yes."

"I'm not so sure you do." He sneered moving close to her ear, the gun now raised to meet at her temple. "Now here is where shit can get a little sticky. I have to decide whether I should allow you to leave or if I should let you experience the same ending as that motherfucker here."

22

"Somebody get that!" Me-Ma stuck her head out of her bedroom door and hollered over the sounds of the crooning negroes in heat music playing on one of those speakers Tallhya plugged her iPhone into. That child had been in a bipolar state for a while now; tears one minute and laughing at some funny memory between her and that no good devil of a husband she married, the next minute. She heard the sound of clopping down the stairs, no doubt it had to be Ginger. She probably had on some ridiculous platform shoes. Ginger loved the way heels accentuated her shapely calves and long legs.

"What?" Ginger gave the messenger the once over and quickly assessed that he was neither rich nor packing any heat in his pants, which accounted for her wanting him to disappear as quickly as possibly.

"Uhm, uhm," the middle aged brother got

all tongue twisted staring up at Ginger. Like so many men he too acted as if he could possibly catch the transgenderitis just from standing too close. If he only knew that he was far from her type so all the begging in six counties couldn't buy him any time with Ginger so he sure didn't need to worry about her getting too close. That was not going to happen. "I'm looking for a Tall . . . hiy . . . aaa," he blurted out all wrong. And like every other person forced to read his sister's name before they hear it out loud he mispronounced it.

"She's upstairs. You can give it to me," Ginger reached out for the manila envelope but the messenger snatched it out of her reach shaking his head.

"She's the only one I can give this to."

"You wait right here and don't you try and steal nothing," Ginger snapped before darting up the stairs. She slammed open the door to the bedroom that used to belong to Tallhya and Walter, but where her sister now lay in a heap crying with some Mariah Carey song playing. Shit had gone from bad to worse.

"Girl you want your delivery you better come and sign for it. Tal, get your ass to the door then you can come right back to this." Ginger hustled her sister out of the room and down the stairs.

"Are you Tal . . . hhhayyie?"

"I'm Tallhya," she stuck out her hand couldn't be bothered tryin'a explain to someone she would never meet again how to pronounce her name. All she wanted was for this person to hand over whatever and to go away. She wasn't done crying and feeling sorry for herself so this interruption was just that; another damn interruption. With all the bodies running around that house, her goal of crying herself silly and wallowing in self pity felt like an impossible task. Ginger came up behind her as the messenger presented her with a clipboard to sign. Once she had finished he handed over the envelope along with something unexpected.

"You've been served," he blurted out and then ran to his car and took off. The man had experienced one too many irate customers to take any chances especially since most of the crazies were Black and Latino women. They reached levels of insanity no man should ever have to deal with when they got served papers. You'd think they'd have no damn idea they were coming.

She tore open the envelope as she closed the door, Ginger stood there trying to figure out the best way to ask for a loan without appearing insensitive.

"Petition for divorce!" She read the top of the legal document in shock. It hadn't occurred to her that this was coming even after she hadn't heard one word from Walter.

"Girl, you better make sure that motherfucker don't try and take your money. Get your ass to that bank and get your money. I don't trust that motherfucker one bit!"

Now she may have been madly in love and grieving, but Tallhya wasn't stupid. She got herself together and went over to that bank to handle her business. Walter had made a fool of her and she'd be damned if she were going to allow him to continue to do so.

"What? What? That is impossible," Tallhya screamed at the bank teller who delivered the bad news. Apparently ole Walter had cleaned out all their bank accounts. A couple of months ago she had added his name onto her accounts in case of an emergency. He'd never so much as touched a dollar and now he had up and taken every single dime she had to her name. Tallhya walked back to her car and just stared at the bank statement the teller printed for her. She kept looking at the zeroes where it said BALANCE. She was overcome with emotions of betrayal. The more she sat there and thought about what Walter had done to her, the more she felt her heart shifting. God knows how long Tallhya sat in her car in that bank parking lot, but when she finally drove home, it was as if a whole new woman was in the driver's seat. A strong woman. A scorned woman. But most importantly, she was a woman with a plan. But before she put her plan into action, she needed to go home and change. She needed a new look to go with her new attitude.

Walter worked at a shipping warehouse over in the industrial part of town. She'd brought him lunch enough times that the guard waved her in as she walked into the building. Tallhya didn't notice that his reasons had more to do with the fact that the security guard was obsessed with watching her scrumptious ass walking past him.

"Hi, I'm here to see Walter Walker," the receptionist knew Tallhya by name and picked up the phone.

"Let me tell him that you're here."

"No," Tallhya panicked then smiled sweetly. "Why don't you let me surprise him?" She winked at the receptionist like they were coconspirators. The woman had grown so bored with the daily monotony that she was excited at the idea of helping out another big girl like herself.

Giving thanks to the Lord for lighting her way as Me-Ma reminded her earlier, Tallhya went back to Walter's office hell bent on accomplishing what she set out to do. When she didn't find him there she closed the door, sat down in his seat and waited. Sure enough a few minutes later who should come sauntering in, with not a goddam care in the world, but her no good husband. The panicked expression of his face shifted to annoyance 'cause this motherfucker was used to ruling over Tallhya.

"What are you doing in my office?" he snarled at her, but unlike the old Tallhya who jumped at his every command the ugliness of his reaction did nothing to deter her from her focus. She snapped open her extra large purse and pushed the divorce papers and her bank statements across the table at him.

"This is what the hell I'm doing here? You stole my money? Wasn't it enough that you made a goddam fool of me? I thought you loved me. I thought you meant your vows when we got married. How could you do this to me?"

"You don't have any money. That's not my problem! Now get the fuck out of my office and don't you ever show up at my job again. Not if you know what is good for you," he threatened. Even after seeing him with that woman, the divorce papers, and him stealing her money, Tallhya still couldn't believe that this person standing in front of her was treating her this way. She couldn't believe this was the same man that she had been so madly in love with just days ago.

"Walter you can't do this. I want my money."

"I done told you that is my money. And I have your signature on a document to prove it. Your dumb-ass legally signed everything over to me without even reading it." He smirked. Walter felt real pleased with how well his plan to con Tallhya out of everything had worked. He and Pamela had big plans with that money as soon as he got untangled from this woman.

"You motherfucker," her arms began to pound into him and she became a mad-woman.

"Bitch, you better remember those special little home movies we made or shall I say that I made when I filmed you sucking my dick, eating out my ass, taking my cum in your face, and doing a whole lot of other things. So unless you want everybody in your grandmother's congregation to get a look at your dick sucking skills, you will walk the fuck out of here and never come back. Do you hear me?"

"Yes," her voice, squeaked as the realization hit Tallhya that she really had just lost everything. And just like that, her newfound attitude had been torn down to nothing.

23

Tallhya's eyes rolled back in her head, not in the praising God kind of way, but in a pissed the hell off to be out of bed this early in the morning when my life is a hot mess and ain't nothing God can do to fix it kind of way. She had been dragged up into Faith and Hope Ministry one time too many with the promise of grace and salvation and since nothing she prayed for ever happened she didn't see any point believing in this mess anymore. But here she sat bright and early in the front row with the unofficial Mayor of this sanctuary, the only person who could convince her to drag her butt up in here, Me-Ma Banks. As much as they tried to be supportive Me-Ma and Simone were sick to death of Tallhya's crying and carrying on like she had lost something precious when in their estimation the only thing she lost amounted to unnecessary dead weight.

"Thank you, Jesus! Can you all say, thank

you, Jesus!" Pastor Cassius, resplendent in his loud-ass royal blue suit. He danced up and down the stage, shouting and praising like something right out of an old fashioned revival. His loyal flock was jumping up and down, shouting out thank you, Jesus like they had just won the Virginia State Lottery and not just another chance to line the pastor's fattening pockets. Simone sat on the opposite side of their grandmother, she also did not want to be there, but in her defense she had a stronger faith than any of her sisters. She knew that as suspicious as she was of Pastor Cassius she would glean at least one take-away from the sermon even if the Reverend made her uncomfortable.

"Good Lord," Ginger's heels click clacked down the aisle as she sashayed her way to the pew where her grandmother sat every single Sunday. Heads turned almost on cue, but like all the Banks girls, she just chalked it up to her exceptional good looks and massive sex appeal. Of course there had been a time not too long ago when Ginger used Sunday service to procure her lovers. She had a particular fondness for other people's mates, she preferred married men and men with money, preferably a lot of it. Ginger always joked that she could write the book on the perfect places to meet the down low brothers in the closeted community and church reigned consistently on the top of her list. Normally though, church and Ginger were not exactly on friendly terms and if it hadn't been for Pastor Street being fine as hell and straight at least on the surface she would have stayed her ass in her bed. Her friends had been whispering about the good pastor for a while so it made Ginger curious enough to find out if she could take the man of God for a spin. Plus she would never admit to it, but her tough act disintegrated when one of her sisters were hurt, so if being in church could make them feel better, then so be it, but don't blame her if she used it as an opportunity to get laid. She slipped in the pew next to her family and paid very close attention to the sermon.

While Cassius led his sermon Ginger spent that entire time imagining him naked and on his knees servicing her 'cause she was a real feminist and preferred to get hers first. Only thing that annoyed Ginger more than being in church was Bunny's absence, her entire focus revolved around her man Spoe. Now she appreciated that Spoe was a keeper who treated her sister like gold, but damn, the Negro could share the girl with her own sisters. Ginger hadn't seen or heard from Bunny since the day they went to the funeral place with Tallhya. Spoe called when they were on their way to eat and whatever it was he wanted Bunny to do must've been important because Bunny canceled all their plans and dropped them at the house like stepchildren. She was acting like she had to go and put out a fire and had not been seen or heard from since. You would think that with Tallhya in a state of crisis her older sister would have picked her head up off of her man's penis and shown up or at least called to check on her.

"Can you see if she's here yet?" Me-Ma craned her neck trying to look clear to the back of the church, many rows back and past a lot of heads, many fitted with fancy hats that could cause a scene at the Kentucky Derby. Simone did a quick look back even though deep down she already knew that her mother would be a no show. She hadn't gotten excited about seeing her mom at church because she knew better than to get her hopes up. She did feel bad for Me-Ma though because no matter how many times Deidra disappointed her, she always kept her hopes up and was destined once again to be let down.

"She's not here," she told her grandmother, again.

288

"This sure is wonderful," Me-Ma smiled feeling so grateful to have three of her four granddaughters there. It was still early so she felt hopeful that Deidra was only running late and would arrive shortly. Her daughter had never been on time for anything.

"Me-Ma, she's not coming," Simone wanted to be realistic and tried to soothe her grandmother's disappointment early. Plus she did not want to spend the entire service checking for her mother whom she figured was laid up somewhere with her latest loser because that was her mother's type.

"She said that she would be bringing this new fellow, Lenny."

"There is always a new 'fellow' or two," Tallhya who had been listening chimed in. Her head and neck going every which way.

"I don't see how you can have anything to do with her Me-Ma. She stole your money and ran out. She's not gonna show up 'til that money is gone." Now whether she was right or wrong, Simone's tone didn't sit any better with her grandmother and since she didn't have children yet she couldn't understand how she felt. For Me-Ma, it was like the saying goes "a mother's love is a mother's love."

"Don't you talk like that about your mother! That is my daughter. My chile you're talking bad about." Me-Ma's voice raised and so be it because she didn't come from this hiding behind your hand whispering generation. She put her stuff right out there and didn't ever care what anyone had to say. If they weren't paying her bills they did not get a vote and that included her grandkids. "Just like I love all of you, I love Deidra. You all with your money, money, money ways don't realize that's not how God intended it. You can't put money over people." Even the choir lowered their voices out of respect for Mrs. Banks preaching. It was Sunday and she sure as hell was giving a sermon. Pastor Cassius must have thought so too because he waved his hand commanding the choir to stop singing, "Precious Lord" mid note.

"Mrs. Banks, you are the elder, me and most of the folks in here want you to have your say. Too often we hush up what the people who have come before us have to say when they're the ones who can teach us the most lessons. We act as if we have invented loud music, short skirts and falling in love with the wrong people. Fellow church members and visitors you need to listen to your elders. Now Mrs. Banks, would you do us the honor of coming up here to share your message with us?" Me-Ma looked around silent. Then she stood up, ascended the stage and took the mic like that was her job.

"I was telling my granddaughters that I don't understand this generation one bit. If you don't know then you will be shocked to learn that when you put anything before God, you will suffer. I'm talking all those fancy Lenny shoes and bags and the stuff you have to spend your money to get." Well, Mrs. Banks was working herself up into quite a frothy lather and she had that Amen corner going. "You need to listen to what I am saying because God loves you." People stood up and starting shouting back in agreement. The reactions really got Me-Ma shouting and pointing her fingers. She had worked her whole life to build a strong relationship with the Lord so she knew what she was talking about and she wanted these people to get it.

"God loves you more than you know. Do you get that?" Well, people kept shouting back agreeing with her. "So you cannot put anything before God and you cannot put anything before your family." Me-Ma took a deep breath sucking in air to expand her lungs before she continued. "Especially those who have strayed from the Lord 'cause those are the ones you need to stay on your knees praying the most for because that is what God would want. When you love someone who has lost their way you never ever give up on them. You nev—" she clutched her hand to her chest. Mrs. Banks's mouth dropped open as her head started to sway back.

"Me-Ma!" Simone's voice raised over the stunned silence as her grandmother collapsed onto stage. Pastor Cassius Street rushed over to her first. The congregation, many who were present when the last pastor died, sat there in stunned silence not believing their bad luck to witness yet another heart attack. Simone, Ginger, and Tallhya raced to the stage as their grandmother took her last breath.

24

"Ms. Banks, so nice to see you back to work. We all thought you left with the money," Gray McPearson, a forty-five-year-old workaholic balding manager snidely remarked as she came through the door. His tone couldn't have been more opposite from the desperate married man hoping to get laid when Simone first interviewed with him. He motioned to her to follow him.

The customers in the bank moved about unaffected by the bank robbery that now was classified as yesterday's news.

"Mr. McPearson, I need to talk to you about my job." She started as he flipped through the paperwork on his desk intentionally ignoring her.

"Yes, Ms. Banks," he began.

"It's Simone. Please call me Simone," she took a deep breath trying to get comfortable being back in this place where she almost lost her life.

"Yes, we do need to talk about your job Ms. Banks," he said coldly. "See, because your first official day on the job coincided with the first robbery this bank has experienced in over six years, I'm feeling a little suspicious of your timing. You undestand why I may be a little suspicious of everything, right?" Simone actually felt shocked that he cut so quickly to the point. It was one thing to want to fuck the new black girl because after all she does have multiple degrees from a second tier university, but when she's suspected of being involved in a bank robbery, well, that just takes things to a completely different level.

"I told Detective Dugan everything he needed to know. I could have died in here and you actually think I'm a part of that crime? Are you accusing me of taking part in the bank robbery? Is this because I'm Black Mr. McPearson?" She paused, "Because I am almost positive that if I was a white woman, that thought wouldn't have even crossed your mind." She stared at him just waiting for this motherfucker to break some law.

"No, that's not what I'm saying," he started to backpedal his ass away from the lawsuit hovering around them.

"Nothing like that has ever happened to

me and I wasn't sure that I would come back to this job. And yes, I knew that it might make me look guilty, but I'm not sure that standing there handing money to the next person holding a gun to my head is the kind of job security that I need." The last thing she wanted was to be classified as a typical ghetto Black girl.

"Well, all our feelings aside, are you planning to return to your job at the bank or not?" Mr. McPearson asked deciding to drop the accusations and just let the authorities handle it.

"Yes, I am, but I can't come back tomorrow as planned. I know that the bank offered me a week off, but there's been a tragedy in my family and I need to take another week."

"Another week? I can give you until Monday." He offered not so generously.

"Fine." She stood up and walked out of the door and was fighting to keep it together as she bumped right into Jackie, the assistant manager.

"You all right?" Jackie held Simone by the arm, leading her away from the offices.

"Not sure you want to be seen with the co-conspirator to the robbery," Simone warned her as they made their way outside. "But I have been better. A whole lot better," she admitted to Jackie, the admission also came as the first she made out loud to herself. Since Me-Ma passed she'd been so busy taking care of everybody else and making the funeral arrangements.

"Honey, all you need for them to be suspicious of you is some extra melanin. That's why even though I been here a lot longer than the last three managers I ain't never going to make it past assistant."

"I'm just so tired." Simone's voice matched her emotions, which made Jackie put an arm around her to offer comfort.

"I know sweetheart. But I promise it's gonna be okay. Just trust in God."

"He thinks he can insult me by basically accusing me of being a thief? That's bullshit," Simone lowered her voice she still heard her father's words in her ear and did not want to be seen cursing in public.

"Look, those men may have known someone, but it wasn't from the tellers because we all know that the best day to take this place down is a Friday. That's when we get the money to cash the Government payroll checks and with the two largest state buildings located a few blocks away that's a whole lot of money. Hell if they were smart they would have waited until Thursday night at six after the armored truck drops off the money. Honey, right now I'm just glad we survived. How are you holding up sugar?" Jackie asked placing her hand on Simon's shoulder.

Simone stared at Jackie and contemplated whether or not to be honest about how she was really doing. Jackie had been nice to her from the day they met and she seemed like a good woman. The way Jackie carried herself reminded her of the nice older ladies from church. Right now Simone really needed someone to be nice to her and so far Jackie had been the only one to ask of her well being.

"To be honest Jackie, I'm a shit!" The word had already bounced out of Simone's mouth before she noticed and too late to stop it, but he was the last person she felt like dealing with today. Detective Dugan stepped out of an unmarked police car and was headed straight toward them. Both women would have had to be blind not to notice him. Plus he had a strong hard body and biceps straining to get out of that shirt that made it hard to look away, too.

"Damn!" Jackie salivated as the detective joined them. "I'm gonna be late from my break."

"Ladies?" The detective nodded his head in greeting as he reached the two, but really he was focused on Simone.

"Officer, I need to clock back in. If you need to talk to me I'm in my office." Jackie quickly excused herself and hurried back into the bank trying to beat the clock. Without a legitimate excuse Simone didn't have any reason to dart away. "Detective Dugan," Simone nodded taking out her car keys. As fine as he was though, she kept telling herself that she had way too much on her mind to be thinking about a man right now. But if her father Simon had still been alive and present he would have been the first one to notice how much alike the two men were, but his baby girl couldn't see it, not yet.

"Ms. Banks, I wondered when you would return to work?"

"Don't you mean if I was coming back to work?" With everything going on Simone felt particularly prickly and took offense that he would assume anything about her.

"My experience has taught me that most people who experience that kind of trauma in the work place aren't in a position to just quit their jobs. I'm not saying it's easy to go back in there, but you do what you have to do. So, not to be presumptuous, but are you coming back to the job?"

"Yes, but I needed to ask for more time

off," she sighed the full heaviness of losing her Me-Ma finally starting to hit. Out of nowhere tears began to well up in her eyes and before she could get a handle on it they began to overflow. Before he knew what was happening his chivalry took over and he had wrapped his arms around Simone in an attempt to comfort her. Something about this girl made the normal workaholic detective want to push the job aside and get to know her. He'd been on this force a good ten years and in his thirty-two years of his life he had yet to meet anyone like Ms. Simone Banks and that included the girls he came across at Norfolk State University where he graduated majoring in Criminal Justice.

Simone could not get control of her emotions. With everything that had happened the last few days, it was as if she had reached her breaking point and everything was spilling out of her. Detective Dugan stood there holding her in his arms without saying a word. In this moment even he felt like he was exactly where he was supposed to be; holding this beautiful, fragile woman in his arms. The familiar way the two of them stood their silently together caused a customer to smile as she exited the bank. She assumed they were in the middle of making up after an argument. She couldn't help, but reminisce about how she and her husband would kiss and make up back in their younger days. The chuckling sound the woman made as she passed by embarrassed Simone who broke away from the detective. Being a private person this show of emotion was so out of character she didn't quite know how to recover after her breakdown.

"You all right?" he asked sensing her discomfort. In his line of work, he was used to handling women that were emotionally unstable, but what he wasn't used to was feeling so attracted to a woman involved in one of his cases.

"It's my grandmother, she passed away two days ago and I just, I don't know I think I'm just —" Her attempt to blow it off failed miserably as Detective Dugan pulled her close again. This time Simone leaned into him letting herself go completely as she closed her eyes listening to his heartbeat. It felt so good if only for a moment to not have to be strong for anyone. The only other man she had ever been able to let herself go like this with was her father. As soon as she started thinking of her dad she completely lost it again as she began to sob while still engulfed in his strong arms.

When she had stopped crying, the detective placed his hands on either side of her cheeks. Even with mascara running down her face and bloodshot eyes, she was still the most beautiful woman he'd ever seen. He found himself taking a step back trying to maintain a professional distance, predicated by the fact that Ms. Banks hadn't been officially cleared of the robbery. Years of investigating perps told him that the reasons she appeared suspect had more to do with six degrees of separation, none of it pointing to her guilt. This made him even more anxious to find whoever had helped to set this up because two dead cops meant somebody was going down for this crime and unless his instincts were way off, he needed to make sure that it wouldn't be her.

"You all right?"

"Yes, I'm fine. I'm sorry I put you in that predicament. Thank you so much, though. I have to go." She darted away. He watched Ms. Banks as she got into a car. He made a mental note about the Dodge. Because it was a mighty step down from the Mercedes she had been driving the day after the incident when she came asking for her keys. She looked so out of place in that car which made him wonder what was really going on with this woman. The next thought surprised him. It was that he'd have to find a way to see Simone again, and soon.

25

As the church imploded with what seemed like the entire congregation coming to pay their respects to Me-Ma Banks, Simone forced herself to put on a brave face and take charge of everything. She kept herself together and helped her siblings deal with loosing their Me-Ma. She stepped up and made all of the immediate funeral and burial arrangements. Luckily Me-Ma had a life insurance policy that covered all the funeral arrangements. Finally, when she could no longer avoid it she phoned her mother to inform her about Me-Ma's death. With Deidra's pockets still full of the money she stole from her own mother Simone knew her mother was too busy spending it to answer or return anyone's calls. After many failed attempts, Simone decided to leave the message she thought that Deidra deserved, "By the way since you won't call me back you should know that your mother is dead."

Simone had been so busy making the arrangements and keeping it together that she felt guilty that she hadn't taken care of her sisters. Thank God the elders of the church stepped forward to comfort them, but Simone almost burst out laughing when she glanced up to see Ginger being comforted by none other than the speaker for the Lord, Pastor Cassius Street. Simone loved her baby sis to the sky, but the way that child could use any tragedy to slip into a straight man's arms should have been taught in a "how to get a man" class.

"Honey, you all right?" Pastor Street had somehow managed to detach himself from Ginger and was standing next to Simone, as she worked her phone trying to handle all the remaining details concerning her grandmother's funeral. In response to the flashy man of God hovering nearby she nodded, motioned to the phone and took off. *Ginger, that is all you,* she thought as she tried once more to reach Bunny who had been MIA the past few days. *Where are you?* She thought to herself. She was beginning to worry because it wasn't like Bunny to disappear for so many days without telling anyone at least where she was going. Simone decided as soon as she had a chance she was going to go to Bunny and Spoe's place in hopes of catching her there.

When Ghostman finally freed Bunny and allowed her to leave, she drove around in a fog not sure where she should go or what she should do. As badly as she wanted to leave with the body of the man she loved as a brother, Ghostman did not give her the option. She thought about calling Simone, but she would probably freak out and call the cops causing a level of trouble Bunny couldn't escape. She couldn't go back home to Me-Ma and pretend like nothing had happened. That woman had some kind of psychic power or a sixth sense that explained why none of her girls had ever been able to hide anything from her since they were little children. It was as if she could sense when one of them was in trouble. Bunny knew that she could not hide this from Me-Ma and there was no way she wanted to put her grandmother's life in danger by telling her what happened. Her grandmother had been through so much, but when it came to Mrs. Banks's family, Bunny knew nothing could keep her from protecting them or helping them, which was why she couldn't go home.

The truth was that there was nothing anyone could do for her. Being alive while

Tariq had been killed in front of her felt cruel. Bunny had been raised in the church with her sisters and had listened to what happens to the eternal souls of people who commit suicide and as badly as she wanted to end her life she couldn't do it.

For three days Bunny lay in bed clutching the T-shirt Spoe had worn before he left to pull off the biggest single heist of his career. He had no idea when he walked out of the door that it would finish him for good. She kept drifting in and out of consciousness only to be reminded when she awoke that the man she loved with every fiber of her being would never come back to her. But she hadn't eaten in days, hell she could barely think straight and the idea of eating made her feel sick. She held the dirty T-shirt up to her nose sniffing for Spoe's scent as she imagined him walking through that door. The bleakness she felt startled her, it went deeper than just pain or despair. It felt like it would go on forever.

"Bunny! Bunny!" she heard someone calling out her name but it felt foggy like it was happening in a dream. "Bunny!" Simone yelled through the door. She knew her sister was home. She'd parked badly in front of her apartment building instead of the garage where she normally left her car. Bunny treated that car like it was her baby and no way would she risk anything happening to it. Meanwhile all the noise of banging and the doorbell ringing started hurting Bunny's head until finally she got up and opened the door.

"Shit! What happened to you?" Simone stared at her sister. She had come there to tell her about their grandmother, but one look at Bunny and now she was so worried about her that she didn't know what to do. She closed the door behind her and led her sister into the living room and sat her on the fancy white couch, the one she picked out of InStyle magazine because one of her favorite celebrities owned one just like it. Her hair was matted up, eyes were swollen and puffy and she smelled like she hadn't showered in days.

"Bunny, what is going on?" a concerned Simone asked her. "Where have you been?"

"I . . . I . . . he . . ." Bunny who could talk shit in a variety of different attitudes barely strung a comprehensible sentence as she collapsed into her sister's arms sobbing uncontrollably. Simone couldn't remember the last time her sister had broken down in tears, not in years.

"What is it Bunny? You can tell me."

"It's Spoe and Tariq. They're dead. Sisi,

he killed them." Bunny went mute her body rising and falling in quiet agony.

"No!" Simone started to cry too and hugged Bunny tightly against her. She couldn't believe all the death surrounding them. For so long they'd been lucky and lately it seemed as if they didn't have bad luck they wouldn't have any luck at all. The two sisters lay together for so long the sun set and the apartment was now covered in darkness. Bunny and Simone never talked about what Spoe did for a living that provided them with foreign cars, designer clothes, extravagant trips and a place that cost nearly ten grand a month. Simone knew it was illegal which was the reason she never took any money from them. Bunny assumed that the worst thing that could ever happen would be Spoe getting arrested and going to jail and then she would wait for him, but she was wrong. Spoe dying was definitely the worst thing that could.

"I don't know how I'm going to live without him Sisi," Bunny's voice sounded defeated, fragile even. A few months earlier Simone had said the exact same thing but about her father and that's how she knew that her sister would learn to survive without the man she loved.

"I need you to come with me," Simone

said, pulling Bunny up from the couch. The last thing that Bunny wanted was to leave this house. It was the one place where she felt connected to Spoe. This was their home and she couldn't leave it.

"I can't. I just want to die." Bunny cried.

"Please bun-bun, we need to go. It's about Me-Ma." Just the mention of their grandmother's name brought a hint of a spark back into her. It hadn't crossed Bunny's mind that anything could be wrong, but the concern in Simone's voice did not go unnoticed.

"Me-Ma?"

"Yes, she was at church on Sunday and . . ." A look of horror covered Simone's face jarring her from continuing.

"What?" Now Bunny was sitting up on her own, staring into her sister's eyes waiting for something bad.

"She had a heart attack."

"No, no, no! This can't be. It can't."

"Bunny," Simone hesitated, "she's gone. Our Me-Ma is gone."

Bunny, who had not eaten or even had water in at least three days simply passed out from the stress and emotional strain.

26

Like a bad penny Deidra always managed to turn up at the wrong time in the wrong way. Two days after Me-Ma's death a friend of a friend managed to track her down in Atlantic City where she and her dick du jour had gone on a five-day bender drinking, partying, and gambling. As soon as they were broke Deidra decided to turn on her phone, that had not been on in days and found out her mother had died. To quote the old folks, Deidra got on the first thing smoking and hurried back to Richmond and her mother's house.

"Don't you make any arrangements until I get there. That is my job," she screamed into the phone as that big girl, Tallhya tried to explain to her everything had already been handled by Simone. She went on to tell her that the final service and burial would happen the next day.

"They just tryin'a get away with something. I don't trust none of them," Deidra complained to her man Len.

"So you gonna get some inheritance, baby?" That was where Len's mind went.

"Hell yeah, I'm the only child so I get everything, the insurance, the house, all those stocks my father left, shit I'm probably going to be paid."

"Baby, that sounds good. Real good." He immediately began counting all the opportunities he would have to help her run through that money before he moved on to his next woman. Len was not what you would call a long term option, hell he must have been getting old because he had been with Deidra a good four months which had to be about ten times that in dog years, or Len years as he liked to refer to time. Deidra jumped out of the car before it could be properly parked and rushed inside the house where she had grown up.

"My mother died and none of you could find a way to get in touch with me?" she hollered as soon as she entered and saw her three and a half daughters, that's how she thought of Ginger — a half.

"Well, we couldn't exactly wait until you needed to steal more money from your mother for you to show up now could we?" Simone who was usually the sweetest of the four got all salty with Deidra, which really pissed her off.

"You did this shit on purpose!" She glared at this disrespectful little bitch. When she got the deed to this property all these freeloading bitches would be sent packing and she didn't give a shit where they wound up.

"Ma, calm down, we did try to find you," Tallhya always the motherfuckin peacemaker tried to insert herself into their conversation.

"Nobody was talking to you. It's little Miss Prissy, I was addressing." Deidra pointed her finger at Simone who had the goddamn nerve to be mugging like she could take her. "Don't get it twisted Miss Thing I am still your mother and I can beat your ass just like I did when you were little."

"Wow, well I'm surprised you were around long enough to give me a beating," Simone snapped back rolling her eyes. The grey eyes that she had the good fortune of inheriting from the mother who she had the nerve to come here just to argue at a time like this. Ginger picked up a program off of a stack on the table and handed it to her mother.

"What the hell you handing me this for?" she perused the paper that had all the information about the funeral written on it.

Bunny, normally the loudmouth had been sitting quietly, but now it was her turn to put her mouth into it.

"In case you want to show up to her funeral. Just know that none of us are expecting you to be there. I mean, you didn't have time for Me-Ma when she was alive so why should we expect you to have time now?" Bunny quipped rolling her eyes at Deidra. Well, that didn't sit well with Deidra so she got right up in Bunny's personal space.

"I'ma tell all you bitches one thing. When I inherit all this shit you are going to have to find someplace else to live. I want all of you disrespectful hookers to get the hell out of my house. So if I were you I would get to packing and don't you take none of my mother's things 'cause all this shit you see here, it's mine."

"You can't do that. Me-Ma wouldn't want you to kick us out," Tallhya said from behind her sister Ginger.

"Me-Ma wouldn't want you to kick us out," Deidra mimicked her daughter adding a whiny tone just to make that shit sound more pitiful.

"It's true. She loved that we all lived together," Tallhya replied in a hurt tone.

"Well, I ain't my mother now am I?"

Deidra snapped as she stormed past them and went up the stairs to root through her mother's things.

"Shit," Tallhya started immediately after she left the room. "It hadn't crossed my mind that mama might end up with Me-Ma's house. What the hell are we going to do? Where are we going to live?"

"This is just so fucked up." Ginger looked at her sisters who had always taken care of her. They were about to be homeless which meant so was she.

"She ain't never been no mother so why would we expect it now?" Bunny asked her voice sounding so far distant even though she sat right there with them.

Simone, as the eldest had always felt that it was her job to take care of her sisters, but even she didn't know what to do. They'd all been hit on so many levels this past week culminating in their biggest loss, the rock who had kept them grounded, rooted to this spot together no matter what.

"I'm broke as a joke," Tallhya added. "Walter done took all my money," she said whining.

"Girl, you gave that man everything. Didn't you learn nothing that Me-Ma taught you about keeping shit for a rainy day? As the youngest y'all should be taking care of my ass. Least Bunny got that money train still rolling fo sure," Ginger laughed bumping her sister and tryin'a make her join in except all it did was cause her to burst into tears.

"Maybe we should just rob a bank or something," Simone joked trying to make light of things.

27

All Me-Ma's granddaughters knew that she would have been proud of the way her service turned out particularly if one didn't include the part where Deidra, no doubt feeling the sting of her perpetual cheerleader now being gone went nuts. They all knew that as soon as Deidra's dramatic-ass got to the church, shit was going to be crazy. And sure enough no sooner had their mother shown up than shit started going sideways. If she had just cried that would have seriously been enough, but she had to go and make sure that everybody in that place knew exactly who she was and that Me-Ma may have acted like the mother to each and every one of them, but she was in fact her only daughter. One of the women in the church stood up and testified to the amazing being that was Me-Ma Banks.

"Me-Ma treated me like family. Like I was her own child," Patricia Hampton who happened to be a peer of Deidra's, cried after the pastor asked if anyone wanted to say a few words about the dearly departed. Well that line snaked all the way down the aisle and out the back door filled with people wanting to share their experiences of grace delivered by the late Mrs. Banks. Sitting in the front row watching all these shows of heavy emotion for 'her' mother got on Deidra's damn nerves. Before anybody could calm her down and stop her she was on the stage shoving the latest speaker to the side.

"Y'all think you knew my mother? You think she wanted to mother all of you? Only reason my mother helped so many of you was 'cause she couldn't save me. I am Deidra Renee Banks. I am her only child. Do you hear me? And since this is my mother's funeral I shouldn't have to hear your lame-ass stories of how you didn't have your shit together and it was my mother that helped you out. You got that? I'm not interested in hearing about how you all took advantage of my poor big-hearted mother, so get the hell off this line and go straight to hell all of you!" She started mean mugging the people in line to the point where they went running back to their seats. Some of them more traumatized by Deidra's accusations darted out of the building.

"Now, now, Ms. Banks I know that you are grieving for your mother, but this is not the way. Your mother would not have appreciated it." The pastor hurried over to Deidra hoping to restore order, but if he knew what her daughters, all sitting in the front row watching this debacle knew, he would have stayed minding his business.

"Motherfucker . . ." Deidra started and her daughters expected and were not surprised with what came out of her mouth next. "You need to go back into whatever gay for pay motherfucking closet you done crawled your shyster-ass up out of —"

"Now wait a minute . . ." Pastor Street began, but he had come up against a professional shit talker and no amount of sermonizing for a living would make him a match against the only child of Me-Ma Banks. Well Deidra lapsed into motherfucker this and motherfucking cock sucker that to the point that Ginger felt so sorry for the pastor she jumped up and dragged her mother off the stage and out of the building. And just so we're clear, that woman put up a hell of a fight. Most of the people were equally shocked that Ginger was strong enough to take on her mother in six inch heels no less.

Of course nobody expected Pastor Street

to show up at the repast especially after the cussing out he got from Deidra and sure enough even though he committed to officiating the event he was ghost to it. No one blamed the man for refusing to be anywhere near the person that had publicly delivered the verbal ass kicking that would take months for him to live down no matter how many sermons he continued to deliver on turning the other cheek. By the third such sermon people were snickering and referring to the cheek as his butt cheek. Lord people can be cruel.

The guest of honor would have been pleased had she seen how many of the ladies of the church went to town on the delicious meals they had donated for the occasion. Me-Ma had reigned supreme as the best cook in Richmond and at least five or six other counties so her repast served as the first chance for the runners up to compete for her now vacant title. There were roast, hams, turkey legs, fried chicken, chitterlings, and every single vegetable you could think of. These ladies had put their foot in the preparation and still everybody remarked on how much they would miss Me-Ma's cooking.

"Everybody all right?" Simone as the oldest, most organized and best mannered grandchild remembered all of her etiquette lessons and made sure everybody had what they needed. Now I'm not going to paint her as some kind of martyr, that girl liked to keep busy so that she could avoid the sadness lurking underneath all those niceties.

"I wish to hell these people would just carry they asses on home," Deidra, nursing her third drink sneered to herself. The only reason she didn't act out again was because she didn't want to break anything in this house that would soon be hers now that her momma was dead. But this would be the last damn time any of these stuck-up freeloaders would enter Me-Ma's house which was another reason she chose not to get out of pocket again. Let 'em have their good time she thought as she strolled around making a mental catalogue of all the valuables, the picture frames, clock collection, and especially the fine china. Deidra had to make sure none of those things went missing with all these sticky fingered guests.

"Mama you all right?" Tallhya the only one of those girls who bothered to check on her asked probably trying to make sure she didn't get thrown out with the rest of them.

"Uh-hum, I'm fine." *Well, she could be as nice as she wanted,* Deidra thought, *but soon as the will was read she would be kicked to the curb just like the rest. Do her good to get out there and fend for herself.* Hell, Deidra had done it and so could the rest of them. She wasn't planning on running no charity, she had raised these girls and now they were grown. Now that her mother was no longer around Deidra chose the opportunity to rewrite history and in her new version she had been a good mother. Three white men entered the living room and Deidra turned to Tallhya who had been hovering near her since they got back to the house.

"Who are those men?" she asked Tallhya. Her mother sure did know a lot of different kinds of people.

"I don't know?" she wandered over to the men dressed in slacks and leather jackets, not like they were planning this visit. "Can I help you gentlemen?" The one standing in the front of the other two asked.

"We're here to pay our respects."

"Oh, are you friends of my grandmother?" she asked as they began to make their way into the room, all eyes turned to them. Before he answered Bunny who must have seen them enter came hurrying across the room.

"No, we're friends of hers." The man took

Bunny's arm and led her outside.

"What are you doing here?" she snatched her arm away from Ghostman, keeping an eye on his thugs.

"We have a problem," he talked to her like a disobedient child who had disrespected her parent. "That money you gave me was sixty thousand dollars short."

"I gave you everything. What do you expect me to do?"

"I don't care," he leaned in close to her and whispered, "But if you don't want to wind up like your friend you will get me my money. Seeing how you're experiencing a family issue I will give you ten days. And don't try and run because it wouldn't help your family."

By the time Ghostman and his thugs pulled away in his Range, Bunny had hit the wall of emotions she was upset and confused, she had never felt so damn alone. He might as well have told her one million dollars because she had no idea how she could get her hands on that kind of money. Bunny had long ago left the sanctity of the church, but that was long after Me-Ma drilled into her that when there is nowhere else you can go that is the perfect time to go to God.

"God, I'ma put this on you."

28

"We're the Bankses and we have a meeting with Mrs. Shelton," a few voices said as one of the most beautiful families of women the receptionist had ever seen approached.

"Can I get you ladies anything to drink?"

"You got cocktails?" the older of the women asked. The receptionist quickly recovered after realizing that the woman was dead serious.

"No ma'am, just water, coffee, and soda," she answered decidedly confused about the cocktail question at ten in the morning.

"Is it free 'cause I know how much these big muckety mucks jack everything up." The older woman complained.

"Ma, please let's just have the meeting and then we can get something to eat or drink," Simone interrupted already embarrassed by her mother's need to prove just how ghetto she was, a source of annoyance to her children.

"Mrs. Shelton will be right with you," the receptionist said after informing Mrs. Shelton of her guests. "You're meeting in the conference room. It's right this way." She led them around the corner and down a short hallway to a large glass enclosed room. Imagine their surprise when they found none other then Pastor Cassius Street sitting with a woman about the same age as Simone.

"Hello, I'm Lauryn Shelton," she got up and came around the table and extended her hand in greeting everyone, but Deidra didn't acknowledged it. She was too busy trying to figure out something else.

"What's he doing here? You did say that this is the reading of my mother's will?"

"Yes, and I need everyone mentioned in the will to be present." She smiled down at Deidra like she was a petulant child. "Everyone ready?" Lauryn went back to her seat that was a little too chummy with the pastor who did everything he could to avoid making eye contact with Deidra.

"We are here today to for the reading of the last will and testament of Marrietta 'Me-Ma' Banks."

"Can we just get to the good part? I'm not planning to be here all day," Deidra snapped making hand motions for Lauryn to hurry the fuck up.

"Excuse me ma'am. I will not have you snapping your fingers or disrespecting me in my place of business." Mrs. Shelton addressed Deidra, "Now please have a seat or I will have security escort you out of the building." This wasn't one of those born with a silver spoon in her mouth attorneys, Mrs. Shelton had grown up in one of the worst housing projects in Richmond and had grown up with a lot of Deidras in her day and she was not about to be talked down to.

"That's right, you tell her Mrs. Shelton! Yes, our mother is not known for her patience." Bunny laughed at the sight of seeing someone shut her mother down, "She is not known for her patience," Bunny added pointing to Deidra.

"Yeah, she has other qualities, like making babies she don't want nothing to do with." Ginger who had had just about enough of Deidra's nasty comments decided she had nothing to lose by fighting back. "Is there any way I can legally make my mother divulge which sperm donor is my father?"

"Please, can we just do this one thing for the matriarch of our family without turning it into some high school drama?" Simone had way too much on her mind like getting back to addressing her health crisis, a possible surgery, going back to work, and probable homelessness, just to name a few.

"I will not be disrespected by none of you little bitches. Mark my words," Deidra snapped and instead of sending her venom in the direction of one of her children she glared at the pastor still not understanding what the hell business he had with her mother. Although Lauryn knew exactly what had been written on the papers since they were executed not that long ago, she made a show of skimming the document as if looking for the right place to start.

"Mrs. Banks left a very detailed will with everyone present represented." Ginger and Tallhya shared a look of glee excited for the windfall when they thought no one was paying attention. Every one of them knew that Me-Ma kept her money tight so there was bound to be a flow in a few minutes. All four of the grandkids would have gladly exchanged whatever she had left them in the will for another week or month or year with the woman who had raised them, loved them, and taught them to believe in the lord even when they didn't want to.

"Go on what did she leave us?" the biggest mouth in the room pushed.

"To my youngest granddaughter, Ginger,

yes I know I gave you a hard time, but I love you just as much as all the others and if that's what you want your name to be then so be it. I leave you my family Bible and that old Louis whoever his name is purse that you told me is worth so much money. I also left you whatever you want out of my closet 'cause your Me-Ma sure had some good taste."

"Wait, she got left some old-ass clothes?" Deidra burst out laughing doubled over in hysteria. "She damn near left you the closet you flew the fuck out of." The rest of the grandchildren had to stand in solidarity with Ginger, which was actually hard because Deidra had some serious jokes. Simone and Bunny shot their mother dirty looks, but all she did was roll her eyes and motion for the lawyer to hurry the hell up.

"To my Tall . . . Tall . . . Tallhaaa . . . Tallha . . ." she tripped over her tongue trying to sound out the name.

"She know her damn name, keep going," Deidra had enough of all this hemming and hawing to last a lifetime. Lauryn turned to Tallhya apologetic before continuing.

"Its not my fault she gave me a name that nobody can pronounce." Her eyes rolled at her mother, who had already made it clear that she was not to be toyed with under any circumstances.

"Your grandmother left you all of her cookware and her recipe books. She also bequeathed you her record collection." Tallhya really just wanted her grandmother back and at the mention of inheriting her recipes, the ones she had taught her to cook by hand she collapsed into a blubbering mess.

"The rest of you might as well join her 'cause none of you are getting anything either."

By the time the attorney got to Deidra she was all but celebrating her good fortune. "Read it and weep you suckers!" she sneered before Mrs. Shelton started reading aloud.

"The house and all of my money I leave to the church, the one place that has given me solace in my life. I would like to appoint Pastor Cassius Street as the executor of my entire estate."

"What the fuck is this bullshit!" Simone screamed out sounding frighteningly like her mother and not at all like herself.

"No! My mother loved me. She would have never left me with nothing. Let me see that paper." Deidra grabbed the paper and tried to decipher what the hell it meant.

"Ladies, God always has a plan and it's

our job as human beings to trust that. This is what Me-Ma Banks wanted so we must respect that." It only took two seconds for Deidra to begin to beat the shit out of him before Lauryn and Bunny were able to pull her off of Cassius who seemed way too concerned with the state of his appearance than the beat down he was about to receive.

"I can't step out of here in a wrinkled suit."

"Ain't this some shit!" Bunny interjected with her outrage, too.

29

Bunny had already lost three days feeling sorry for herself. The clock was already counting down and she knew that Ghost-man would not be up to giving her more time. He had that shoot your ass over nothing vibe as it was witnessed by the way he killed Tariq over messing with his money. After the complete nightmare of the reading of the will she decided to drive back to the apartment hell-bent on getting out from under this mess. There had to be some kind of solution and she was intent on finding it. Nobody knew that Spoe was dead so she decided to work that in her favor. As she pulled into the garage the sight of Spoe's car parked in his space, like he was about to get into it and go about his day broke her all the way down. She had to sit in her car dry heaving tears streaming down her face until she could compose herself enough to move. That's when this thought hit her. She would sell her car.

Thirty minutes later she pulled into the Porsche dealership on the Midlothian Turnpike. She hadn't parked good when two hungry salesmen rushed out to greet her smelling their latest mark.

"I'm looking for Rusty Johnston," luckily she had found the card of the salesman that sold the car tucked inside a manual in the glove compartment.

"Nice to see you again," the salesmen said. The guy didn't remember that the car had been a surprise and he'd never laid eyes on Bunny in his life. That being said, no one is saying he wasn't happy to see her though.

"I'd like to sell my car." An accomplished liar Bunny spun some story about needing to leave town and that's why she had to sell the car.

"I'm sorry, but you don't own the car," he explained this basic fact to a stunned Bunny who remembered the day five months ago when Spoe had opened the garage and shown her the matching Porsches.

"But it was a present. You can't loan somebody a present."

"No, but Mr. Thomas thought you would want a new car next year so he paid off the three year lease agreement up front. That way you can keep it that long if you wanted, but in case you wanted to upgrade or get a new car you could."

"So I don't own the car?" Bunny sounded stunned and honestly, didn't get it. The guy was obviously loaded and he paid in cash, which any good salesman knows not to question even if it appeared really suspicious.

"No, ma'am."

"Did he lease his car, too?"

"Yes, ma'am he did."

"Thank you," Bunny got up, ignoring his suggestions to check out the latest models. And for the first time since she got the car when she got in it all she thought about was what a worthless piece of shit it had turned out to be. She had to find out a way to come up with that money.

When Bunny got back to the house she started looking around for any and everything that she could sell to make money. There were so many guys that tried to bite Spoe's style. He lived for Gucci, Louis, Guiseppi, and Tom Ford, which made sense because he and Bunny liked to floss. He has mad style and a wallet to satisfy his appetite. Lots of other men were hating on him and Bunny realized they would probably pay top dollar for his clothes until it hit her that she couldn't run around selling his things. That would look really suspicious. No, she had to be smart about this and not run around half cocked looking crazy. She had already showed her hand to the car salesman so the last thing she could do now was to have one of their leased Porsches go missing.

She remembered that in Spoe's watch box there were half a dozen of the finest time-pieces money could buy; a Rolex, two Cartiers, a Franck Mueller, Hublot, and a Patek Phillippe his crown jewel that was totally iced out. She crumbled at the idea of parting with them and emotionally felt herself start to crumble inside. She didn't know why she hesitated to sell these, but she had been with Spoe each time he had purchased one and the look on his face, a kid buying a new toy had been priceless. Selling these watches felt like she was giving up a part of Spoe, but as hard as she tried to find a solution in the end she didn't have a choice. She knew a pretty good fence that could get her top dollar so she gave him a call and they arranged to meet the next day.

That next morning Bunny was getting herself ready to meet with Billy the fence when her phone started blowing up. Ginger called worried about her because she'd just seen on the news that two bodies had been fished out of the James River.

"One of them is Spoe's friend Tariq. Where is Spoe?"

"I don't know, where he is."

"Do you think, his body could be in the James River too and maybe it's washed down to the Bay? I know that happened to one of my lover's cousin's homeboys."

"I don't know. All I know is that Spoe and Tariq left together, going on a job."

"Are you all right?" Ginger told her sounding more upset than Bunny, but of course she already had this information so it didn't come as a surprise.

"Yeah, I know," she answered sounding weary as someone started banging on her door. "Ging, let me call you back." She hung up and opened the door unaware of the shit storm the information about Spoe's death would start.

"All right bitch, get the fuck out of my son's apartment," Spoe's mother, Wanda screamed as she stood in the doorway glaring at her. "That is unless you want me to throw your skinny-ass out?" Spoe's family had never much cared for Bunny especially since Spoe stopped paying all their bills and giving them as much money as they ungrateful asses felt they were entitled to. They felt that since there was a change in his behavior shortly after he and Bunny officially got together, it was because of her. Before she shacked up with Spoe he spoiled his mama, two sisters, and their numerous kids no matter how obnoxious they were. He didn't seem to care that they were using him and always had their hands out demanding he buy them more things, pay their rent and send them on trips. To be perfectly honest they treated him like shit and it wasn't until Bunny came along and showed him how he was supposed to be treated that he stopped caving in to his family's demands. She not only took care of him, but worried about his well being and showed him a kind of love he never got from his family or even his mother.

While his family didn't care how he got his money Bunny did and would remind him that they had enough and that he should think of quitting that life and going straight. She forced him to reevaluate the selfishness of his family, which led to him having a real come to Jesus moment that culminated with him pulling away from his family and cutting them off from the Bank of Spoe. When Spoe stopped coming around and wasn't taking their call, they all blamed Bunny. To say they were salty or bitter about being cut off was an understatement. As more time passed and they saw Bunny driving around town in her flashy car, they hated her with all their might.

"You heard me bitch. You ain't deaf are you?" his mother sneered. Now under normal circumstances Bunny would have whipped her ass right there, but Bunny wasn't a dumb bitch. Wanda had both of her ghetto-ass daughters with her and Bunny knew she couldn't fight all three of them. They all stood there frowning, itching to take her down.

"If you don't get the fuck out of my face," Bunny said wanting to slam the door on them, but before she could stop them they had already pushed themselves inside. "Get the fuck out of here."

"All this shit in here belonged to my son and we're going to take all of it."

"That's right you gold-digging bitch!" Shanay, Spoe's oldest sister placed both hands on her hips, staring down Bunny.

"Let's just kick her ass," Li'l Moni, the baby balled up her fist and tried to scare Bunny.

"You come near me and that shit will not end well!" Bunny warned them. She had already gone through too much and wasn't about to let them intimidate her. "This right here at this moment is not what you want. I'm trying to compose myself out of respect for Spoe but right now you need to just leave me the fuck alone!"

"Now, I know that Spoe loved you and would want you to have some of his things, but you are not going to threaten me."

"Bitch probably took all his money, too," Li'l Moni snapped trying to rile up her mother and older sister.

"We should call the police," Shanay insisted to the mother. "Throw this greedy-ass thot up out of here."

"Really?" Bunny sneered. "And how exactly are you going to explain your brother's income? I can prove that I live here so there is nothing you can do to get me out."

"That's the way you want to play this?" Wanda remarked giving her the stink eye.

"We are taking everything that belongs to Spoe so you need to move your ass out of the way." Li'l Moni faked like she was about to hit Bunny whose hands shot up in defense. They all burst out laughing clowning her. Then they shoved passed Bunny and stormed into the bedroom and started grabbing all of Spoe's things.

She couldn't believe these vultures. Less than an hour after hearing about his death they were there stealing all his shit.

"Dammit!" Bunny said to herself freaking out at the realization Spoe's jewelry box was within reach. She had taken it out earlier to get everything ready to meet up with Billy so it wasn't in the safe where it normally would be. She grabbed the box and was about to throw it under the bed when Wanda snatched it out of her hand.

"You tryin'a be sneaky bitch?" Wanda said as she pushed Bunny to the floor. She sat on the bed and looked in the box. She didn't say a word, but the look on her face was as if she had just won the lottery.

30

"OMG! OMG! OMG! What the are you go-ing to do?" Simone screeched. Bunny had just explained to Simone everything that happened with Tariq and Ghostman. She had just told Simone she had no idea how she was going to meet Ghostman's de-mands. They were sitting in Me-Ma's kitchen eating their way through the moun-tain of food the ladies from the church had brought over earlier. They were grateful that those women now saw it as their job to take care of the four Banks girls as homage to their recently departed sister. "This shit is fucking crazy and fucked up!"

"I don't know. I just don't fucking have any idea." She shook her head. She knew Simone was upset because she had only heard her sister curse two times in her life. The first was when her father died and the second being this one. "There's no way I can get my hands on that kind of money."

It all just seemed impossible to her because Ghostman didn't care about her herculean efforts, all he gave a shit about was his money and he was not about to play on that.

"But what about all the clothes and jewelry? Spoe really had serious high-end shopping habits. Can't you sell some of his things?"

"That's what I planned on doing. I even had a fence set up to exchange his watch collections for so much money that even after I paid off the debt I'd still be flush.

"So what happened?" Simone inquired.

"His jealous money hungry mother and sisters happened. They pushed their way into our spot and took everything I coulda made some cash on. Girl, they even tried to take his Versace drawers. But what the fuck could I do? Wasn't like we were married and I had some legal right to all his illegally gotten goods."

"That is so messed up," Simone sympathized with her sister feeling incredibly hopeless about the whole thing.

"They were damn lucky I didn't cap one of 'em. The only reason was because I knew even though Spoe had stopped talking to them, he still loved his family. He would have wanted to know they weren't left out there with nothing."

"But what about you? Why didn't he make sure that you were taken care of? That just so fucked up."

"Look, he had my back the same way that your dad had yours. Shit don't always work out the way it's planned. I know Spoe had my motherfuckin' back!" Bunny lashed out at Simone for insinuating that he didn't. Her anger, frustration and fear were threatening to overflow onto the next person to get out of pocket even if it was her favorite sister.

"I'm sorry. I shouldn't have said that. I know how much he loved you," Simone offered backing off. She hadn't meant it the way her sister had taken it. This entire thing was really traumatic and she was worried about her sister. As the oldest Banks sister, Simone thought it was her job to help her siblings out of their messes, but this one was way above her head. The fact that she couldn't help her sister in her time of need pained her.

"Yes, he did love me," Bunny said her voice sounding fragile and strong at the same time. Unlike Simone's father who had died of cancer, Spoe had been killed. He had been taken from her and if it was the last thing she did, Ghostman would pay.

"We have to figure something out."

"No, this isn't on you. It's my problem. I just needed to vent Simone." Bunny had always prided herself on being able to handle her issues alone, but loosing Spoe was too much for her to keep to herself.

"We're sisters so your problem is my problem. You weren't there when Me-Ma spoke to the entire church, but this is exactly what she meant when she got up on that pulpit and preached. It was about the gift of family and how we don't get to just leave each other flailing in the wind when they have a problem. We have to stick together and not just when good stuff is happening," Simone reached over and hugged her sister.

"What about the cars?" Simone shouted excited to have figured out her sister's problem.

"The cars are leased so I gave his over to his mother 'cause what good is it going to do me since I can't sell it?"

"What about your stuff? All those expensive bags and clothes?"

"I went into one of those expensive-ass resale stores but since I didn't have the receipts for none of it the woman didn't want to fuck with me. Everything was paid in cash so they couldn't look it up with my card and I never saved the receipts. So there was nothing she could do. I'm fucked. And the consignment shop, basically after it's sold and they take their cut, it would be like I was selling my stuff for crackhead prices." Bunny shoved her plate of food across the table. There was no way she could have an appetite anymore.

"It's not like I can go to the bank and get a loan. They want collateral and since they don't mean last seasons Chloé bag or Chanel shoes the only other thing I can put up is my ass." The two of them shared a look 'cause they were thinking the same thing. "You think if you had a fake ass you could take it to the bank and use it as collateral?" Well, that was enough to make them smile.

Lucky for the Banks sisters God spared no expense when it came to making sure they were fine, they all had booties that men salivated at even fully clothed.

"That would be classic." The sisters finally laughed to keep from crying and high fived each other they were clowning so hard.

"Sisi, you work at that bank. You wanna slide your little sister about one hundred grand? You know to save my life?" Bunny actually started laughing, which proved contagious because before long both sisters were in hysterics.

"Hell yeah, you and everybody else. Just come to my register and I will personally hand you the money. You need cash to buy a new pair of Louis for a party? Well here is three thousand because you're going to need a new bag to go with it too." Simone mimed handing over the money.

"Well, I really need money to get my nails done . . . in Paris," Bunny spurted out barely able to form the words, but Simone played her part to the hilt sounding like the straight laced bank employee.

"Paris, France or Paris, Texas because whatever you need I got your money right here." She laughed before continuing, "The way that damn manager treated me today I should just give you all the money. I told you how he acted toward me when I went today, right?" Bunny nodded.

"Bwwaaaa!" Simone broke out into gleeful laughter. "Could you imagine his face?"

"I would give anything to see that!" Simone said, her face growing serious. Bunny noticed Simone's expression change and their eyes met. The two of them grew silent, their thoughts traveling from one to the other.

"Then why don't we just do it?" Bunny spoke first and instead of arguing or disagreeing Simone broke into a smile.

"And I know exactly how it would go down." Simone said smirking.

"Why not right? Let's fucking go in there and get that money." Bunny raised her hand to high five her sister who just sat there staring at her.

"I was kidding. You do know that don't you?"

"Well, I'm not. This is the perfect solution," Bunny argued sounding really adamant. Simone gave her a look to let her know that she thought this was crazy, but she knew her sister and once Bunny made up her mind it may as well have been set in stone.

"You're crazy if you think you can pull this off? Forget it." The doorbell ringing stopped her from telling her sister in detail how insane she thought her idea actually was. What did she think she could do, burst in and rob the bank all by herself?

"Who the hell is that at this hour?" Bunny got up to answer the door just as Tallhya came flying down the stairs.

"Maybe it's Walter?" she blurted out. Simone and Bunny raced in front of their sister to the door just as Ginger joined them stretching from her nap.

"Hello ladies, may I come in?" Pastor Cassius Street stood on the doorstep in a royal blue suit. Ginger was pissed to be seen in booty shorts and a cropped top without her hair done right.

"Sure, come on in Pastor," Simone offered giving her best imitation of Me-Ma who would always welcome people into her house with a smile, even if that person had been the devil which this man had already proved to be. The pastor entered taking a good look around.

"How are you ladies holding up with your grandmother's passing?" he asked in his best caring concerned man of God voice.

"We're doing just fine Pastor," Bunny snapped refusing to pretend this leper was a welcomed guest. What she really wanted was to give him a beat down for manipulating their grandmother.

"So, I wanted to have a little talk with you ladies to say that what your grandmother did, donating all of her money and property to the church was an amazingly generous thing."

"We're not entirely sure that she did. With all due respect Pastor, we find it a little bit suspicious that she had only had the papers drawn up a week before she passed," Simone told him trying to keep the rage out of her voice. She had been taught early on that it was better to catch with honey than with flies and right now she wanted to catch this snake in his lies.

"Well, anyway," the Pastor continued, ignoring their concerns, "I think your grandmother would have preferred it that one or all of you have the opportunity to buy this house from the church. Wouldn't that be lovely? To keep it in the family?"

"Wait? That's some bullshit!" Ginger's words mirrored what they had all been thinking.

"We need to have our attorney look into this," Simone told him. "The will has to pass through probate before anything can be done with our Me-Ma's things Pastor."

"Yes, that's right Ms. Banks. So that will take thirty days and by then this property might have already been listed with multiple offers. I just wanted to do the right thing by you ladies and to give you first dibs." He had the nerve to act like he was actually doing them a favor. Simone had to grab Bunny before she went upside his head. Ginger was already balling up her fist ready to wop him when Tallhya pushed the pastor toward the door.

"Thank you Pastor. We will call you," Simone grabbed him by the arm and hurriedly walked him out of the door, and closed it behind her. "That fucking crook!"

Simone was disappointed in herself that she was cursing as of late, but she was reaching her boiling point. "He is not going to steal Me-Ma's money and get away with it," she stated. The rest of the sisters all nodded agreeing, but none of them had a solution.

31

"How's it going?" Jackie checked in with Simone as she handed over her daily cash with a receipt she needed to check off and hand back after she validated that the count was correct.

"I will tell you at the end of the day," Simone said with a smile. "So far things are going well, but the bank hasn't opened yet so it's going to depend on how many guns I have shoved in my face," she told her only half kidding.

"We have added extra security measures. There will be another security guard posted outside of the bank between the hours of nine and five. All the studies show that the last hour is the safest. Also from now on we are going to rotate and distribute marked bills so that way nobody has them every day. You will know they are the marked ones by the green band holding them together. And last week they had three more cameras installed that are linked to the police station. There is a button near station four that when it's pushed, sends a signal in case of emergency." Jackie pointed at the button on the station next to her.

"That makes me feel a whole lot more secure."

"So the next time somebody thinks they can just rob this bank they will be on candid camera and the police will have surrounded this place in seven to ten minutes."

"Wow, that's great," Simone answered thinking how she couldn't wait to tell Bunny this so she can stop with her crazy thinking. Just then Mr. McPearson stopped in front of her station and added his ten cents.

"We want our employees to feel safe and to know that we're protecting them. What happened at this bank will never happen again. I'm actually looking forward to the next time someone thinks they can just come in here and steal from me," he said with a pompous attitude. Simone didn't know if she was being paranoid or if this man had actually just indirectly dared her to try something.

"That's good to know." She gave him her best fake smile. *What an asshole,* she thought before turning back to keep counting her money.

"Don't let him bother you. Just be grateful that you don't have to live with his ass." Jackie elbowed Simone to make her laugh.

The rest of the morning went relatively quick and painless with no major issues before lunch at least. When Simone counted out her bills to make sure all her numbers added up she was actually pleased that it equaled out perfectly. Last thing she needed was for Mr. McPearson to accuse her of stealing ten cents.

"You can take lunch," Jackie told her. "I ordered a pizza and there is still half left in the lounge."

"Thanks, but I need to get some fresh air. Thought I'd head over to Starbucks and grab something." After a quick lunch, she returned to the bank and as luck would have it, walked in just in time to come across the last person she wanted to see.

"Oh, look who finally got a job," Marjorie quipped under her breath as Simone passed. She decided to ignore her and went to clock in and return to her station. No sooner had she opened her window than Marjorie came over no doubt to mess with Simone. She waved a handful of hundred-dollar bills, money that probably belonged to Simone in the first place.

"What do you want Marjorie?"

"I just wanted to see what it looked like when a princess actually worked for a living. Your father would be so proud especially after he paid for three college degrees and the best job you could get only requires a high school diploma. Things must really be tough out there in the real world?" She laughed waving the money in front of Simone's face.

"Look, why don't you do us both a huge favor and walk away." Simone had to do everything she could to keep herself from punching Marjorie in her smug face.

"I see you're not so big and bad now are you? After all you don't want to risk the only way that you know how to make money now do you? Because I'm not giving you any of mine." She taunted Simone loving the fact that by being at work her wings were basically clipped so she couldn't fight back or sucker punch her like last time.

"Walk the hell away from me!" Simone hissed in a low voice trying to keep her composure and not alert the other tellers.

"Maybe if you hadn't been such a Class-A brat all those years twisting my husband around your little finger I might have been more generous to you. But I never liked you. Not for one single second. Your father may have thought I did, but that was just great acting on my part honey. See I knew that if I were going to manipulate your father into marriage I had to at least pretend to be the loving stepmother. And I did damn well for all those years, which is why all this money is mine. It's the least I should get for putting up with your boring-ass, lousy fuck father, and his second rate beauty pageant brat. So as you're slaving away at this little job just know that I am somewhere having a great life spending all your dumb-ass daddy's money and getting the shit fucked out of me on our bed." Well, Simone had taken all she could.

"Fuck you!" she seethed at Marjorie who now had her stepdaughter exactly where she wanted her.

"Excuse me? What did you say to me?" she raised her voice intentionally sounding insulted.

"You heard me," Simone stared so enraged at her stepmother that she was not paying any attention to the amount of ruckus she was causing. The other tellers and the customers were starting to stare in her direction, but the biggest problem was walking straight toward her window. "I said fuck you! You bitch!"

"Ms. Banks!" Mr. McPearson arrived at her window in time to get an earful of the words she had just spit at Marjorie who could not have been more pleased with the outcome.

"Is this how you train your employees to speak to your valued customers? If this is the case then I may have to take my seven figure account elsewhere." Marjorie admonished the bank manager who shot Simone the dirtiest look.

"I'm so sorry about that ma'am. I will have my associate finish your transaction with us today. I hope this does not interfere with our business relationship and as a courtesy we will waive this month's account charge. I will assure you this will not happen again." Mr. McPearson said as he turned toward Simone. "Ms. Banks, I need to see you in my office right away." He stated before walking away.

"Dammit!" Simone could not believe that she had walked right into the perfectly orchestrated trap that witch had set especially for her. As furious as she was at Marjorie the person she really wanted to slap was herself for being that gullible. She braced herself walking into Mr. McPearson's office.

"You do understand that you are still under a ninety day probation period Ms. Banks? That means you are not a permanent employee with the bank and that your behavior during that period is closely monitored. It also means that at any moment we can let you go without a disciplinary hearing. What you said to that woman is more than enough grounds for you to be dismissed do you understand?" Mr. McPearson barked at Simone as she sat in front of his desk.

"I really need this job," she pleaded not knowing how she would deal if she were fired and all because of that damn Marjorie.

"When I hired you it was because not only were you educated, but your qualifications made me think one day you could graduate to management. But what I've seen since the robbery makes me think you're not the kind of person who can handle this job. Maybe it's best for you to go back to sitting on your couch or whatever you did before you bothered to get your first real job at almost thirty. I mean I never really delved into it but what did you do for a living?" He insisted. As badly as Simone wanted Mr. McPearson to be the second person she told off today she held her tongue.

"Mr. McPearson I really need this job."

"I'm just not certain that you're the working type. At least not this kind of work." Simone got that she had just been called a hooker, but she tried to pretend that's not what this asshole manager was suggesting.

"I can handle it. I just . . . I can not explain in detail my problem with Marjorie, but I really am sorry. And if you give me one more chance you will not regret it, sir." But the look he gave her meant she was out of chances.

32

Simone exited the bank to find Detective Dugan leaning against his car parked in front of the bank.

"Can I walk you to your car?" he asked but instead of answering first she glanced back toward the bank to see if her boss was watching her. The last thing she needed after talking her way into keeping her job was to see her talking to Detective Dugan and have McPearson start to think that she's being sneaky or keeping something from him. The detective saw her reaction to him being there and figured out what she had been thinking. "I already talked to the powers that be in the bank and explained that every one of their employees had been cleared of any involvement in the robbery."

"That's nice. A relief," she told him although she knew she was innocent it helped that her boss wasn't still thinking she may have been involved. Something told her that he didn't need another excuse to dislike her. "Is that why you're here?" Dugan who normally felt self-assured found himself a little nervous in front of Simone. Maybe it had to do with the reason that he had to see her.

"Uhm no, would you like to get a quick coffee?"

"So you're here to invite me to coffee?" she asked not convinced that was his real intention.

"No," he had to laugh at himself. "You got me. I actually came to ask you to dinner. To ask you on a date," he told her shuffling from one foot to the other like some adolescent teenager.

"Wait so I went from being a suspect to being a possible dinner date?" she asked him trying to keep a straight face. She was struggling to keep from laughing. She found it a bit comical that Detective Dugan was asking her out after the hard time he had given her.

"Hey look, I was just doing my job," he explained trying to reason with her.

"And you did your job well," she added.

"All right I get it. This was a bad idea. I'm sorry if I offended you." He took a step back trying to gather himself. It wasn't his habit to mix business with pleasure and he sure wasn't used to getting turned down even if it was by the most beautiful woman he'd met in ages.

"You think you offend me?" Simone asked putting her hand over her chest acting as if she was surprised.

"I'm sorry Ms. Banks. Really, can we forget I ever stepped over the line and made a real fool of myself asking you out? I get it." He had that look on his face of sheer embarrassment and Simone was really enjoying his discomfort a little too much.

"Get what? That a really cute police officer actually thought I was guilty?" She had to fight to keep herself from laughing.

"No, I didn't say that I thought you were guilty . . . wait? You just called me cute? Like baby puppy cute or like I should get to know him cute?" He broke out into an infectious smile.

"So where are you taking me on this date?" Simone asked letting him know exactly what kind of cute she had been talking about. It had been a long time since she'd actually agreed to a date, but she had been thinking about the detective more than she wanted to admit.

"You want to grab a quick coffee and talk about it? I mean I did drive all this way and waited for you to finish with work." She had been listening but that was before a Brinks armored truck pulled up in front of the bank. Two armed guards exited and went into the bank. "Hello? Hello?" the detective broke Simone out of her trance watching the money being loaded into the bank. She glanced down at her watch, five-thirty.

"What is your first name Detective Dugan? I cannot go out with someone when I don't even know his first name," she smiled teasing him a little more. *Damn, this girl is gorgeous,* he thought to himself.

"It's Chase, Chase Dugan."

"Yeah, that sounds about right. You look like a Chase. So Chase, you want to go and have a coffee?"

"Sounds good. There's a place around the corner. It's not Starbucks, but I think it's a little more quaint," he told her as Simone allowed him to lead her down the street. So many things were swirling in her head, but one of them was definitely how good it felt to have a man this fine want to get to know you better. There was something about the detective that reminded her of someone, but she couldn't put her finger on who that could be.

33

By the time Simone and Chase got back to their cars it was way past eight. They'd spent so much time talking about their families, mostly him and their lives that time had gotten away from them. He had grown up in the area, went away for college, and retuned determined to make a difference in his hometown. The whole ride home she kept replaying their conversation and thinking about how comfortable they were together.

When she walked in the door Bunny was sitting in the kitchen alone making notes in a book. She didn't even look up when Simone walked into the room.

"What are you doing?" she asked concerned because her sister had an intense expression on her face when she entered.

"Nothing," she answered without glancing up. Simone came around the table and stood over her shoulder. An immediate feeling of sheer terror shot through her body as she caught a glimpse of what had captured Bunny's attention.

"You can't do it."

"Yes. I'm going to. I don't have a choice." Bunny gave her sister a look of such resignation that she knew there was no way to change her mind.

"This is like when I told you that Marla Thompson was bullying me in third grade and you threatened to beat her up. No matter how much I tried to talk you out of it you wouldn't listen and you beat the girl up anyway. My little sister came to my rescue," Simone said reminicing.

"Yup, that's exactly what it's like Simone. You can't stop me," Bunny said without looking at her.

"I couldn't stop you then and I can't stop you now, huh?"

"No, you can't."

"Then I'm going to do it with you."

"No. You must be crazy if you think I'm going to let you do that."

"I'm the insider. I can actually make sure you don't get arrested or killed." Bunny stared at her sister and began considering what Simone had just shared, but in the end she fought against it.

"No. And I mean it, Sisi. I can take care of myself. I'm the one that was living in the fast lane with a man that ripped people off for a living. Sure they were drug dealers, but this is my mess to clean up. You never even got a driving violation. You do things the right way and follow all the rules. I couldn't live with myself if I got you caught up in any kind of trouble."

"And look where being a Miss-Goody-Two-Shoes has gotten me? Working at a bank for a boss who thinks I'm some ghetto thief anyway. I might as well make sure that he's right."

"I'm not going to let you destroy your life. You're better than this," Bunny said trying to do whatever she could to talk her sister out of this.

"So who are you going to get to help you? Some of your friends? Bunny, where are all those girls now that your money is running low? You think they won't turn you in if it came to them or you? Family is the only thing you can trust. I will have your back."

"I know why I am willing to risk my life Sisi, but you can't. I won't let you do this for me." But Bunny knew that Simone was just like her when it came to being stubborn. She knew once Simone made the decision to do something, nothing would stop her from it.

"Well, don't flatter yourself. I'm not doing

it for you." Simone answered, looking into a confused Bunny's eyes. Now it was time for her to share something, "When my father died and that bitch stole all his money she took something else, that I need. She cut me off from my medical insurance and . . ."

"What? Sisi, tell me!" A red flag went off and Bunny knew that whatever her sister was holding back had to be huge.

"I need to have all these expensive tests and I need them done soon. The doctor thinks I might be very sick and unless I get these tests I won't know how bad things are and what the best course of action for me to take is."

"Wait, what? Sick, how sick do they think you are, Simone?" a now worried Bunny asked her.

"Pretty sick Bunny," Simone said trying to keep it as vague as possible, but her sister wasn't having it.

"How sick Simone? Stop beating around the fucking bush Simone!"

"They think I might have cancer," Simone said in a low tone.

"Cancer? No! I can't lose you. Not after Spoe, Tariq, and Me-Ma. Please God, no," Bunny cried out at the injustice.

"I know, but I'm going to be fine as long

as I get the money to handle the medical tests."

"So I guess we're going to do this?" Bunny asked gazing into her sister's eyes.

"Look, I saw that robbery go down and I can tell you everything those men did wrong. They were total amateurs. They didn't even know the bank routines or the best time to rob the place. They just thought that if they busted in like bad asses they would be able to take the place. And those stupid masks were ridiculous."

"We need to hire a driver," Bunny started to flip through her mental rolodex trying to find someone that they could trust.

"And at least one more person. And we need weapons."

"I got guns. Spoe kept all his equipment in a storage place and nobody knows where he kept them except me and him so I'm sure they're all still there." Bunny's eyes started to water thinking about Spoe. Simone glanced up and saw her sister's damp face.

"Everything will be all right, baby sis." She gave Bunny a squeeze trying to comfort her.

"I'm all right. Maybe doing this, exactly what Spoe use to do is going to help me in more ways than one. Because you work there you need to draw the inside of the bank and make a list of all the employees and how many guards."

"And we have to make damn sure that nobody has the chance to put a dye pack inside the bag when they're putting the money in there. That stuff does not come off. And we need the robbery to happen on a Thursday evening."

The two of them were so busy caught up in the details of the robbery that neither noticed Tallhya standing in the doorway her eyes wide from shock. She cleared her throat dramatically attempting to get their attention. They both looked up surprised expressions on their faces.

"So now you bitches think you're Bonnie and fucking Clyde?" she asked raising her voice loud enough to wake the neighbors.

"Shhh! Are you fucking crazy?" Bunny snapped at her.

"Me? You're asking me? You two are the ones that sound crazy. Y'all bitches think this is the movie, *Set it Off* or some shit and if Me-Ma was here she would beat you both with those wooden spoons over there." She pointed to the jar of spoons on the counter that their grandmother used to discipline her unruly charges when they were young.

"We don't have a choice. Or do you have

a whole lot of money hidden that we don't know about?" Bunny questioned her and then added a hostile stare for effect.

"No," Tallhya said looking down at the floor, "in case you two forgot, that no good husband of mine stole all my money and the bank says I have to sue him to get it back so I don't have shit," she said looking from one sister to the other with tears in her eyes.

"Look, just don't say anything to anyone please. If we had a choice we would, but we don't," Simone said with pleading eyes.

"I don't think you two can do this alone. I know that for sure."

"We don't care what you think as long as you keep this shit to yourself," Bunny said with an attitude. They both waited for Tallhya to agree, but she didn't.

"Guess I'm going to have to help since I don't want to visit you in the state pen." Tallhya's words shocked her sisters.

"What?"

"Y'all are not the only ones sick and tired of being a damn doormat having everything go wrong. Hell, just less than two weeks ago I had a husband who I thought loved me and a nice size bank account. Now here I am single and broke. Hell yeah, I want in. The way I see it Simone needs to be at work so it doesn't look suspicious, Bunny and I will rob the place so now all we need is someone to drive the getaway car." All three looked at each other realizing that neither of of them were the best drivers in the family.

"Ginger!" they all said in unison.

34

Bunny drove her sisters to Hopewell, a little town about thirty minutes outside of Richmond to the spot where Spoe and Tariq kept all their equipment for the robberies. Spoe knew that he had to make sure they weren't ever spotted with the weapons or clothing from the robberies. Luckily he trusted Bunny and made her come out with him to learn how to shoot the guns. He didn't ever want her in a situation where she couldn't protect herself so she went from being a novice to an expert marksman.

"Where the hell are we going?" Ginger raised her voice looking around at the country road with nothing but miles of trees on either side. Occasionally they'd see a small house pushed back from the road, but this was too densely populated for the sisters. "This can't take all day 'cause I got places to go, people to do and more people to do." Ginger laughed high-fiving Tallhya.

"You stoopid," Bunny shook her head at their youngest sister.

"Not too stupid for you bitches to need me to save your asses. See y'all can't be talkin' about Ginger and treating her like the pain in the neck little sister when she got skills to pay the bills." She snapped her fingers to solidify her point.

"Whatever," Simone laughed grateful they could always count on Ginger for some comic relief.

"I'm about to be one bad bitch with a gun in my hands. Then I'll be packing in more ways then one," Ginger joked.

"Ew, stop! Just stop!" Bunny yelled then proceeded to shoot Ginger a dirty look in the rearview mirror. "Thank God, we're here," Bunny pulled Simone's beat up old Dodge into a hidden driveway and drove a ways down a road until they came to a shack with a garage.

"I'm not going in there," Tallhya shook her head and Bunny just gave her a look so fierce she jumped out of the car without any more complaining.

"This is serious!" Simone stood there in shock as Bunny unlocked the huge metal cabinet that held a shitload of artillery. Tallhya and Ginger raced over each grabbing a gun like they were toys. Tale held a semi-automatic pistol, but of course the youngest had to have the biggest and went straight for a machine gun.

"Bam! Bam! Bam! Motherfucker, take that you're dead," Tallhya shouted to her imaginary victim who her sisters assumed was Walter. She shot at the cans Bunny had lined up outside on a wall and missed all three of them. Simone brandishing a Glock came up next to her and hit all three cans.

"Now Walter is dead for real," she said winking at Tallhya. Thankfully her father had always made sure that she knew how to defend herself. She had taken shooting once a month since she was thirteen.

"How could I have been so stupid?" Tallhya whined.

"Good dick will make you do some dumb shit," Bunny laughed thinking about all the things she had done with and for Spoe.

"Ain't that the motherfuckin' truth," Ginger sighed.

"I know," Tallhya started, "but it wasn't even that good." She confessed and they all burst out laughing 'cause that made it sad.

"All right we need to get serious," Simone interrupted them breaking off the fun. "This is a real big deal so we need to be focused and ready. No thinking about men or dick or heartbreak or any of the people who messed us over. Not now. The slightest mistake can cost us our lives or our freedom so the time to joke and have fun is done. You hear me?" She glanced over at her sisters even Ginger who always had a snappy comeback remained mute and serious. "We are ready to run through what we need to do because once we —"

"I got this Sisi," Bunny interjected, cutting her off. "I know you're the big sister and you're used to being in charge, but this is my thing."

"No, it's not. You have an immediate need that makes you too invested to take the lead. The other reason I'm going to lead is because I'm the one working at the bank. Do any of you know where the security is stationed? What measures have been put into place recently in order to thwart another bank robbery? Do you even know the best day in order to get the most cash? No. So if you want me involved you need to let me take charge. I will get you in and out of there safe."

"Fine, but something goes wrong and it's on you!" Bunny announced throwing up her hands. Simone waited until the wrath of her sister's threat dissipated before continuing.

"Every one of us is going to have a job to do. First off, Bunny and I know how to use guns so Tale and Ginger you both have to learn marksmanship. While I'm at work the next two days you both need to come out here and work on your aim and comfort levels. You can't have any fear. Bunny is going to come up with our disguises and outfits for the hit. Also, Bunny it's your job to make sure we have the right weapons and burner cell phones. Tallhya you have a memory like an elephant so I need you to come to the bank and to do a visual walk through. You need to make sure that no one notices you checking out the bank.

"What about me?" Ginger always wanting to keep up with her sisters interrupted her mouth pressed into a pout.

"You need to find a car that no one will notice and we can use for the heist."

"That's easy."

"So everybody has their assignments. My job is to draw a map of the bank and to give you all the details you need to pull this off." Simone surprisingly took to the whole criminal thing. She liked finally being in control.

"You really think we can pull this off?" Bunny whispered to her older sister.

"Yeah, I do. In fact I know we can do it," she smiled, taking her sister's hand.

35

"Girl, what the hell are you wearing?" Ginger asked then she physically blocked Simone from leaving the bedroom. "Tall-hyra, Bunny come quick!" she hollered down the stairs for reinforcements.

"Stop playing we need to do one more run-through before I leave," she insisted try-ing to maneuver around her sister. Ginger folded her hands across her chest and gave her the once over before shaking her head at this pitiful display.

"What?" Both Tallhya and Bunny crowded into Simone's bedroom.

"Look at this hot mess!" Ginger pointed at their older sister's outfit, a pencil skirt, a button down shirt, a blazer and a pair of pumps.

"What? I like this outfit," she said defend-ing her outfit.

"If you were tryin'a be a librarian or a receptionist you would definitely get the job," Tallhya sassed.

"Its not that bad," Simone insisted staring at her image in the mirror.

"Unless you are trying to blow someone off, this is not a let's take it to the next level kind of outfit. This is a shut that shit down 'cause you ain't getting none." Bunny laughed.

"That cooty cat is on some Fort Knox security level." Ginger snapped again.

"But I don't know him enough to sleep with him." Simone insisted getting uptight about her first date with Detective Dugan.

"How the hell are we related? If he's fine, employed, and interested then sex is usually on the agenda. How are you even Deidra's child? Our mother likes to fuck, we all like to fuck except you." Bunny glanced at her oldest sister who looked embarrassed at this uninvited attention to her sex life.

"It's not that. I like sex just as much as the rest of you, but I want to know that it's not just about the sex. I want a guy to respect me," she told them.

"Girl they can respect me, but if the sex ain't poppin' then I'm not going to respect them and the shit will be over. Done. Dead. Finished," Ginger explained complete with finger snaps.

"Awwww, somebody really likes this guy,"

Bunny teased Simone. "And if that's the case you don't have to fuck him, but you do have to make sure he wants to fuck you and that's not going to happen in that outfit." The sisters wore her down and finally convinced her to change her outfit to a fitted black wrap dress that was both classy and sexy. She had an hour to kill before Chase picked her up so they went over their plans for tomorrow and gave Simone some dating tips too. When the doorbell rang, they all felt ready for the next day and Simone was ready for her date.

"Hello," Simone blushed as she answered the door to Chase who looked damn fine in a pair of dark jeans and a light blue button down shirt open at the neck. She tried to hurry out before the girls embarrassed her but that didn't happen.

"Don't do nothing I wouldn't do," Ginger joked batting her eyelashes and acting a fool. After lots of funny remarks she managed to get them out of there and into his car.

"Have fun you crazy kids," Bunny teased them as they got into the car. As soon as they were gone, the sisters got to talking.

"Damn he was fine as hell," Ginger exclaimed. "I would have let him arrest me just so he could pat me down."

"You better leave your sister's man alone," Bunny laughed.

"I'm happy for her," Tallhya added. "Lucky bitch!" They all started laughing and even though Bunny's man had been killed and Tallhya's had left her they really wanted their sister to find love and to be happy.

"Your sisters really love you," Chase said as he glanced to look at Simone.

"Yeah, they especially love embarrassing me."

"I wish I had siblings. Being an only child, I never had moments like that. I wish I had older or younger siblings. You're really lucky to have each other."

"It's definitely never boring," she confessed as he pulled away from the curb. Then unexpectedly, Chase turned toward Simone, grabbed her hand and kissed it. This was a first for Simone and she blushed like a little schoolgirl. As he began to drive them to a hip Gastro pub downtown, Simone did not let go of his hand until they reached their destination. After he parked, he insisted she stay in her seat as he came around and opened the car door for her. Simon had always treated his daughter like a princess, opening her door, expecting her to sit before he had been seated along with great table manners and he always told Simone that if she ever found a man that treated her the same to make sure she hold on to him because good men are hard to come by.

"Can we grab a booth?" Chase asked the hostess before they took a seat. Simone liked the way he took charge as he sat down beside her. Damn, she wanted to grab him and make out right there, but she didn't. She kept it clean at least for now.

"So, now I want to hear more about you?" she asked staring into his eyes.

"Then you're going to have to stop looking at me like that because I can't even think. And you have to stop biting your bottom lip like that," he demanded before leaning in and kissing her. Simone felt herself gasp as his lips touched hers. The electricity between them cause the two to pull back and stare at each other a full minute before they could recover.

"Wow," she exclaimed touching her lips where his had just been.

"Wow, is right. Damn woman, what are you trying to do to me? I'm trying to be all PG, first date and that kiss took me sailing right passed rated R." She lowered her eyes afraid he'd see that they were in the same place. Chase placed his hand on her chin and brought her to his eye level. "I like you Simone Banks. I really, really like you. Now if I wanted to get laid that's easy. Way too easy and I'm not trying to sound conceited, but it's true. I want to get to know you first and foremost. And whether we wind up in bed today, next week or next month it doesn't matter because I'm still going to want to get to know you. So we can take this as slow as you like or as fast, but I'm on this ride with you." His words rang true to her, but they were also scary. Her whole life Simone had been waiting for a man to be real, honest and to not try and play her. Basically she had been looking for a man that reminded her of her father, but those kinds of men didn't come around every day.

"I hear you," she answered knowing that she couldn't hide the vulnerability in her eyes. She wanted so desperately to believe him and to trust him, but she'd been burned more than once by a brother who came on hard, got what he wanted and was out.

"I'm not asking you to just believe me. Not some surface bullshit, but deep down at the core. Look, I know how this sounds and I'm the one saying it. What I do for a living requires me to take everything I hear and weigh it, but to never just trust it until

I've ruled out all other possibilities. Well, I'm telling you that what I'm saying to you I haven't said to a woman since I was in college and I fell in love freshman year. The relationship lasted three years, but it wasn't forever so we moved on and we're still friends." He leaned in and kissed her again causing her to get wet in between her legs. She felt so exposed that when she glanced up there were tears glistening in her eyes.

"I . . . I just don't know . . ." she stopped herself getting tongue-tied.

"Yes, you do," he started and they both froze to allow the waiter to deliver their food although at the moment neither felt any hunger.

"Thank you," they both said to the waiter when he finished.

"If that kiss didn't mean anything to you I need to know now."

"Of course it did, but this is crazy we just met each other," she began. "You don't just go from having gone out for coffee to having dinner and talking about serious commitments in just a few days. Yes, I have feelings for you that I can not explain considering we barely know each other and the circumstances in which we met, but this is crazy. It's love craziness," Simone told him as she shook her head.

"And what's wrong with crazy love," he demanded staring into her eyes and making her feel so weak and desperate for him. What the hell had happened to her? Simone had never allowed herself to go there with a guy, not this quick, and probably not ever. God, this man was sexy. Before she could stop herself, her emotions took over and she leaned in and kissed him. She stopped caring if this were real or not and decided that either this would be the biggest heartbreak or that she had finally gotten her love story.

"You think we should eat dinner?" he laughed when they pulled apart.

"Probably," she answered grinning from ear to ear.

"So what made you become a bank teller?" he asked.

"Desperation. If it were up to me I'd probably be one of those perpetual students always traveling, taking classes, and learning new things, but my circumstances had changed and I needed to get a job. I don't think taking that kind of job is fueled by some kind of romantic longing. It was pure necessity on my part, but I've met some interesting people since I started so it hasn't all been bad." She laughed flirting with him.

"And she flirts," he teased her. "When I

first met you I thought you were one of those women that needs a man to make at least six figures to get your attention."

"Really? Maybe I am?" she couldn't help joking with him. "I need to see your Dunn & Bradstreet rating, your tax returns for the last five years, and I need to go to your house to make sure you're not living with some woman."

"Check!" Chase held up his hand dramatically to flag down the waiter who came running.

"Yes?"

"We need to get the check ASAP." The waiter raced off to handle this request.

"You're kidding right?" Simone asked curious about this.

"No. I want you to see where I live. Let's go," he said taking her hand.

"Wait. Wait. I believe you."

"So you don't want to see my house?" he asked challenging her.

"Oh, I'm going to see your house just not tonight." Simone had a big day tomorrow and if all went well then she and the detective would have plenty of opportunity to get to know each other.

"So you're chickening out?" he laughed.

"No, I'm not. As a matter of fact the next

time we see each other I'm going to your house."

"Tomorrow? What are you doing tomorrow?" he asked her waiting for Simone to wriggle out of it, but she wasn't trying to do that at all.

"Working and then I'm going to your house," she said matter of fact. He leaned in and kissed her, the both of them getting turned on. "Yes. I'm definitely coming to your house."

36

All day Simone had to stop herself from watching the clock, remembering that everything that she did was filmed. She knew that she would probably look suspicious if anyone studied the tapes, but that didn't stop her. The bank manager had been particularly pleased with his job at heightening the security as the day wore on without incident. Everything had been going exactly as it should thanks in part to all the new measures he'd put into place. *Yes, this was about to be another great day,* he thought as he saw Detective Dugan enter the bank at 5:12 p.m. It certainly helped morale that the Richmond Police Department were making extra rounds into the bank these days.

"How's it going?" Chase surprised Simone when he appeared at her window. She almost had a heart attack and not because she was excited to see him which would have been the case at any other time except right now she was freaking the fuck out about how close this visit was.

"Great," she answered. "To what do I owe this visit or were you here for another reason?" She tried to fix her face so the smile wouldn't come off as fake. *Don't look at the clock,* she told herself knowing that it was ticking down to the moment she and her sisters had worked on for the past week.

"No, I came to tell you that I had a great time last night. I didn't want to be rude and text you. I've always felt texts are so impersonal. Plus we said we'd see each other today and I wasn't sure if you'd remember," he said. Boy did this brother do all kinds of things to her Simone thought just watching his juicy lips moving.

"Sure. I remembered. I'm suppsed be going to your place for dinner." She smiled, but inside she was trying to figure out how to get him the heck out of there.

"Yes, I can't wait."

"Detective Dugan," she heard Mr. Mc-Pearson call out coming toward them. She noticed that he had that look as if he wondered if she were in some kind of trouble.

"Mr. McPearson, I'm just checking on things. Making sure everyone is safe." He winked at Simone as he walked over to greet the manager.

Go, go, go, go, the mantra kept ringing in her head as she watched the two men having a conversation about nothing. Dammit. She needed him to get out of there or they all would wind up in prison and that was real.

Meanwhile ten minutes away . . .

"Who's gonna run this town tonight, we're gonna run this town tonight . . ." Jay-Z and Rihanna's voices filled the old model Suburban as the three girls inside prepped themselves.

"This is hot as hell," Tallhya complained about the extra padding she had been forced to wear so that she would look like a dude. They did not want to appear to be three women. Even Ginger had her boy clothes on. This was not the place for five-inch heels and killer nails and remarkably she did not complain.

"Can you slow the fuck down Speed Racer!" Bunny hollered at Ginger who was having way too much fun in her new role. She had always felt like she wasn't needed in the family and like she didn't have anything to offer then so the fact that she was needed by her sisters gave her a rush and made it well worth the risk to her.

"Ooops, sorry," she commented as she eased her foot off the gas.

"Okay, so you all know the plans. Tallhya, I do all the talking. Don't deviate from what we choreographed. You hear me?" Bunny demanded.

"Yes, now calm the fuck down," Tallhya ordered her sister as she snatched her Hillary Clinton mask off the floor in front of her and grabbed her beanie. They all shoved their ponytails under the hats.

"Pull over right here," Bunny pointed to a side street.

"Why are we stopping?" Ginger questioned. "That was not in any of the run throughs that we practiced."

"We need to get rid of all the evidence. Anything in writing has to go." Bunny got out of the car with the papers where Simone had drawn the inside of the bank. She took out a lighter and lit the papers and waited until they burned before getting back in the car.

Back inside of the bank . . .

Simone breathed a sigh of relief as she checked the clock when Chase started to walk toward the exit. He looked over his shoulder and gave her a little smile that no one else would have picked up on. He held the door for the Brinks guys who entered right on time and handed the bags of money over to the bank manager. He would normally take about twenty minutes to take it down to the safe and lock it up. Once it was in the safe the chance of getting the money was gone.

"Can I have that in all fives?" a sweet old lady who might have been one of Me-Ma's friends requested of Simone. As she began to count out two hundred dollars in fives she felt anxious and really hoped this lady was out of the bank before the robbery took place. The last thing she wanted to do was to be responsible for this old woman having a heart attack. Simone watched the Brinks guys leave the bank as she finished with the old lady.

No sooner had the old lady stepped out of the bank then three people entered the bank wearing Hillary Clinton masks.

"This is a motherfuckin' robbery," Bunny speaking in a deep gravelly voice began. "Rat ta ta ta!" her machine gun made a noise as she pointed it at the ceiling and popped off a couple of rounds. She needed to make her point as Tallhya and Ginger, weapons in hand hurried over to the registers to keep the tellers from pushing buttons. Simone was glad that they looked like dudes and not women. "Do what I say and no one will get hurt. Now any of you motherfuckers want to be brave then that will be your funeral. Everybody down on the floor now."

All the bodies lowered, fell or jumped down onto the floor except the manager who thought it might be a good idea to reason with them.

"Look, please don't hurt anybody," Mr. McPearson begged as he held up his hands and moved toward Bunny. Luckily there were only four customers in the bank, three tellers, two managers and one security guard. The other guard always went home at five which is why Simone told them to wait until five fifteen. Bunny took the butt of her gun and slammed it into McPearson causing him to go down. She wanted to say, "that's for fucking with my sister and for treating her like shit," but she knew better. He went down without a complaint. Bunny had to stop herself from glancing toward Simone in fact she made a point not to make eye contact with her sister. *Stick to the plan,* she told herself.

"See those bags?" Bunny pointed to the bags Ginger and Tallhya held in their hands.

"Fill 'em up," she screamed at the tellers. "Move!" she yelled. "And don't touch none of those buttons because I'm looking for an excuse to use this piece." She waved her gun in their directions.

"Oh my God!" Simone cried just as they had rehearsed.

"Bitch one more sound out of you . . ." Bunny aimed her gun on Simone. ". . . and I will make damn sure those are your last words. You understand?" she barked. Instead of answering, Simone appeared terrified as she shook her head up and down. Then Tallhya slipped into the manager's office where the two huge bags of money were sitting. She grabbed the bags and started walking toward the exit door. Bunny went to the tellers and swooped up the bills they had at their registers and all the while Simone was staring at the clock. This was getting close. Too close. Simone knew she had to take the chance so she coughed. Bunny looked at the clock, grabbed the money and headed for the door.

"Five minutes. Do not move for five minutes and all of you tellers put your motherfuckin' hands up in the air." And just like that, Bunny, Tallhya, and Ginger were out the door racing to get into their car. A good two minutes later they could all hear the sound of sirens. Simone knew that it would take them five minutes to get to the second car.

"Everybody get up," Mr. McPearson told all the people lying on the floor. Jackie got up and went to check on the tellers.

"You guys all right?" she asked.

"All the employees nodded, a few that had just experienced the last robbery and murders of their coworkers were breaking down. Simone pretended to be affected shaking as she started crying along with two other tellers. She imagined her father's funeral so that she could make herself cry. She really was worried though. Until she knew for sure that her sisters were safe she would not be all right. She glanced at the clock. Normally she would be getting ready to leave, but right now the employees were waiting for the detectives to show up so that they could be interviewed.

37

"Detective, these robbers were in and out before we arrived. Not at all like the last ones. It's as if they had a playbook that was the exact opposite of the one those four guys used. They even used a similar mask for all three of them, Hillary Clinton as if they were taunting us? I mean this may have been the perfect crime." The officer finished as Simone glanced up and saw that he'd been talking to Chase who must have just walked in.

"There is no perfect crime. We need to look at the tapes." Chase told the detective. Simone froze where she was standing as she worried about what they would find on the tapes.

"We need to set them up in a room. Right this way," Jackie led the men toward the back of the bank.

Simone watched the clock and waited as every single person had been interviewed.

Almost an hour passed while she waited too nervous to call her sisters. The plan was to all meet back at the house. There was no telling if her phone was bugged after that last robbery so she wasn't taking any chances. It's the little dumb things that get you caught. As she glanced around she saw one more employee going into the office, which meant that they were almost done. She wondered why they had left her for last.

"Ms. Simone Banks." A female officer approached without waiting to confirm if it was the right person. Everybody else had been allowed to go home so who she was was obvious.

"Yes, that's me," Simone volunteered and followed the officer down a hallway and into a back office that had been set up with Chase and another detective.

"You all right?" Detective Dugan questioned and smiled as she entered, his attempt at comforting her.

"I'm just really tired," Simone told the detectives.

"This must be hard for you? Especially after that last robbery. And this one right behind it just doesn't make any sense. At least no one was shot this time."

"Yes, thank God. I couldn't have handled that."

"So Simone . . . I mean Ms. Banks, this is my partner Detective Franklin," he motioned to the middle age white guy leaning against the wall watching her with an intensity that made her nervous.

"Hi, nice to meet you Ms. Banks," he says all the while staring at her.

"Nice to meet you, too," she answered trying not to avoid him. She knew that the detectives would look for signs of guilt.

"We need to ask you some questions about the robbery," Chase said, starting to interview her. After last night this seemed so weird.

"Yes, of course. What do you need to know?"

"It doesn't make sense that anyone would hit the bank this soon after the last one. The one thing every one seems to agree on is that at least one of the suspects was a female, but there is a question about the others. Not everyone agrees on all of the suspects being female." Simone didn't dare mention what had just gone through her head, which was that Ginger would go ballistic if they dared to suggest she wasn't a female even if she was pretending to be male.

"Yes, I thought it was two girls, too," she agreed.

"Our first thought is that these might have been connected to the male bank robbers?"

"You think so?" She hadn't thought of that as a possibility.

"We were looking at the surveillance tapes and we couldn't help noticing a couple of things Ms. Banks," Detective Franklin commented. She glanced over at Chase and saw him attempt to offer his support with a weak smile.

"Yes, what is that?" she asked trying to stop her voice from shaking and revealing that she was scared shitless.

"We noticed that for at least an hour prior to the robbery you kept glancing at the clock," the detective questioned her. Simone had to think quick on how she would explain herself out of that.

"I had special plans tonight and I guess I couldn't wait. I spend a lot of time being independent not allowing myself to like anyone and the truth is I had a date last night with someone I liked and we were going out again tonight." She caught Chase's eyes as he looked up at her curious about how much she would say.

"Really? So you were watching the clock because you had a date?" Chase jumped in and asked her.

"Yes, I guess my secret is out. I was

anxious about my date tongiht," she coughed and then had to take deep breaths to stop herself from choking. She wasn't entirely lying. She really was looking forward to her date tonight, but she knew that wasn't the real reason she kept looking at the time.

"You all right?" Chase rushed over to the door. "Can you grab us some water?" When he returned he handed Simone a bottle of water.

"I just have this cough that comes and goes."

"Wait. Ms. Banks, the reason you were looking up at the clock had to do with your excitement over a date? So you must really like this guy?" Chase questioned her watching her closely to see if she were embarrassed. Simone scrunched up her face, trying not to die of embarrassment.

"I like him enough to not want to talk about it. I don't know him well enough. I mean he could be a player for all I know."

"But you like him?" he asked again while Detective Franklin watched the two of them like a tennis match. Suddenly it was as if a light bulb went off.

"Yes. I think so," she admitted.

"Thank you Ms. Banks. That will be all. Partner why don't you walk Ms. Banks to her car. We can get in touch with her if we have any more questions."

"You sure about that? I don't want to step away if you need me?" Chase questioned his partner no doubt feeling self-conscious.

"I'll go and gather my things," Simone explained and left the room with the two detectives watching after her.

"She's a beautiful woman Chase," his partner teased him.

"Look, I only asked her out after she was cleared from the last robbery. I had no idea that the bank would get hit again and this would become an issue."

"You like her, huh?" he asked putting Chase, who preferred to keep his work and business life separate on the spot. The two men worked exceptionally well together over the past four years, but where Franklin was married with children his partner could and had been accused of being wedded to his work, but the way he looked at Simone gave his partner some hope. He'd been talking to him about the importance of balancing work and home life and he hoped this meant that he was actually willing to make a change and to give this woman a chance.

"I do like her, but maybe it's a bad idea trying to mix these two things."

"If I thought that was a problem I would

be the first to tell you to proceed with caution. But there is no way that young lady had anything to do with this robbery I'd bet my badge on it. If you like her and from what I just witnessed I'd say that you do then you should go out with her. Hell, I haven't seen you light up at the sight of a woman in years and the way they throw themselves at you I would know."

"You're right. But you really think it's going to be all right?"

"What you don't trust me now?" He gave his partner a stern look to go with his response.

"I'll be right back," Chase agreed.

"Go. And take your time I want to look at this tape again." He motioned his partner out of the room. It was nice to finally see something other than work on his mind if only for five minutes because they had a lot riding on this case.

Chase met Simone at the door.

"I'm around the back in the employee parking lot this time. I thought it was time I followed the rules. My boss isn't exactly team Banks." Simone told him as they went around the building to her car.

"Look about tonight?" he began and she could tell that his mind was heavy so she finished his thoughts.

"It's not going to work for a date?" She smiled up at him. "I know you have your hands full." She smiled at him again.

"I do. You have no idea. The FBI is threatening to take this case away from us if we don't find the suspects within the next twenty-four hours," he sighed looking real stressed about the situation, which made her feel torn because she knew that she was the reason for his problems.

"It's all right. I can have dinner with my sisters. I really need to get my mind off today," she lied because what she needed was to help Bunny give Ghostman his money tonight.

"So now you're cancelling on me?" he looked a little confused and that actually confused her.

"But I thought that you were cancelling on me?" she answered and even though she wanted nothing more than to spend time with him she had something much more important on her plate at the moment.

"I might be a little later than I originally planned, but I will let you know. You're not getting rid of me so easily." He leaned in and gave her a kiss that turned passionate reminding them both of the chemistry they'd had last night.

"Wow?"

"Was that okay? I don't know after everything you went through today I thought it might —"

"Might what?" Simone asked cutting him off.

"Be nice. A reprieve from the heavy stuff we're both dealing with not to mention that I've been wanting to kiss you all day."

"Good, because to me that is the best reason." She smiled suddenly wanting to be wrapped up in his arms somewhere far away from this bank. Hell, far away from all of it if that were even possible.

"I got to get back in there. I will call you as soon as I can." He opened her car door and waited until she got in and pulled away before heading back into the bank. The detective couldn't remember the last time he'd spent this much time thinking about anything besides work. Yes, Simone Banks certainly intrigued him, but even more than that she made him feel at home he thought as he reentered the crime scene.

He kept asking himself how the hell had the same bank been hit in such a short time?

"Nice of you to join us Detective," FBI Agent Jonathan Marks, Detective Dugan's contemporary and nemesis quipped when he saw that Chase had come and appeared annoyed to discover him surveying the crime scene.

"What? You're not honoring the twenty-four hour threat your superior gave us? Is that how the FBI works these days?" Chase sneered at the man who proved to be a consistent thorn in his side always taunting the local police that they were inept when it came to doing their jobs.

"Oh, I'm so certain your team will fuck this up that I'm making sure none of the evidence is compromised."

"Your blatant disrespect is getting old, Jonathan." He looked down at the agent pleased to have a good four inches on him.

"You don't have a problem with it do you? Because I could call your Sergeant and talk to him?" he quipped watching his team collect whatever they could from the scene. All Detective Dugan could do was to watch the smug officer who had made a habit of stealing his cases to the point that he couldn't help but take it personally. Sure he'd been the one to make detective before Marks and that made him quit the police force and join the FBI, but you'd think making that leap would have satisfied him.

"I've got work to do," Chase stepped around him and went to find his partner.

"Detective Dugan, tick-tock," the agent warned him as he stormed off as much to get away from him as to try to find the bank robbers.

38

Simone left the bank and drove straight home. She knew that if for some reason the cops hadn't bought her story and put a tail on her she needed to go where she said she would be. Her nerves were completely shot as she pulled up in front of the house and parked.

"Dammit!" Simone noticed a new large for sale sign spiked into the grass in front of the house. She hated that damn Cassius Street and promptly added his name to the list of people she planned to make pay for their betrayal one day.

"We did it!" Ginger raced outside and jumped all over Simone as soon as she stepped out of her car.

"Stop!" she snapped at her sister. "We need to act cool in public." She rushed Ginger inside the house.

"What happened at the bank after we left?" Bunny hurried down the stairs at the sound of Simone's voice.

"Well, Chase and his partner interrogated me for what seemed like forever. But then I could tell that they ruled me out."

"Chase? We like Chase," Tallhya kidded as they entered the living room. Simone blushed at someone else mentioning his name.

"Stop!" she warned her. "So as far as I could tell they didn't think it was three women. They thought that it could possibly be one woman and two guys."

"See I said you two hoes act like men," Ginger laughed clowning his sisters. " 'Cause I'm the only real woman around here."

"Ginger shut up. What else happened?" Bunny demanded. Simone understood why her sister sounded more stressed out than the rest of them, but she needed to fall back. This whole thing had taken its toll on her today.

"They did everything I said that they would, fingerprints, tire prints, they separated all of the employees, and interviewed us. It was like they were trying to catch us all in a lie, but they didn't know that I was the only one that knew anything."

"So it was that easy?" Tallhya sounded shocked.

"Maybe it was beginners luck," Ginger suggested.

"We can't ever do it again," Simone preached to them. "This was so scary. My nerves are shot right now. You all have no idea how worried I was sitting in the bank after you three left. I just kept wondering if you were going to get caught and all of us would wind up behind bars. We risked our lives. I still can't beleive we did it."

"But we did it for Bunny. Me-Ma was the first one to tell us that we needed to stick together and take care of each other no matter what," Tallhya added.

"Shit, Me-Ma would not be okay with this, but it ain't like we had any other choice. We can't let somebody hurt our sister," Ginger added, getting emotional as she went to hug Bunny.

"Thank you so much all of y'all. I can't believe we pulled it off. I mean this motherfucker would have no problem taking me out the way that he did with Reek, and you all saved me."

"Shit, after what that asshole Walter did to me I needed to do something badass on some *Set it Off* shit. This new Tallhya ain't about to take no shit from nobody so jokers like Walter better watch their fucking backs."

"Amen, my sister!" Simone, Bunny, and

Ginger exclaimed as they went in for a group hug with Tallhya. There was just one thing left to do before they could put all of this behind them.

"Guess it's showtime," Bunny got up and went upstairs to get herself dressed. Simone didn't want to let her go alone, but this wasn't about to happen without a fight because her sister invented stubbornness.

"Either I come with you or you're not going and he'll have to come here to pick up his money," she insisted, as Bunny stopped to weigh what she said before taking a deep breath and answering.

"Fine you can drive with me, but you can't come inside," Bunny demanded as she strapped on a pair of black tight jeans and black patent leather flat Louboutins.

"Damn, I wanna go," Ginger came into the living room whining. The adrenaline of the day had her going nuts. She was ready to race all over town like a bat out of hell and cause all kinds of trouble, which is why her big sisters clipped her wings at least for the night.

"You need to stay put," Simone warned.

"Damn, Sisi, you are getting in the way of my shit," she complained. "If I hadn't robbed a motherfuckin' bank like a real pro

I'd still be going out and getting my swerve on."

"Well, then it's good you're being forced to take a break," Bunny snapped giving her face and attitude. "Give your jaws a break from all that dick sucking."

"And we need to let the heat cool down off that cash, too." Simone piped in.

"So let me get this straight? All the money is too hot to mess with so that little shopping spree I wanted to go on is not going to happen?" She pouted at the idea that she wasn't going to be as fly as she had been earlier.

"Girl, stay your ass home. We can watch reruns of the news," Tallhya came in from the kitchen eating a slice of peach cobbler pie. She plopped down on the sofa and television flipping the channels for the news stations.

"So we good Bonnie?" Simone asked but it came out like more of a warning than a question. All three sisters turned to stare at this new version of their sister who had always been the rule follower with her head on straight.

"I hope you calling her Clyde 'cause my ass is Bonnie," Ginger just couldn't stop herself from being drama, but they lived for her quips as they all broke out laughing.

"Bunny? You're going to pay off the thug who probably killed your boyfriend not a date," Simone reminded her rolling her eyes.

"Yeah, well I want to keep him distracted so that he don't know what the fuck hit him until it's too damn late."

"All right. Hurry up! Let's go."

"Somebody is tryin'a get back in time for a late date," Tallhya kidded her sister. "I can't believe that after everything that went down today you of all people got dick on the brains?"

"What's that supposed to mean?" Simone asked getting all huffy and bothered after all she was a living breathing female. Three sets of heads swiveled in her direction and served her some serious side eye. "What?" she asked still not getting why her sisters were messing with her. "I like him."

"All we know is for the longest time we thought you were adopted, or Deidra had stolen you or something." Tallhya tried to sugarcoat what they had all been thinking.

"Girl, what she trying to say is that your mama Deidra is a ho and her fine-ass daughters are not that far behind her and we always wondered why your ass wasn't giving it away, too," Ginger told her snapping her like it was just a given. Bunny jumped in with her piece.

"Well, I might not be as big a ho as some of you," she said shooting looks at Ginger and Tallhya. "But we all got dick sucking skills in the blood and like to fuck except you 'cause you be so damn prissy. No biggie. We love you like a sister," Bunny winked trying to make her laugh, but she was not pleased.

"For all your information I might look like a good girl in public, but I'm a real freak between the sheets. And if we were in a contest I would win on fellatio alone."

"You can't even say sucking dick in public in case somebody hears you being inappropriate so I know you can't beat me," Ginger teased loving the look of embarrassment on Simone's face.

"Can we go?" Simone rolled her eyes. "Later for all y'all and when I go on my date tonight I will remember this."

"Why does she get to go out when I can't?" Ginger complained, but Simone turned to her, all attitude.

"Because I am going to find out exactly where they are with the case tonight and if that happens after the best sex I've ever had then great." She laughed shooting a smug look at Ginger as she headed to the door. "That's why."

The two sisters stepped out of the house

and got into Bunny's Porsche. She hit the pedal and they were off. They had to stop and get the money from the storage place Ginger had rented earlier in the week. They had Ginger dress in men's clothing to rent the space as Gene in order to cover their tracks. Bunny had to give it to Simone since her Type-A Virgo personality made sure every single detail of the robbery had been covered.

Bunny left her car in the parking lot of a supermarket and they slipped into the store and came out the back exit where they got into an old Hyundai, a Craigslist purchase that Gene had also gotten for them. They drove the car to the storage locker and once they were inside Simone cut on the camping light she purchased a few days ago. There sitting on top of some crates were the bags of money.

"You need to check inside the bags to make sure there is no dye," Bunny instructed her sister. "I can't get it on my hands because that would be it." When all the money had been laid out Simone spotted the marked bills and grabbed them as they counted out the hundred grand.

"I want that motherfucker to pay," Bunny seethed talking about Ghostman.

"Let's just make sure he doesn't kill you."

They shoved the money in the plastic grocery bags and left. Bunny took out her phone and dialed.

"I'm on my way."

39

Bunny felt nauseous as she entered the house where she had last seen Tariq alive and dead. She couldn't believe how terrible it felt in her gut as if she were reliving the whole thing all over again. Instead of the bodyguards that she had been expecting Ghostman answered the door himself. Bunny felt her gun rub against her side and wanted desperately to take it out and blow this asshole away.

"So nice of you to come, and right before our little deadline at midnight," he smiled as if they were about to sit down to a lovely dinner.

"Not like you gave me a choice. The way I saw it either I get you the money or you shoot me and my family is dead," she responded in the exact tone he had just used to speak to her.

"There is always a choice," he reminded her.

"Yes, well, I don't exactly see death as a choice. It's more of a sentence imposed onto you or an unlucky kind of fate."

"So, is that my money?" he asked reaching out for the bag she handed over to him.

"It's not groceries," she snapped back.

"Normally I'm not okay with smart-asses, especially women. I prefer my women silent, naked, and submissive at least when I am about to fuck them," he said leering at her as if he were imaging her in his ideal scenario, naked ass up bent over his coffee table.

"I wasn't trying to be a smart-ass. I brought you the money now can I go?" she asked knowing that this was not the kind of man who honors his word; at least not unless he wasn't given a choice. He walked into the dining room and spilled the contents of the bags onto the table. A huge grin began to spread across his face.

"So you're happy?" she questioned him.

"Happy? No, but I'm relieved for your sake that you brought my goddam money that your thieving bitch of a friend stole from me."

"Aren't you going to count it?" she asked him trying to figure out how to accomplish what she needed to do.

"No, I don't need to count it. Unless you

have a death wish, you better have made sure every dollar is there. I know where you live and you know firsthand that I make good on my threats," he shouted, the saliva from his mouth spraying Bunny as he moved closer to her.

"I would never ever try and con you. You told me what I owed and gave me a deadline and here I am. That's all."

"Yes, here you are little Bunny rabbit." Ghostman ran up on Bunny and pressed her against the wall. He took his hand and rubbed it over Bunny's breast. She did not even flinch as he moved his hand lower rubbing between her legs. But she did begin to imagine him dead. "You like that?"

"Please, I have to go," she told him her voice quivering.

"Go? Bitch, you owe me for allowing you to live. Yes, you brought the money, but now you have to give me something for being generous by sparing your life. By allowing you to live I am taking a risk. What guarantee do I have that you will not try to rob me the same way that your 'friend' did?" he asked with a negative emphasis on the word friend. Bunny had to work overtime to keep from freaking out.

"Take off that jacket!" he growled at her. "I want to see what is under that." As she began to remove her jacket he snatched it off of her. "Now spin around!" He motioned for her to twirl and she knew that if she did he would spot the gun sticking out of the band of her tight skirt. Slowly she turned and he was all smiles and bullying until he spotted the gun. He grabbed her by the waist wrestling the gun away. "Is this supposed to be some kind of threat? Were you trying to kill me? You bitch!" He backhanded her knocking Bunny to the floor.

"Nooo! I was carrying a lot of fucking money and nothing was going to come in the way of me getting this money to you. I had to have protection. What if someone had tried to rob me?" she cried becoming hysterical as she lay on the floor constricting her body into a tight ball.

"Get up! Come on get up!" he shouted waving her own gun at her as she slowly stood up to stand.

"I swear I wasn't trying to hurt you," she pleaded with him knowing it would mean nothing for him to kill her right there.

"You're right. I have a tendency to overreact." He placed the gun on top of the bag of money basically letting her know that he now claimed it. "It's a personality flaw, my temper, but it's one I hope won't get in the way of us getting to know each other better," he cooed sounding as if they had just had some lovers' spat and not him threatening her life. "Come here!" he crooked his finger in her direction.

"Please. I have to go." She took a step back pleading with him.

"What? You're not going anywhere." He grabbed her and began groping her body, his hands moving in different directions, feeling her breasts with one hand, his other palmed her ass. "Damn, you could make some real fans if you got up on the pole, baby." Bunny felt ready to throw up, but instead she pulled away from him and violently kneed him in the balls sending him flying backward onto the floor. She knew that if he caught her he would torture and then kill her so she took off like a bat out of hell flying to the door. She flung it open and raced outside and down the street. By the time he recovered and reached his front door he didn't see any sign of Bunny.

"I'm ready! Gooooooo! Go! Go!" Bunny told Simone as she got into the car. Simone immediately grabbed the phone that was on the passenger seat and dialed the number she already dialed on the burner phone.

"I need to speak with Detective Dugan?" Bunny spoke into the phone using a strong southern accent. A man answered with a deep voice.

"Detective Dugan."

"Hello, I would like to report a man with a gun. He's been bragging that he held up the Metropolitan Savings and Loan National Bank. The address is 777 Palm Drive. Hurry, he's armed and dangerous!" she screamed into the phone as she slammed it shut.

"Now we wait." Simone smiled at her sister, as they stared into the rearview mirror at Ghostman's house.

40

Chase hung up the phone and raced out of his office into his partner's where Franklin sat staring at the computer. They'd been checking out all the bank robberies in the area within the last year trying to find some kind of pattern. With the FBI breathing down their necks they desperately needed this call.

"We got a lead," he informed his partner, who looked up with questions spilling out of his mouth.

"Viable? I mean do we trust it?" he asked standing up and getting his gun and equipment.

"I don't know, but it's the only lead that we have. The caller said that apparently this guy is armed and dangerous. We should take at least two cars with us to check this out just in case."

"Let's go!" The two headed into the squad room.

"Captain," Franklin called out as he came into view. "We got a lead says it's our guy and that he's armed. Not sure if the other perps are there or even if this is real, but we need to follow it."

"I agree," the Captain glanced around at his room, "Take Manfred and Douglas, Turner and Reilly, and O'Brien and Anderson. And Palley and Hopper," he called out igniting the officers who all hurried and grabbed their things.

"I sure hope this is it," Dugan said sharing his concern with Franklin who nodded letting him know that he was right there with him.

"This thing between you and Marks it's getting old. That guy he has such a hard on for you that its become a real problem."

"Tell me about it," Dugan agreed as they got into their car. The four standard cop cars led by the detectives' Chevy formed a convoy as they sped in the direction of the address.

The whole thing had taken seven minutes to organize and already Simone and Bunny were worrying that Ghostman would somehow get away. The women were parked a block away with a pair of binoculars watching the house.

"There they are," Bunny shouted to her

sister excited when she saw the caravan of cops fanning out in front of the house.

"I want four of you to spread out in case anyone tries to run. Franklin and I will go to the front door, the other four of you follow us," Dugan led them up the steps where he rang the bell. Usually this is where the threats began in order to convince a perp to open the door, but Ghostman made it so easy for them when he swung the door open thinking that Bunny had come back.

Ghostman was so relaxed because in his mind, women usually begged to be with a man of his influence and he didn't expect her to be any different, so imagine his surprise when he opened the door to the cops.

"Hi, can we come in?" Detective Dugan waved his badge at Ghostman who reacted quickly by trying to slam the front door in their faces. Dugan and Franklin caught the door before he could close it. Ghostman turned and ran to the table grabbing Bunny's gun and aiming it at the cops.

"Come any closer and I will shoot," Ghostman hollered as he stood across the room with his gun pointed at them.

"Let's talk about this?" Dugan spoke in that calm voice under pressure that took many years to perfect.

"Fuck you! I don't want to talk to you," Ghostman cocked back his gun.

"Blam! Blam! Blam!" It sounded as if fireworks were going off inside the house from where Simone and Bunny were located.

"Blam! Blam! Blam!"

"Nooooo!" Detective Dugan screamed as Ghostman's body was riddled with bullets sending him falling to the floor. He'd taken the first shot at the detective who returned the hit, but the four officers running in behind them finished it.

"Dammit," Franklin and Dugan shared a look. This could be bad. Really bad.

"We need to find evidence that this is our guy!" Franklin shouted to the cops. They all fanned out in different directions in the house desperate to locate whatever could tie this man to the robberies.

"We better hope like hell that this guy had something to do with the robbery. Because if this is just some random crazy person we are so fucked," Dugan said commiserating with Franklin.

"Detectives?" one of the officers shouted from upstairs. They went running upstairs and into the home office. Right there on the table sat a bag containing neat bundles of money. The bag also had side pockets and when Dugan unzipped them he found three Bill Clinton masks.

"Bingo!" Dugan and Franklin slapped their palms together. They were damn near jumping up and down. And this was just the beginning of the haul.

"Wait." Dugan stopped to stare at a painting. He went over and moved it slightly placing a hand behind it.

"What?" Franklin questioned. He knew his partner and he didn't miss one thing. That's what made him so good at his job.

"It's a safe."

"We need an entire team."

"We need to get some forensic specialist, also someone who can break into this safe and should we invite the FBI for shits and giggles?"

"I can't wait to see a certain someone's face when we show him that we've got this case sewn up."

"That is going to be so damn sweet. I can't wait to see it." The two men shared a look delighted that their bad luck when it came to solving cases was finally turning around.

41

Simone and Bunny had just pulled off from watching the drama at Ghostman's place when her phone started to ring. Bunny snatched the phone out of the cup holder and showed it to her sister. Simone pulled over and grabbed the phone as a look of complete fear passed between the two as their worst case scenarios swirled in their heads. Did they find something in that house to tie them to the bank robbery?

"Hello," Simone answered trying to keep her voice level and normal when every part of her was quaking with fear. Bunny placed her hand on top of her sister's to calm her from shaking.

"Ms. Banks?" Detective Dugan spoke into the phone using a formal greeting instead of the playful one he had used this afternoon. Simone's face registered her worry. Bunny's hand went to her mouth fighting back her own concern.

"Detective?" she responded trying to keep the worry from overpowering her words.

"You will never guess how things unfolded after you left," he told her, but she was distracted by Bunny's hands moving questioning her. She shrugged her shoulders turning back to the call.

"Really, what?"

"We found him."

"Found who?"

"The guy who hit the bank. Now we haven't yet identified his accomplices, but it's definitely him." Simone couldn't help but smile, relieved to be in the clear and touched by the excitement in his voice.

"Did you arrest him?" she asked looking directly at Bunny who pressed herself close to the phone to hear the other side of the conversation.

"No. We had an altercation and he shot at us and my men wound up killing him, which was obviously not what we wanted. If he were alive he could have led us to the others and now we may never find them. But forget all of that for a moment. We had a date tonight?"

"Yes, we did," she couldn't stop herself from smiling and knew that he could see it through the phone. Bunny moved away watching her sister.

"Can we rain check it for tomorrow?" he asked.

"Really?"

"Yes. I want to come to your door, pick you up, and take you out on a date and not have either of us worry about getting up to go to work in the morning."

"Oh," she answered feeling way more girly than she had in ages and really turned on.

"Unless I'm being presumptuous?" he asked.

"No, you're not and that sounds perfect," she told him then proceeded to give him her address.

"I can't wait and Simone, we really deserve this break," he told her before hanging up.

"So you're going on a date tomorrow?" Bunny asked fluttering her eyelashes at her sister in jest.

"I guess I am." She laughed.

"We better go and get our money then," Bunny cheered.

"I can't believe we did it!" Simone shouted.

"No. I can't believe how badass my sister is," Bunny boasted as the two hugged relieved to have gotten away with their crime.

42

Simone and Bunny decided to surprise their sisters on their way home. They stopped and got Chinese food, champagne and of course the money which they had already switched into grocery bags.

"Your ass went grocery shopping," Ginger complained as they came through the door with their packages.

"Shut up!" Bunny snapped back taking the champagne out of the bag and passing it to her.

"Oh, hell yeah," Tallhya cheered.

"It's done. Ghostman took the fall and to make it even better, he's dead. Fool tried to have a shootout with the police," Simone told them.

"We saw it on the news and they found the marked bills," Tallhya told them as they all danced around.

"And the gun that was used in the robbery matches the gun that Ghostman used to shoot at the cops," Ginger added.

"How the hell did you know it would work out like this?" Bunny asked Simone who was pouring them glasses of champagne.

"I didn't, but it just made sense. I knew the cops would not give up on finding the bank robbers and Bunny needed this guy to pay for what he did to Tariq so it made sense," she confessed.

"Now if we can only figure out how the hell to make Walter pay then that's what's up," Tallhya joked.

"Oh, that is going to happen along with my Step Monster getting exactly what she deserves along with my father's ex-partner," Simone said as she passed the champagne around.

"And don't forget that bitch-ass, fake nigga, Cassius Street. He needs to know that we are coming for him," Ginger added.

"Oh, absolutely. And anybody else you want to add to the list let me know because I am forming a plan as we speak," Simone said so calm that it actually sounded more scary than a threat.

"Your ass is just a straight up criminal." Bunny raised her glass to their oldest sister. "Here is to the greatest criminal master-mind in our family."

"I know that's right." Ginger toasted

before they put down their glasses and dived into the money throwing it up in the air.

"Woo, we are rich bitches!" Tallhya shouted as they danced around playfully. They were so distracted having a good time that they didn't notice someone had entered the house and was standing in the doorway watching them a look of shock slowly turning to pleasure.

"Well . . . well . . . what do we have here?" They all turned to Deidra smirking at them an expression of pure joy lighting up her face. "Now you know good and well, even you can do that FED time waiting on you or run me some of that cash. As a matter of fact. All of that cash in those bags."

The sisters looked at each other and on three they were about to tackle her, but then Lenny pulled out a big-ass machine gun while Deidra collected the brown paper bags.

"Didn't Me-Ma tell ya! Easy come and easy go?"

ABOUT THE AUTHOR

Nikki Turner is the author of *The New York Times* bestseller *Black Widow*, the #1 *Essence* bestseller *Forever a Hustler's Wife*, and the *Essence* bestsellers *A Hustler's Wife*, *The Glamorous Life*, and *Riding Dirty on I-95*.

The employees of Thorndike Press hope you have enjoyed this Large Print book. All our Thorndike, Wheeler, and Kennebec Large Print titles are designed for easy reading, and all our books are made to last. Other Thorndike Press Large Print books are available at your library, through selected bookstores, or directly from us.

For information about titles, please call:
(800) 223-1244

or visit our Web site at:
http://gale.cengage.com/thorndike

To share your comments, please write:
Publisher
Thorndike Press
10 Water St., Suite 310
Waterville, ME 04901